"Is this a confes[sion]"

Burk grinned.

"Well, sort of," she said slowly.

"Have you murdered somebody?" he asked.

She blinked in astonishment. "Of course not!"

The grin disappeared as quickly as it had appeared. "Would you be marrying me for my money?"

"Oh, Burk, no! If I marry you, it will be because I love you with all my heart, but—"

"Then I don't want to hear whatever it is you feel you must confess."

Kate was stunned. "But you don't even know what I'm trying to tell you."

He shook his head. "The past doesn't matter. We're both old enough to have made a few mistakes, but I'm not going to tell you mine, and I don't want to hear yours. We'll start fresh and concentrate on making each other happy in the present. Okay?"

Kate was so tempted to believe they could do that....

Dear Reader,

The holiday season has arrived—and we have some dazzling titles for the month of December!

This month, the always-delightful Joan Elliott Pickart brings you our THAT'S MY BABY! title. *Texas Baby* is the final book in her FAMILY MEN cross-line series with Desire, and spins the heartwarming tale of a fortysomething heroine who rediscovers the joy of motherhood when she adopts a precious baby girl. Except the dashing man of her dreams has no intention of playing daddy again....

And baby fever doesn't stop there. Don't miss *The Littlest Angel* by Sherryl Woods, an emotional reunion romance—and the first of her AND BABY MAKES THREE: THE NEXT GENERATION miniseries. Passion flares between a disgruntled cowboy and a tough lady cop in *The Cop and the Cradle* by Suzannah Davis—book two in the SWITCHED AT BIRTH miniseries.

For those of you who revel in holiday miracles, be sure to check out *Christmas Magic* by Andrea Edwards. This humorous romance features a cat-toting heroine who transforms a former Mr. Scrooge into a true believer—and captures his heart in the process.

Also this month, *The Millionaire's Baby* by Phyllis Halldorson is an absorbing amnesia story that's filled with love, turmoil and a possible second chance at happiness. Finally, long-buried feelings resurface when a heroine returns to unite her former lover with the son he'd never known in *Second Chance Dad* by Angela Benson.

All of us here at Silhouette wish you a joyous holiday season!

Sincerely,

Tara Gavin,
Senior Editor

Please address questions and book requests to:
Silhouette Reader Service
U.S.: 3010 Walden Ave., P.O. Box 1325, Buffalo, NY 14269
Canadian: P.O. Box 609, Fort Erie, Ont. L2A 5X3

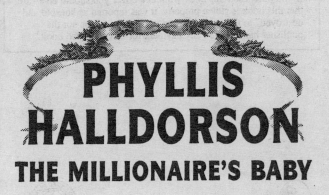

PHYLLIS HALLDORSON

THE MILLIONAIRE'S BABY

Silhouette®

SPECIAL ▼ EDITION®

Published by Silhouette Books

America's Publisher of Contemporary Romance

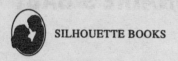

SILHOUETTE BOOKS

ISBN 0-373-24145-3

THE MILLIONAIRE'S BABY

Books by Phyllis Halldorson

PHYLLIS HALLDORSON

met her real-life Prince Charming at the age of sixteen. She married him a year later, and they settled down to raise a family. A compulsive reader, Phyllis dreamed of someday finding the time to write stories of her own. That time came when her two youngest children reached adolescence. When she was introduced to romance novels, she knew she had found her long-delayed vocation. After all, how could she write anything else after living all those years with her very own Silhouette hero?

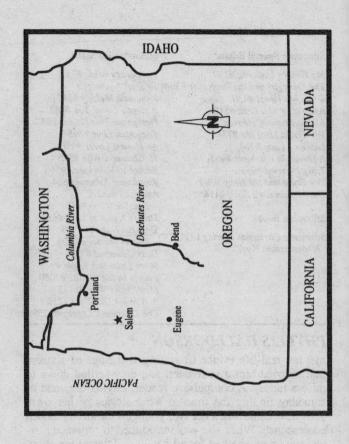

Chapter One

The gale force winds howled with rage and shook Katherine Brown's lightweight compact sedan. Pelting rain slashed across the windshield in such volume as to render the wipers useless.

Kate clutched the steering wheel so tightly that her knuckles were white. She'd slowed to little more than a crawl, but she didn't dare stop on this highway high in the Cascade mountain range of Oregon. Visibility was practically zero, and if anyone was coming behind her they'd rear-end her and send her car out of control for sure.

"Damn! Damn! Damn" she muttered aloud as she noticed that the rain contained particles of sleet. It was spring! The weather wasn't supposed to turn nasty in the spring. Not even at almost six thousand feet in the Willamette National Forest.

When she'd left Bend this morning the sun had been shining, and the forecast for the higher altitudes had been for overcast skies with the possibility of rain. Rain! Not deluge! She'd expected to be in Portland by early afternoon, but at this rate she'd be lucky if she got there before dark. Or if she got there at all.

Thank heavens there was a guardrail that she could see along the outer side of the road. She'd follow it until it ended, but then she'd have to pull over and stop. She couldn't drive when she couldn't see the highway in front of her!

What rotten weather. If she'd had any idea she'd run into anything like this she'd have stayed on Interstate 84 and taken the easier route from Denver to Portland, but her best friend, Holly, had pleaded with Kate to come by Bend and spend a couple of days with her before going on.

Kate and Holly had been friends since they were seven years old. That's when Kate had come to Portland to live with her grandparents after her parents were killed in a boating accident in the turbulent waters off the coast of Northern California where they'd lived at the time. The two girls had gone through school together, including college at Lewis and Clark, and had become separated only when Holly married and moved to Bend with her husband.

They hadn't seen each other in the five years since Kate had left Portland in disgrace. At least, in disgrace with herself and the journalistic community that she had dishonored. Not to mention Burk Sinclair!

Even now, five years later, she shuddered when she thought of what he'd do if he ever caught up with her.

She'd messed up royally, and she was deeply ashamed. That was why she'd never come back. Grandma visited her in Denver at least once a year, but Kate hadn't been able to face the idea of returning to the scene of her tragic mistake.

An especially vicious blast of wind tore Kate's thoughts away from her musing and it took all her strength to keep the auto from veering into the middle of the roadway. It was then she realized that the guardrail at the side of the road was no longer there, but she continued driving until she caught a glimpse of a stand of trees through the rain and knew it was safe to pull over and stop.

But before she could, the sudden roar of an engine startled her and all hell broke loose!

The roar materialized into solid metal and slammed into her car, sending it skidding out of control across the road. At the same time she was totally engulfed in something huge and pliable. Her only thought was "Thank God for the seat belt" as her body was thrown against it.

With another jolting crash the sedan hit something and stopped, although she kept bouncing around in the confines of her seat belt and what she now realized was the air bag. Just before she blacked out she knew beyond doubt that without them she would have gone headfirst through the windshield.

She never totally lost consciousness and even before her vision cleared, she smelled smoke, but it was more like burned rubber smoke than fire smoke. Groggily she fumbled with the seat belt until it unbuckled. She noticed that the air bag had deflated and she was no longer pinned by it.

There was something that looked like a big wheel poking through the roof and windshield on the passenger side of the car, only inches from where she sat, and her only thought was to escape before one or both of the vehicles caught fire. She struggled with the handle, trying to open the door, before she remembered it was locked.

When she finally pushed it open, it threw her off balance and she tumbled out and into a big prickly bush before sprawling in a puddle of water on the wet ground. For a moment she just lay there trying to catch her breath. She was aware of the icy rain pummeling her back, and she shivered with cold.

She raised her head and the back of it hit a branch. Ducking back down she squirmed to the side and tried again.

This time she was able to sit up, although there were trees and underbrush all around her. At least she was somewhat sheltered by them.

She was shaking badly. Even her teeth rattled. Pulling her knees up under her chin she wrapped her arms around her legs in an effort to stop trembling. She was pretty sure it was more from shock than from cold or injury, but whatever it was, she had to calm down and get help.

Her gaze turned toward the car and she froze, then blinked. Surely she was hallucinating.

She blinked several more times but the image stayed the same. There was a huge motorcycle embedded in the side and roof of her car!

For a moment she just stared, trying to assimilate everything that had happened in the past few minutes. Where had that motorcycle come from? She hadn't seen any indication of a side road, but then, she hadn't been able to see much of anything past her own car.

Why would anyone be out in a storm like this on a motorcycle?

Then it struck her. There had to be someone riding that monstrous machine, but where was he…or she?

A surge of panic revived her somewhat and she slowly pulled herself to her feet with the help of the nearby shrubbery. She didn't seem to be injured—at least, nothing was broken. But her trembling legs threatened to give way any minute, and she clung to the sturdy branches of the bush for support.

The rider had to have been thrown off the bike, but where had he sailed to? And how seriously had he been injured?

She decided it had to be a man. No woman would be out, unprotected from the elements, on a motorbike in a storm like this. Only a macho-driven male would attempt such a stupid thing.

She shuddered at the thought. Had he been wearing a helmet? Was he badly crushed? Or worse, was he dead?

The only thing she knew for sure was that she had to find him.

Forcing herself to let loose of the branch she'd been clutching, she took a tentative step. Her knees buckled, but she grabbed for support again and managed to stay on her feet.

Dammit, she didn't have the leisure to give in to her shocked nervous system. She had to find the idiot who didn't have sense enough to come in out of the rain. He might need immediate care such as resuscitation or pressure to stop severe bleeding....

She tried taking a step while balancing herself with the bush, and this time her legs still felt like rubber but didn't give way. Encouraged, she took another step, and another, still holding on to the brush and trees for support.

She decided to check the highway first in case he'd fallen off before the vehicle left the road. If so he could be run over if another car came by.

By straining her eyes she could see to the other side of the road and up and down it for a few yards. There was no sign of a body, so she turned in the direction he'd have been thrown if he was tossed through the air when the motorcycle hit her car.

By now her balance had returned and she could walk unaided. Deep in the underbrush she found what she was looking for. The body of a man sprawled on his stomach on the ground under a tall redwood tree.

Kneeling down beside him, she checked the pulse in his neck. It was erratic but beating! Breathing a sigh of relief she noticed that he was also wearing a helmet, but her relief turned to anxiety when she saw that the helmet was badly dented and cracked. He could be severely injured even with the protection!

Now what was she going to do? She'd had enough first

aid to know she shouldn't move a patient with a head injury until he'd been examined by a doctor or paramedic, but she couldn't leave him out here in the pouring rain and sleet, either.

On the other hand there was nothing else she could do until the storm let up. She already knew that she was too far out of range for her car phone to work. She'd tried it when she first ran into the bad weather.

As far as she knew there were no cabins or homes nearby. At least, the visibility was too limited to see them if there were. And what were the odds, really, in this weather, of another car coming by, which could be flagged down for help?

While all this was going through her mind she'd been examining the rest of his body for injuries, but he didn't seem to have any broken bones. He had a magnificent body though. Hard and muscular.

Quickly she discarded those thoughts.

She was going to have to turn him over onto his back whether it was advisable or not. He was lying facedown in the rain-soaked ground cover that would be a puddle very soon. He could drown in just a few inches of water!

"Dear God, help me," she repeated over and over in a litany of prayer as she struggled to turn the unconscious man. He was deadweight and heavier than she'd thought, given his slender build. He was also wearing a warmly lined leather jacket and gloves, faded jeans and thick-soled boots.

She wished she'd worn something heavier. She'd wanted to look nice when she arrived at her grandmother's house later in the day so this morning she'd dressed in her new lightweight beige slacks and jacket as well as matching low-heeled leather pumps. All of which were now soaking wet and coated with mud.

She positioned her hands at the man's shoulder and waist and tugged him as carefully as she could onto his side. He twitched and groaned, and she stopped. "I'm sorry," she said, not knowing whether he could hear her or not. "I don't mean to hurt you, but I have to turn you over. It would be easier if you could help. Can you hear me?"

He didn't answer but rolled over onto his back, emitting an involuntary cry of pain, and clutching at his helmet-covered head, his eyes tightly closed. He fumbled with the strap under his chin, but she placed her hands over his to stop him. "No, don't take off the helmet yet. I'm going to have to move you, and I don't want to chance hitting your bare head again."

He was bleeding from the nose, but there didn't seem to be blood anywhere else. "I'm so sorry," she repeated, and squeezed his hands. "Can you tell me if you have a lot of pain anywhere other than your head?"

He blinked open his eyes. They were a golden brown in color but he wasn't able to focus them. "Wh—who...? What...?" he stammered.

At least he was conscious again, or nearly so. "I'm Katherine Brown," she told him. "Your motorcycle collided with my car and threw you headfirst into this tree we're under."

She knew that was what had happened because she could see the place where the bark on the trunk had been broken by the collision. "Do you know if there are any people living around here? I need to find a telephone and get help. You need medical attention."

He moaned and closed his eyes again, and she released his hands. She was afraid he'd slip back into unconsciousness or go to sleep, and she needed him awake. "Please, stay with me here," she pleaded. "Don't black out on me again. I'm trying to get help for you. Are you from around here? Are there people living close by?"

He opened his eyes with an effort. "Across the road," he murmured thickly.

Kate's heart pounded with exhilaration. Was it possible

there was assistance that close? "Is there a cabin over there?" she asked cautiously.

"Yes," he breathed, almost inaudibly, and closed his eyes again.

She couldn't let him drift away. She put her hand on his shoulder and shook gently. "Come on, stay with me. I can't get you over there by myself. Do you think you can stand up and walk if I help you?"

He grimaced. "No...stay here."

She felt a wave of tenderness. She couldn't blame him for not wanting to expose himself to that much agony, but she had no choice. "We can't stay here. It's cold and pouring rain. We'll catch pneumonia or worse if we don't get dry and warm soon. Are you sure there's a cabin over there?"

"Yes." His voice was getting a little stronger. "Bring...keys...from Harley."

"Harley," she repeated uncertainly. "Is that your name, Harley?"

He grimaced again. "No. Motorcycle."

Of course, how could she have been so dense? Her mind was still fuzzy, too. He wanted her to bring him his keys from his motorcycle.

She got to her feet carefully and found to her great joy that her legs were once more firm and strong. Gingerly she climbed to the top of the wreckage of twisted metal and found the keys in the ignition of the Harley-Davidson. Pulling them out, she hurried back to her patient and again knelt beside him to put them in his hand.

He opened his eyes, and this time he was better able to focus. "No...you take," he said. "Open cabin."

Was he trying to tell her the place belonged to him? "Is it your cabin?"

"Keys fit," he said without actually answering her question.

"Okay." She could question him later. "Now, can you try to sit up? I'll help you."

She held out her arms to him. He ignored them and turned onto his side, then slowly pushed himself upright, grimly cursing with pain with every move. Putting her arms around his shoulders, she held his head against her chest, terrified that he'd fall down and injure it even more.

He allowed the intimacy without protest and sank into the softness of her breasts. The movement had taken all the strength he had, and he panted for breath.

"I'm sorry to put you through this," she murmured, "but there's just no other way. I know I asked before, but do you hurt anywhere other than your head? I felt you all over, checking for broken bones when I first found you, and I didn't feel any, but—"

"Wish I'd been...awake to enjoy that," he mumbled, startling her so that she laughed.

"Bless your randy male libido," she said happily. "That's the first full and coherent sentence you've uttered since I found you. Do you think you can get up and walk?"

"For you...anything," he answered weakly. "Never had a guardian angel before."

Her arms tightened around him. "You don't have one now, either. Just ignorant me. I'm a technical writer—I know nothing about nursing. I may be doing you more harm than good, but we've got to get to shelter."

Prodding him to his feet was agony for him and hard work for her. Fortunately they were close enough to the tree that he could pull himself up by the trunk with a lot of help from her. When he finally accomplished it, he had to clutch the tree trunk and catch his breath as well as try to get oriented.

His face was white and pinched, and she saw his eyes begin to turn up. "No!" she yelled, and wrapped her arms around both him and, as far as she could, the tree. "Don't faint! Take a deep breath and hang in there. I'll never get you up again if you fall.''

She could feel the effort he made to straighten up and not black out. If he lost consciousness he'd be deadweight and she wouldn't be able to hold him upright. She had to keep him talking.

She said the first thing that came to mind. "I told you my name, but you haven't told me yours yet. You do have one, don't you?'' she teased.

For quite a while he didn't answer, and she was about to ask him again when he finally spoke. "No. Call me Buddy.'' His voice was weak again.

Buddy? Wasn't he a little old to be called buddy? Did he mean no, he didn't have a name? Or no, he wasn't going to tell her what it was?

Oh, well, this was no time to start an argument. "All right, Buddy, now keep on talking to me and try to focus your thoughts. What were you doing riding a motorcycle in this storm?''

"Going home.'' This time it came out a little stronger.

"And where is home?''

"Portland.''

Before she could prompt him again, he spoke on his own. "The earth's...stopped spinning now. Think I can walk. Help me.''

Needing all the reinforcement she could muster, she stepped away from him. "Stay propped against the tree and turn to face me, but be careful not to fall.''

Slowly he unwound his arms from the trunk and turned, keeping his body against the tree for support.

She stepped in line beside him. "Now, put your arm around my shoulders, and I'll put mine around your waist. You're tall, but I'm five foot seven and strong. I should be able to brace you if you can stay on your feet and walk. We're going across the highway to the cabin you say is there. Are you ready?''

They put their arms around each other and took the first step. Kate was familiar with the adage that a journey of a thousand miles starts with the first step, but she'd be grateful if they could make it only as far as the cabin.

It was a grueling trip. Several times he stumbled and almost brought them both down, but by taking it slowly they finally got across the road. At least they didn't have to worry about traffic.

The wind and rain had tapered down a little, and from the new vantage point she could catch glimpses of the so-called cabin through the driving rain. The image was blurred, but it looked more like a log house to her, and was set several yards back and up on the side of the mountain from the highway. There was a long driveway leading back to it. That must be where Buddy had come from on his Harley.

The man beside her tottered, and she turned to put both arms around his waist as he similarly embraced her. "Hold on just a few minutes longer," she pleaded. "Can you make it up that hill?"

"Sure," he said, breathless from the effort he'd been exerting. "If you stop…and give me a hug…every once in a while."

She liked his teasing. It showed that he was aware of his surroundings and thinking straight. "The pleasure will be all mine," she assured him as they started walking again.

It seemed that they stumbled along forever, and they did stop for him to get his balance and his breath several times, but at last they made it to the covered porch and blessed partial shelter from the storm.

Kate propped him up against the rugged log front of the structure while she found the right key and opened both the storm door and the heavy oak one. Buddy's legs started to give way just as she reached for him, and again she grabbed him in a tight embrace.

"Just a few steps more," she assured him. "Then you can sit down."

He groaned but let her half carry, half drag him inside, where he literally collapsed in the first chair they came to. It was a thickly upholstered one, covered in Naugahyde—fortunately—since he and his clothes were muddy and dripping wet, as was she.

It was also fortunate that there were no carpets on the floor, only a large hand-braided scatter rug, which was rapidly getting drenched and dirty but hopefully could be washed.

"Are you going to be okay?" she fretted as he slumped precariously in the chair.

It was evident that he was dangerously exhausted as well as seriously injured. She was afraid to go very far away from him for fear he'd lose consciousness and fall out of the seat, but the room was darkly shadowed and she wanted to turn on a lamp. The windows were shuttered and there was little natural light because of the storm.

"Just…just help me get this helmet off," he said as he reached up to unfasten the strap. She saw that his hands were shaking badly.

"Here, let me do it," she said and unsnapped it, then carefully pried off the bulky and battered headgear.

It was a tight fit and he stiffened and clutched the chair arms with both hands as she maneuvered it. Apparently his head was swollen from the battering it had taken.

He slumped even more when she finally relieved him of the helmet, and she sat on the arm and once again cradled him to her breast. He snuggled against her, breathing heavily from the exertion, but was too wiped out to even lift his arms and hold on to her.

Now that his helmet was off, she could see that there were no open injuries to his head. Only his nose was bloody, and the blood was no longer flowing. There was also no bleeding from his ears. That was a good sign, but she knew it didn't necessarily mean there was no damage to his brain.

He needed medical care and quickly. Much as she'd like to sit here holding him and soothing his pain, she had to get him to a doctor.

"Buddy," she murmured against his short, dark brown hair. "Is there a telephone here?"

It took him a moment to answer. "Kitchen."

"I need to call for help," she told him. "Do you want me to assist you to the couch?"

The sofa was perhaps fifteen steps away, but she wasn't sure he had the strength to make it.

Apparently he wasn't, either. "No...I'll stay here."

She wasn't certain that was a good idea. "You'll call me if you feel light-headed or dizzy?"

He raised his head and looked up at her. His eyes focused well now. "You think I'd...pass up a chance...to cuddle with you?" He still had trouble catching his breath.

She smiled and stroked his cheek. "I can see there's nothing wrong with your reflexes," she joked, then released him and stood. "I assume the kitchen's in the back?"

He shifted to a more comfortable position. "Yes."

She felt for a light switch on the wall as she walked from the living room, through the dining room and into the kitchen, but she didn't find one. The kitchen was brighter than the living room due to a skylight so she decided to make the call before searching further for the switch.

She picked up the phone, dialed 911 and waited. Nothing happened, and she realized that it wasn't ringing on the other end. She jiggled the hook then held the phone to her ear before dialing again. There was no dial tone. The phone was dead!

Dear Lord, what was she going to do now? She spotted a light switch on the wall under the kitchen cabinets and walked over to turn it on. Nothing! In a panic she switched it on and off, on and off, but nothing happened. The electricity was off, too! Did that mean they had no heat, either?

A wave of desperation washed over her. What on earth were they going to do? They were soaking wet and chilled to the bone, with no way to warm up and dry out. The air in the cabin was chilly and damp. She was grateful for the shelter, but they had to get out of their drenched clothes.

Fighting back her fear, she decided to explore the rest of the house. She'd noticed a stairway to the second story next to the front door, and now she found a laundry room off the kitchen, and a short hall off that, which led to a bedroom and bathroom. The double bed was made up and there was a shower. Upstairs were two more bedrooms, but the beds were not made up and there was no extra bedding.

Investigating further she found a few men's and women's clothes hanging in the closet, and underwear in the dresser drawers. Did that mean Buddy had a wife? She'd noticed that he wasn't wearing a wedding ring. Oh, well, at least they could change out of their wet things.

Taking a deep breath she went back to the living room to confront him and found him dangerously close to going to sleep and slipping out of his chair.

She hurried over and put her arms around him. "Buddy, wake up! Don't go to sleep, I need your help."

He roused and pushed himself up in the seat. "Sorry," he muttered.

"Can you tell me how this place is heated?" she asked. "Is it oil, gas or electricity?"

He leaned his head against her. "Electricity."

She blew out her breath. "I was afraid of that. The electricity is off and so is the telephone."

He leaned back to look at her. "But it can't be. Both of them...were working...when I left here."

"And when was that?"

"Just before...I ran into you." He leaned against her again and closed his eyes.

Acting on impulse rather than careful thought she stroked the side of his head and his exposed cheek tenderly. "Well, neither of them is working now, so I'm afraid we're going to have to improvise."

"Mmm-hmm," he agreed contentedly.

"Was there hot water this morning?"

"Mmm-hmm," he repeated, and put his arms around her waist.

"Then it will still be good and warm," she said and knew what she had to do to ward off pneumonia for both of them. It would be embarrassing, but that couldn't be helped.

Gathering up her courage, she nuzzled the top of his head with her cheek in hopes of distracting him from reacting to her next statement. "I apologize in advance if I offend you for even thinking of this, but I..."

She swallowed then hurried on before she lost her nerve. "I'm going to give you a shower."

Her ploy didn't work. That woke him up, but quick!

"You're going to what?" he roared, and jerked his head up, then swore with pain and again buried his face in her softness. "Dammit, woman," he muttered, his words muffled, "I'm not...an invalid. I can take...my own bath."

Kate knew that wasn't true, but this called for a bit of diplomacy. "Of course you can, but the hot water will be limited, and we're going to have to shower together in order for both of us to get warm. With no heat we'll never warm up and dry off otherwise."

His answer was so long in coming that she was afraid he was refusing to discuss the matter, but then he sighed. "All right, but...you're not going...to wash me like a baby."

She stifled a giggle. It wouldn't be the first time in her twenty-eight years that she'd showered with a man, and given this one's good looks, personality and apparent age, it wouldn't be his first encounter with a woman, either. So why was he acting like an outraged virgin?

Chapter Two

The man who called himself Buddy silently cursed his helplessness while at the same time reveling in the tender care of this young woman who had come out of nowhere and very probably saved his life.

If only he could think straight, but his mind was mushy. So was his memory. It was filled with holes. He knew where he was and what he'd been doing up here in the mountains, but he couldn't remember his own name, or whether or not he owned this cabin! He knew that he lived in Portland, but couldn't remember his address or phone number.

Now this sweet guardian angel who said her name was Katherine wanted him to shower with her. He should have been ecstatic, but instead he wasn't even sure he could stand up. The excruciating pain in his head was driving everything else out of it. It pounded and throbbed and every move was agony. He wished she'd just keep pillowing i between her soft breasts until the stabbing torment went away.

"I hate to make you move again," she said apologetically in the vicinity of his ear, "but it's imperative that we get out of these wet clothes and under the warm shower before the water in the tank cools off."

The very thought of trying to get back up on his feet again made him shudder, but right now she had him so bewitched that he'd do anything she asked him to, no matter how much it hurt. "Can you...help me up?" he asked, disgusted with his halting speech. He couldn't think fast enough to form coherent sentences.

"Yes," she said, moving carefully away from him, "in a minute. But first I want to take off your boots. No sense in tracking mud over all these beautiful hardwood floors."

He'd noticed that she'd already stepped out of her flimsy pumps.

Kneeling down in front of him, she tugged off one boot and peeled away his sock, then did the same with his other foot while he just sat there, dependent as a baby. He hated it. Not that he disliked her undressing him, but the fact that she had to do it because he couldn't do it for himself was demeaning.

"There," she said, and stood up. "Now let's get you out of that jacket."

That was something he could do for himself, and he reached up and unzipped it before she could, but then he couldn't figure out the moves to get it off his arms.

Bloody hell! He hoped his motor reflexes hadn't been permanently damaged!

She stood by and let him struggle for a few seconds, then quietly pulled it off him one arm at a time without making a comment. She was kind and empathetic, but that only frustrated him all the more.

Underneath the jacket he wore a red-and-black-plaid flannel shirt, which was fairly dry since the leather jacket was waterproof, and when she started unbuttoning it, he had sense enough to let her do it and not argue.

Under the flannel shirt was a white T-shirt, and again he dutifully held up his arms and let her slip it over his head leaving him only in briefs and jeans. He knew without a doubt that she'd have to peel him out of those, too. He couldn't even bear to think of bending over with his head down!

"Okay, now you'll have to stand up and walk into the bathroom," she announced as she leaned over and put her hands under his armpits.

He'd been through this before and wasn't looking forward to a replay, but there was no way to get out of it. Grimly he grabbed the arms of the chair and with her help managed to stand, but then he had to grasp her again while he waited for his head to stop pounding and the room to quit spinning so he could regain his equilibrium.

Not that embracing her wasn't almost worth it. She was an armful of pure bliss. Just the right height to fit against him in all the important places, and curvy enough to be soft instead of angular, pliable instead of bony.

She had her arms around his waist and her feet spread apart to provide balance in case his trembling legs gave way. His groin nestled against hers as though they'd been made for each other.

Damn! Even with the tormenting headache he could feel the start of an arousal. Time to take a hike!

"I think...I can walk now," he told her, then released her. He hoped he didn't sound as reluctant as he felt. He'd like nothing better than to stand there and hold her, but he didn't want to embarrass them both with a full-fledged erection when she took off his pants.

"Fine," she said and dropped her arms, too, then turned so they were standing side by side instead of face-to-face. For a moment he thought he heard regret in her tone also, but dismissed it as wishful thinking on his part.

They put their arms around each other's waists and made the slow, torturous trek to the bathroom. Inside she propped him against a wall next to the door and reached for the snap on his trousers.

To his great relief he was too out of breath and pain-ridden by the exertion to respond to her again. Shyly she averted her eyes as she unzipped his fly and pulled down his clinging wet jeans, but there was no awkward encounter. He had trouble keeping his stability when he stepped out of them, but together they finally got them off.

He girded himself for the ordeal of controlling his response again at the thought of her putting her fingers inside the waistband of his briefs to strip them off, too, but to his relief she didn't.

"We'll leave our underwear on while we shower," she told him somewhat shakily, and he knew this was embarrassing and difficult for her, too.

She turned on the water in the glass shower stall and adjusted the temperature, then turned on the spray and helped him step under it. She told him to hang on to the shower head while she undressed.

He could hear her in back of him shedding her saturated clothes while the blissfully hot water poured over his shivering body, and in less than a minute she joined him under the stinging spray.

He had water in his eyes and didn't see her immediately, but when his vision cleared he couldn't pull his glance away. It wasn't as if he'd never seen a woman in skimpy underwear before, but this one was an original! She had all the standard equipment, but somehow hers was more shapely and enticing, to say nothing of soul-stirringly sexy.

She was wearing a pink-and-rose-printed silk bra and matching panties with cream-colored lace trim. Her breasts were full and gave the impression of spilling out of their confinement without actually doing so. Her waist was small and trim, and her hips and butt burgeoned gently under the flowered silk covering, sending his imagination into over-drive, picturing the delights they promised.

To his horror his own equipment sprang to pulsating life. He turned away from her abruptly so that she wouldn't see what she did to him and almost lost his precarious balance in the process.

"Be careful," she warned as she grabbed him around the waist from the back. "If you fall in here you'll almost surely do more damage to your head."

That wasn't the only place that was going to be damaged if he didn't get his libido under control! Her bare flesh pressing against his was an oasis of heaven amid the flames of Hades.

By the time the water was cool, he was presentable again. They got out of the shower stall, and she handed him one of the thick terry towels hanging on the rod, then wrapped herself in the other one.

"Put that around you," she said, "then sit down on the closed commode lid while I find us some dry clothes."

She looked at him. "Is this your house? Are the clothes in the closet and dresser yours and your wife's?"

She caught him off guard, but he answered without having to think. "I don't have a wife."

Somehow he knew that was the truth, and he decided there was no sense in trying to hide his memory loss from her. "I don't know...if the clothes are mine...but they'll probably fit."

She frowned. "What do you mean, you don't know?"

"Just what I said. I'll tell you...after we get dressed."

She hesitated a moment, then turned and walked out of the room, closing the door behind her to keep the steamy warmth in the bathroom as long as possible.

He pushed his briefs down over his narrow hips, then sat and worked them down his legs and onto the floor. At least she wouldn't have to perform that indignity for him, he thought as he dried himself, then wrapped the towel around his waist.

Kate pulled the big thirsty towel closer around her as she stepped out of the warm bathroom and into the cold hall. In the bedroom a hurried search of the closet and drawers turned up two fleecy sweat suits, several pairs of woolen ski-type socks and long thermal underwear, and a pair of men's fur-lined bedroom slippers. All but the slippers were a generic size large.

Quickly she tossed her towel across the footboard of the bed and climbed into her half of the garments. They were big and bulky but blissfully dry and warm.

She picked up the rest of the clothes and headed for the bathroom. As she reached for the doorknob she hesitated. After all, the poor guy in there deserved some privacy. So far she'd given him precious little. She knocked instead.

"Come on in," he called, and she did.

He was sitting there with the towel wrapped around his hips and his soaked briefs lying on top of the other wet clothes on the floor. The knowledge that he had nothing on under that towel sent a flush of embarrassment through her, and for a moment she just stood there, unsure of how to proceed.

He needed help putting the clothes on, but would he welcome it from a woman he'd known less than a couple of hours? And for that matter, was she up to performing such an intimate function for a buck-naked male hunk who was a stranger?

Well, why not? She'd undressed him.

But not all the way.

She'd showered with him.

But they hadn't been totally nude.

He must have sensed her confusion, because the corners of his mouth turned up in a half smile. "I think I can manage...by myself," he said softly and held out his hand.

"Just hand me the clothes...and turn around. That way you can catch me...if I fall."

Kate felt both relieved and guilty. What was the matter with her? She was no teenage virgin, and he didn't seem especially disconcerted by the idea of her seeing his...his maleness. Besides, he had a head injury and was in pain. He probably didn't even think of her as a desirable woman, just a bossy nurse intent on tormenting him.

Still, she took the out he offered and handed him the set of long johns. "Here, put these on and then I'll help you with the sweat suit."

Still disgusted with herself, she picked up the pile of wet garments and put them in the sink, wiped up the puddle of water on the floor with another towel, then turned her back on him and waited.

It took him quite awhile, and a couple of times she asked if he needed assistance, but he insisted on doing it himself and finally told her she could turn around. He was wearing the thermal underwear, which he'd gotten on a little crooked here and there, and a frustrated look.

"I never would have thought...that putting on underpants and shirt...would be so difficult," he panted irately.

She smiled and picked up the sweatshirt. "Don't forget, you've been injured in an accident. I think you're doing wonderfully well, considering. Now, let me get this on you, then we'll tackle the sweatpants and socks."

It didn't take her long to finish dressing him, and then they took the slow trip back to the living room. When they got there, she arranged pillows at one end of the long couch so he could lie down. He sank onto it with a groan, and by the time she found a heavy blanket and covered him with it, he was asleep.

Kate sat down on the edge of the couch and looked at him closely, something she couldn't do when he was awake, without making them both uncomfortable. He was an extremely handsome man—now that she could see him without that helmet. His hair was dark brown, cut short and parted on the side, or it had been until he tousled it with the towel to dry it. His face was alarmingly white and drawn, but he seemed reasonably coherent.

Careful not to wake him, she slid her fingers along his throat until she felt a pulse point. She kept them there. The beat was fast but steady. She couldn't time it because her watch had been broken.

Reluctantly she took her hand away. She liked touching his bare skin. It had felt firm and a little grainy when she'd stripped his wet clothes off him, and in the shower it had felt warm as it did now.

She closed her eyes and relived the scene. In nothing but briefs, he had left little to the imagination. He had a body that would rival any sculpture, and his was warm flesh instead of cold marble. It was also muscles that rippled and arms that held her tenderly even as he leaned on her for support. His hands were big and the palms rough, but they handled her gently.

A wave of heat coursing through her blood jolted her, and her eyes flew open. My God, what was the matter with her? She was getting turned on by a stranger who was only partially conscious and wouldn't even tell her his name!

Quickly she rose and headed for the kitchen to try the telephone and light switch again. Neither of them worked. What was she going to do? She was a city girl who hated camping, and had never felt the need to take a course in wilderness survival. Without a phone and electricity she literally couldn't function!

Candles! Surely there must be candles around here somewhere. Even she knew that utilities could be pretty unreliable in a mountain storm, so people who had summer cabins usually kept auxiliary appliances on hand.

But not candles. Lanterns! That's it! Battery-operated lanterns.

She searched the house again and found three of them

in a cupboard in the laundry room. She turned them on and they worked!

Although the storm was still venting its fury, and the day was getting darker, she could see well enough to get around, so she turned the lanterns off. She didn't dare run the batteries down. Heaven only knows how long they'd be without power, and she didn't want to spend the night in total darkness.

She took the lanterns into the living room, and it was only then that she noticed the fireplace. A beautiful stone one that took up one full wall. Actually, she remembered seeing it when they came into the house, but she'd been so worried, upset and uncomfortable that she hadn't comprehended its importance.

It could provide both light and warmth.

On closer inspection she saw that a fire had been laid and was just waiting to be lit, while on the raised hearth stood a hammered copper box of extra logs.

She walked over to examine it more closely. It had a gas starter, but the pilot was off. She needed matches to light it, and found them in a decorated tin holder on the mantel.

It wasn't long before the fire was burning brightly, and she couldn't resist standing in front of it for a few minutes to let the heat penetrate the chill that seemed to have permeated all the way to her bones. Maybe the fire would dry out the air in the cabin and banish some of the dampness.

She spotted a redwood battery-operated clock on the wall ahead of her, and according to it the time was 3:30. She couldn't see out because of the shutters over the windows, but she could hear the wind and rain and knew that the storm had let up somewhat but was still raging.

For the next hour she divided her time between searching the cabin to familiarize herself with the food and medical supplies available, keeping an eye on her patient to be sure he was still breathing normally and checking to see if the phone and electricity had been restored. They hadn't.

By five o'clock her apprehension about Buddy had reached the unbearable stage. She was almost sure he was asleep, but he could also be unconscious, and the only way to find out was to wake him up. She hated to do that. If he was asleep at least he wasn't suffering, but if he was unconscious—!

She wasn't even going to think about that until she knew for sure one way or the other. She approached the couch and sat down on the edge of it. He had hardly moved at all, but his breathing was still even.

She reached out and put her hand on his forehead. The lamp wasn't lit, and she'd deliberately kept the fire low so as not to use the logs up too fast, but she could see that the flesh around his closed eyes was dark.

Black eyes! It looked as if someone had hit him and blackened both of them. She hadn't noticed that before. Did it have any significance? She seemed to remember reading that sometimes happened with a head injury.

The fear that had been ever present but controlled clutched at her again. When were they going to get the telephone lines fixed? He could die without medical care, and there was nothing she could do about it!

His forehead was cool, but he looked bruised and beaten.

Fighting back her terror, she put her hand on his shoulder and shook it gently as she called his name.

He moved restlessly and turned his face away from her.

Encouraged, she repeated the effort. "Buddy, it's Kate," she said softly. "Wake up. I need to know that you're all right. Please, open your eyes and talk to me."

He rolled his head back toward her and slowly blinked his eyes open. She saw no recognition in them.

She stroked his cheek, hoping he might remember her touch, and tried again. "I'm Kate. Remember? Your motorcycle smashed into my car on the highway. You have a head injury."

He raised his arm out from under the blanket and put his

hand over hers, imprisoning it against his cheek. "Katherine?" he muttered, and she remembered that she'd introduced herself as Katherine Brown.

Weak with relief she smiled. "Yes. My name is Katherine, but my friends call me Kate."

He smiled back. "I remember," he said faintly, and cleared his throat. "You're...not easy...to forget."

Thank God he was coherent! He didn't seem to have lost any ground while he slept.

"Is your headache any better?" she asked anxiously.

He closed his eyes and grimaced. "No."

"I found some acetaminophen tablets in the medicine cabinet in the bathroom. I'm pretty sure it would be safe to give you a couple. I'll get them."

She got up and went after the pills. When she returned with them and a glass of water, she found him sitting on the edge of the couch with his elbows on his thighs and holding his head in his hands.

In her anxiety she slammed the pills and glass on the coffee table when she sat down beside him. "You should have waited to sit up until I was here to help you."

Her tone was strident, but it was from fear rather than anger. "You could have fallen."

"I'll be all right," he groaned. "Just give me a minute."

Feeling contrite, she put her hand on his arm. "I'm sorry. I didn't mean to scold, but I'm so worried about you."

He raised his head from his hands and looked at her. "That...that's very kind," he said softly. "But you shouldn't. The accident wasn't your fault. I'm the...the irresponsible bastard who ran into you. Remember?"

He looked so remorseful that she couldn't trust herself to answer without her voice breaking. Instead she picked up the pills and glass and held them out to him. "Here, take these. They're not very strong, but they might make the pain more bearable."

He took them from her and swallowed them, then set the glass on the table.

"Now, why don't you lie down again while I rustle up some supper?" she suggested. "I haven't had anything to eat all day and I'm hungry."

"Fine," he said, "but will you help me...walk to the bathroom first?"

"Sure," she said, and reached down to help him stand.

She left him at the bathroom door and went into the kitchen to find something that could be eaten without being cooked.

She came up with a can of pork and beans and another of sliced peaches, as well as a box of wheat wafers. There was a six-pack of beer still cold in the refrigerator, but she wasn't going to mention that to him.

The advisability of giving him the medication was iffy, but she knew he shouldn't have alcohol.

She heard the bathroom door open and hurried to help him back to the couch, but when they got there he wouldn't lie down again. Instead he insisted on sitting up.

"I can't eat lying down" was his excuse. "I see you...built a fire in the fireplace."

"Yes," she said, "and it really helps. It doesn't throw the heat very far, but it makes this room a little warmer and a lot more cheerful."

She found a hand-operated can opener and within a few minutes had the meal, such as it was, dished up, and she carried it into the living room on a tray. She set it on the coffee table and handed him a plate, then sat down beside him with her own.

"It's not exactly a banquet, but it's the best I could do," she apologized.

He swallowed a spoonful of beans. "Tastes fine," he assured her. "Mom always insists we restock...the cupboards after we've been up here."

Kate pounced on that admission. "Then you do own this cabin." It was a statement, not a question.

He looked momentarily surprised. "Yes...I guess we do. It belongs to the...the family."

She was more than a little put out with him. Why all the secrecy? "Whose family?"

For a moment he hesitated. "Mom and Dad...Diane, Douglas and me." He rattled the names off as if he'd just memorized them and wasn't sure he'd remembered them right.

"Are Diane and Douglas your brother and sister?"

He picked up his bowl of peaches. "Yes," he said, and put a spoonful of the fruit in his mouth.

Why was she having to drag this information out of him? It wasn't as if she was asking him to reveal secrets about national security.

"Why didn't you tell me this when I asked you earlier?"

He closed his eyes for a moment. "Because I...I couldn't remember. I...I don't remember my name, either. Or my address...except Portland."

A new wave of anxiety mixed with compassion washed over her. This was a complication she hadn't anticipated and had known nothing about. "I'm so sorry. That must be pure hell."

He looked at her, and she saw the anguish in his expression. "It is. At first I...I didn't want to tell you."

She felt guilty about her earlier impatience. "I'm glad you did tell me. These are things I have to know so that at the very least I don't do you any harm. I'm sure your memory will come back soon."

She tried to sound encouraging, but she had no idea how much devastation had been wrought to his head by his collision with the tree.

She picked up her plate again, but her appetite had fled. "Kate, I know I had a...a billfold in my jeans pocket.

My driver's license…and credit cards were in it. Is it still there?''

It hadn't even occurred to her to check his pockets, but then again, she'd even forgotten to look for her own purse. She hoped it was still out there somewhere. "I don't know but I'll see," she said, and put her plate down again as she stood up and headed for the bathroom.

She rummaged through the pockets of his dripping clothes, but found nothing in his jeans, and only a fountain pen, a handkerchief and an army knife, the kind with all sorts of gadgets on it, in a zippered pocket in his jacket. No billfold, either with or without identification.

"The wallet must have been thrown out of your jeans on impact. It's probably lying in a puddle at the accident site," she told him when she returned. "I'll go over and look for it in the morning, but I doubt any of the contents will be legible after the soaking they're getting."

After that, they ate in silence until he put his plate down with at least half its contents untouched.

"Don't you like baked beans?" she asked.

"It's not that," he assured her. "It's just that my…my stomach's a little queasy and I don't feel hungry."

Alarm flooded through her, and she put her plate down, too. "When did that start?"

He reached out and took her hand in his. "Don't worry," he said. "It's all right. It's not unusual to be nauseated…after a head injury."

She liked the feel of his big hand engulfing hers. "How do you know?" she asked suspiciously.

He grinned. "I used to be a Boy Scout. Went clear up to…to Eagle, and took several…first-aid courses on the way."

"You could have told me," she muttered.

He squeezed her hand. "Why? I had no complaints. You're doing just fine. Hope they don't…fix the phone…till we get better acquainted."

"Oh, please, don't say that!" she cried, superstitiously afraid that if he joked about his injury, he would be tempting fate. "A blow to the head is nothing to make light of. We've got to get you to a hospital—"

Before she could suspect what he was going to do, he'd put his arms around her and cradled her close against him. "Whoa, Katie, I didn't mean to upset you. I know it could be serious, but I don't think it is. You've been taking such great care of me that I'm not worried. I enjoy your tender loving attention, and I'm not in any hurry to give it up."

She couldn't believe what she was hearing, and it wasn't just his declaration, but she was too befuddled to figure out what. "But the pain—"

His arms tightened around her and he leaned against the back of the sofa, taking her with him. "Ah, yes, the pain," he murmured. "I admit I could do without that, but those pills you gave me helped quite a lot. Besides, it will probably go away on its own in a few days even without treatment."

As he spoke, Kate began to realize what it was that puzzled her. It wasn't what he was saying, it was the way he said it!

"Buddy, listen to yourself!" she commanded.

He stopped abruptly. "What?"

"I said, 'Listen to yourself!'" she repeated. "You've been talking nonstop for the past few minutes with never a stammer or a hesitation. You're speaking normally again."

His eyes widened as he looked at her. "Well, I'll be damned! I was so eager to reassure you that I didn't have time to think about what I was going to say. It just came tumbling out. Is that a miracle or what?"

Kate cuddled against him. "Well, I wouldn't go that far," she said, "but I think it's a good sign."

He rubbed his cheek in her hair. "Whatever, I hope the cure is permanent."

Kate would have liked to stay in his arms all evening, but she knew that getting too chummy with him was a stupid thing to do. Sure, they were strongly drawn to each other, but it was based on sympathy on her part and gratitude on his. They were both needy after the shock of the accident and would have been attracted to anybody who offered comfort.

Reluctantly she muttered something about stirring up the fire, and stood.

By eight o'clock Kate was exhausted and beginning to ache from the shaking up she'd endured in the accident. Although he wouldn't admit it, she could see that Buddy was tired and aching, too. Also, in spite of the fire, it was getting colder inside as the temperature dropped outside and the wind and rain, although abating, continued on.

At first he argued against her insistence that she would sleep on the sofa and he could have the roomier bed in the bedroom. She finally convinced him that since she was uninjured, and her reflexes were quicker, she was the one who should keep an eye on the fire.

"I won't build it up again," she said, "but it will take quite awhile for it to go completely out, and even with the screen in place I'll feel safer if I'm out here to watch it."

He grumbled but acknowledged that she had a point and allowed her to help him get ready for bed. They agreed that for warmth they should sleep in the clothes they had on, so when he'd finished in the bathroom she helped him into the bedroom and took off his slippers.

"Did you take your pain pills?" she asked as she leaned over the bed and pulled the blanket and quilt up around his shoulders.

"Yes," he said tersely.

"And do you promise to call me if you need anything during the night?" She knew she was treating him like a child, but she had to be sure he understood that he wasn't to try getting up and wandering around by himself in the dark.

"Yes, Mama," he grumbled. "And will *you* call me if there's anything you need?"

She knew he was being sarcastic, but she also understood that by being so dependent on her his pride was taking a beating.

"Of course I will," she said tenderly and caressed his cheek with her hand. "Good night. Sleep well."

Before he could respond, she straightened and was gone.

Although she was tired and aching, Kate found it difficult to sleep. She kept dozing off then waking up, and every little noise startled her; she was afraid it was Buddy needing help.

As the fire burned lower, the house got darker until, as the blaze was replaced by ashes, the cabin was pitch-black. It was also icy cold, and she hadn't been able to find more blankets.

She'd left one lantern on the bedside table for Buddy and had another one on the coffee table beside her, but she didn't want to turn it on. She couldn't risk having it burn out in case his condition deteriorated during the night and she needed all the light she could get.

Kate dozed, then was wakened again by a noise. Could it have been Buddy?

She listened for a while but it wasn't repeated. It was probably just mountain forest noises from outside—nocturnal animals coming out to play and scrounge for food, or maybe something rustling in the trees.

As she lay there listening, she realized what it wasn't. It wasn't the storm. There was no sound of wind or rain.

Maybe the power was back on!

Quickly she sat up and felt for the lantern. Turning it on, she scrambled off the couch, threw her blanket around her shivering shoulders and took the lantern with her to the kitchen where she picked up the telephone.

Her heart sank. Still no dial tone. The same with the electricity. No lights.

She hadn't yet identified the source of the noise so she picked up the lantern and tiptoed into the bedroom to check on Buddy.

He was lying quietly under the covers, but when she got to the side of the bed she saw that his eyes were open and he was watching her.

"I heard a noise," she told him. "Are you all right?"

"I'm cold," he said, "and I know you are, too."

She pulled her blanket closer. "Yes, I am. I'd hoped it wouldn't be necessary to start up the fire again, but..."

"There's another solution," he announced.

She was surprised. "Oh? Do you know where there are more blankets?"

"No, but I know that two bodies generate more heat than one." He turned toward her and held up his covers. "There's no sense in both of us freezing. Come to bed with me, Katie, and we'll keep each other warm."

Chapter Three

Kate stared at Buddy, too surprised to react. What was going on here? Just what was he suggesting?

"Come on, Kate," he said impatiently. "Stop looking at me as though I were proposing something kinky, and get in here before we both freeze. I can assure you I'm really not up to an orgy tonight."

He was right, of course. Now she was the one who was behaving like an outraged virgin.

Quickly she spread her blanket on top of the quilt, turned off the lantern, set it on the floor and climbed into his waiting arms. He held her with one arm while he adjusted the covers over them with the other.

"Now, isn't that better?" he asked as he wrapped her in both arms and cuddled her close. "I promise not to come on to you."

Better? It was fantastic! His clothing was warm against hers, and his embrace was strong but tender. He'd held her several times today while she struggled to keep him upright and walking, but this was different. The storm was over and they'd be able to reach help soon. Desperation was gone, along with the battle to survive, and they were both relaxed and at peace.

"I know you won't," she assured him. "It's just that you took me by surprise. I've been propositioned before by men I hardly knew, and I just automatically refuse...."

"I'm sure you have," he murmured. "I'd be surprised if you hadn't. I don't seduce women I don't know well, but you have no way of knowing that, so you were right to hesitate. This is a matter of survival, though. I think we can both remember that."

Kate wasn't so sure. So far, this man who had come out of nowhere and nearly killed them both was fast winning not only her approval but her admiration, as well. A few more days alone with him and he wouldn't have to go to the trouble of seducing her. She'd do *her* best to entice *him*.

"Sleep well, my angel," he whispered against her ear just before she felt him relax in sleep.

It took her only a few minutes to do the same as she snuggled into his blessed warmth.

Twice after that she was vaguely aware of their changing positions. Once he curled around her back, and the other time she curled around his, but she didn't wake up again until the cabin was filled with the light of a sunny morning. Even though the shutters on the windows were still closed, she could almost feel the warmth of the sun.

So strong was her imagination that she even thought she smelled fresh-perked coffee. She turned her head to see if Buddy was still sleeping.

The bed beside her was empty!

"Buddy!" she yelled, terrified that he'd gotten up sometime during the night and fallen. "Buddy, where are you?"

She threw back the covers and jumped out of bed just

seconds before she heard him call back. "I'm all right, Katie, I'm in the living room."

The sudden movement brought an onslaught of pain from tormented muscles, especially across the shoulders and neck, that had knotted up during the night. Obviously she wasn't going to come out of that accident as undamaged as she'd thought. While she slept, her ligaments had tightened in protest of the shaking and pressure they'd received earlier.

She grimly ignored it and raced across the cabin to find Buddy sitting in one of the recliner chairs by the fireplace with a mug in his hand.

"What are you doing up?" Her irritation was evident in her tone, although relief was the stronger of the two emotions that warred within her. "I told you to call me if there was anything you needed."

He smiled at her. "I would have, but there was no need. I'm getting around better this morning, so when I checked the electricity and found it on, I turned up the heat and made some coffee."

"The electricity's on!" she gasped. No wonder it felt warmer in here. "And the telephone? Did you call 911?"

"No, sorry. The phone lines are still down, but at least we can cook and keep warm. Why don't you get a cup of coffee and join me?"

Instead, she crept closer to him, concern still outweighing his assurance. "Are you really feeling better? Did you sleep well last night?"

He grinned and drew a cross with his finger on the left side of his chest. "Cross my heart," he said. "And once I got you in my arms I slept like a baby. But that doesn't mean I don't still need you. I'm not a bumbling invalid anymore, but I can get around without help only if I'm slow and careful."

For some reason his admission that he still needed her made her feel better. She rationalized it by telling herself it was because it would make him easier to handle. If he agreed that he still needed help, he wouldn't be so insistent about doing things for himself.

She went into the kitchen to get some coffee and checked the phone again. Still no dial tone.

When she came back to the living room she realized it would be a lot more pleasant in the house if the window shutters were opened.

"Is it all right if I open the shutters?" she asked.

He frowned. "You'll get your feet wet if you go outside. You haven't any dry shoes."

She wasn't going to be deterred by that. "It's okay. There are more clean dry socks in the drawer."

She put her mug on the coffee table, then walked over to the door and opened it. "I'll just push back the ones that front onto the porch," she assured him.

The view outside was breathtaking. The clear sky, the brilliant sun and the forest of green trees still dripping raindrops from their leaves and needles all belied the rampaging storm of only a few hours earlier.

The cabin wasn't set up as high as it had seemed yesterday when they were struggling to get up the hill, but it was elevated enough to get a sweeping view of the area with the highway winding through the bottom of it.

She couldn't see the wreck from her vantage point. It was hidden by the trees and brush, and she wondered if passengers in the cars that went by could see it from the road. If so, surely someone would call to report it. There was hardly any traffic now, but it was bound to pick up later in the day.

On the other hand, even if it was reported, would the highway patrol check the cabins nearby? They were set quite a way off the thoroughfare, and since there were no bodies or injured people at the crash scene, they might assume it had already been investigated and not bother.

With a sigh Kate opened the shutters and hoped the phone would be fixed soon.

Back in the house she was delighted by the difference the sunlight made. The living room was bright and cheerful and seemed much larger. The view from the wide window expanded their horizons and chased away the feeling of being closed in and confined.

"Excuse me while I change my socks," she said as she hurried through the living room on her way to the bedroom. "Do you feel well enough to eat now, and do we have anything that resembles breakfast food?"

"I'm starved," he called after her. "There's cereal but no milk, and no eggs or bacon, but there is bread and orange juice in the freezer."

Kate put on dry socks, then went back in the living room and picked up her coffee mug to take with her to the kitchen, but he stopped her before she could leave.

"Sit down for a minute, and I'll tell you my good news," he said gleefully.

"Good news?" She turned toward the kitchen. "Do you mean the phone's finally working?"

"No, no," he said hurriedly, "it's nothing like that, but it's almost as welcome. I woke up this morning with my memory intact!"

That *was* good news! It meant that the damage to his thought processes wasn't permanent.

"Do you mean you know your name and who you are now?" she asked as she sank down on the sofa and picked up her cup.

"Yes. My name is Burk Sinclair, I'm thirty-six years old and president of the family business in Portland."

Kate's hand jerked, as did all her other muscles, and she dropped her cup, spilling coffee over the table and onto the floor.

Burk Sinclair! No, that's not possible!

"Katie, what's the matter?" He pushed down the footrest on the recliner and started to get up, but she quickly reassured him.

"No, please don't get up! I'm sorry, it just slipped out of my hand. I'll wipe it up." She was on her feet and into the kitchen before he could reply.

Her knees shook and she clutched at the sink for support. That man couldn't be Burk Sinclair! The odds against their literally running into each other like this were astronomical. It couldn't happen. There must be some mistake.

Besides, Buddy didn't look like Burk Sinclair. She'd never seen him in person, but she'd seen pictures of him. He and his family were VIP's in Portland. They owned a chain of computer stores and even developed and manufactured a computer under their own logo. They were rich and he and his wife...uh, ex-wife...had frequently been pictured in the newspapers and on television at various charity fund-raisers.

Burk had a short beard. At least he did five years ago when he more or less ran Kate out of town! However, if he'd shaved it off, that would change his appearance.

He'd never seen her, either, nor did he know her name, but she'd never forget the terror she'd felt as she hid in the conference room adjoining her editor's office and heard his threat.

"You son of a bitch." His tone had been low and menacing. *"You can't go around wrecking peoples lives and calling it the public's right to know. I'm going to ruin you and that reporter you're protecting. It doesn't matter that you won't tell me who he is. I'll find him and make him wish he'd never messed with me."*

Burk had thought the reporter who exposed his secret plans was a man. That was undoubtedly the only reason he hadn't caught up with her in the intervening years.

She'd moved to Denver and given up journalism to get away from him, and now, five years later, they'd been physically thrown into each other's arms!

Coincidences like that didn't happen—it was too far-out.

His voice from behind her made her jump. "Katie, what's the matter? Are you sick?"

She whirled around so fast that her head began to swim, and she tottered. Buddy caught her in his arms. "Honey, what happened? You're trembling."

He was Buddy, not Burk. She couldn't, mustn't think of him as Burk. "I—I'm sorry," she stammered. "I guess the trauma of yesterday is just catching up with me. I'll be okay—"

"Damn right you will," he growled into the side of her throat. "I'll see to it. Where do you want to go to lie down—the bedroom or the living room?"

All she wanted was to stand here and let him hold her. She felt safe in his arms. If only she could just melt against him and let him protect her.

Yeah. Sure. Protect her from himself? He was the only person who threatened her security, and he'd be bent on doing her real damage once he found out who she was!

She forced herself to push away from him. "I'm not sick, really. It was just a momentary dizziness. Let me help you back to the living room and clean up what I spilled, then I'll fix us some toast and orange juice."

Before he could protest, she put her arm around his waist and led him out of the room. She settled him back in his chair, all the while ignoring his insistence that she didn't have to wait on him anymore, then cleaned off the coffee table and fixed their breakfast.

While they ate, she encouraged him to talk about himself. Her grandmother had kept her up-to-date on what was public knowledge about the Sinclair family. She knew the tabloid had mysteriously gone out of business shortly after that, but to the best of her knowledge he'd never found his ex-wife and his little girl.

Kate still felt a surge of guilt when she thought about it. She'd done him a terrible disservice. How he would hate her if he knew who she was. She had to get away from him as soon as possible! The growing attraction between them could destroy them both if it wasn't nipped in the bud.

"I believe you said you have brothers and sisters?" She knew the answers to her questions, but didn't want him to know that.

"Yeah, a younger sister, Diane, and brother, Douglas. Di is divorced and has a daughter, and Doug has a wife and two small sons."

"And your parents?" Kate prodded.

He took a sip of his coffee. "Dad's CEO of the business, and Mom's a retired high school English teacher. She keeps busy now as a volunteer tutor in the poorer school districts."

Kate remembered that the senior Sinclairs had been the moving force behind several charities and civic projects. They were a nice family. No public scandals except for Burk's ill-fated custody suit, and that was Kate's fault.

One wrong decision and she had cost Burk his daughter!

She wrenched her attention back to the present. It hurt too much to think of the past. "That's very generous of your mother," Kate said, and meant it sincerely.

"I don't think she looks at it that way." There was affection and pride in his tone. "She loves kids and she likes teaching, but she didn't want to do it full-time anymore. How about your family? Hey—I forgot to ask. You're not married, are you?"

She laughed. "No, I'm not and never have been. I don't have much family, either. Just my grandmother. I was an only child, and my parents were killed in a boating accident when I was seven. Grandpa and Grandma took me in and raised me, but Grandpa died ten years ago, so now there's just Grandma and me."

She saw compassion in Buddy's—*Burk's* expression. "I'm sorry. Family can be a pain once in a while, but mostly they're a blessing. We all go our separate ways a lot, but everyone gathers around when there's trouble or a loss.''

She knew he spoke from experience. His family had stood beside him all during the bitter custody hearing, and afterward when he'd set out to extract revenge through the civil suit.

She nodded and hurriedly changed the subject before he could ask another question. She didn't want to give him much information about herself. That could be downright dangerous if he ever suspected she was the reporter he'd been looking for all these years.

"Excuse me," she said, and stood up. "I'm going to try the telephone again."

This time she got a dial tone!

She practically shouted the good news to Burk as she dialed 911 and got an answer. She explained the situation to the operator and asked for a helicopter to take them to a hospital.

"They're coming," she called as she raced back to the living room. "The highway patrol will be here in a few minutes, but the Medevac helicopter is coming from Eugene so it will take about half an hour. I'll straighten up the house—"

"Don't worry about the cabin," he ordered. "Mom has a housecleaning service from Bend that will come in and clean it. I'll call them as soon as I get home."

Kate tried to argue but he was adamant, and the whole conversation was moot a few minutes later when a highway patrol officer knocked on the door.

They invited him in and he took their report while another officer surveyed the scene of the wreck. One thing Kate learned during the questioning was why Burk was out in that storm on his motorcycle. She'd been so upset on finding out who he was that she'd forgotten to ask why he had been at the cabin.

"When things get too noisy and hectic at the office and at home, I sometimes come up here just to get away from it all," he told the officer.

"Sounds like a great idea," the policeman replied. "But why were you out in that storm?"

Burk made a self-deprecating face. "Just plain stupid on my part. I had an important date Sunday night, and I'd promised the lady I'd be home in plenty of time. When the storm showed no sign of letting up, I decided to leave anyway. I figured I'd run out of the bad weather not too far down the road.

"Frankly, I didn't realize how severe it was until I was out in it, and I misjudged the distance of the driveway. I was on the highway before I realized it and slammed the Harley into Ms. Brown's car. Thank the Lord she wasn't hurt!"

Kate felt a twinge of dismay. So that was why he'd been in such a hurry to get back to Portland. He had a heavy date. Was she his fiancée? His significant other? Did he love her? If he was involved with another woman, why hadn't he told Kate?

That last sentence brought her back to her senses. What right did Kate have to expect him to tell her about his love life? She was nothing to him but a ministering "angel" whom he needed to lean on until help arrived.

Now help was coming, and within hours he'd be reunited with the woman he'd been so eager to get back to that he'd nearly killed himself and Kate in his hurry. Kate would probably never see him again after he was admitted to the hospital and she was sent on her way. Their insurance agents would handle any claims.

The muted hum that had been buzzing in Kate's head finally got through to her, and she recognized it as the sound of a helicopter. Help wasn't just coming, it was here!

"That'll be the paramedics," the officer announced, and stood up to look out the window. "Our men are blocking off the highway now. They'll land there and bring a stretcher up for you.''

He turned to look at Kate. "Are you going with him, ma'am?''

Burk answered before she could gather her thoughts. "Of course she is. She was badly shaken in that accident, and will need medical attention, too.''

It hadn't occurred to her that she might not be flown to the hospital with him, but actually there was no need for her to go. She wasn't injured, and she knew his insurance company would rent her a car. She could get a ride back to Bend with the highway patrolman and pick one up there, then drive on to Portland.

"Oh, I don't think that will be necessary—'' she protested, but Burk cut her off.

"It's necessary and it's nonnegotiable, Katie,'' he insisted. "As soon as we've been examined by a doctor in Eugene, I'll make arrangements for a charter plane to fly us back to Portland.''

She wasn't wild about his proprietary tone, but it was the quickest and easiest way to get home. "If you're sure that's what you want...''

His expression relaxed and his tone softened. "It's what I want. I'm not going to let you get away from me until I'm sure you're all right.''

The corners of his mouth turned up in a half smile. "Besides, I need you. I told you that this morning. Remember?''

Remember? How could she forget? Waves of heat washed over her when he said things like that, and she felt a powerful yearning to give him anything he wanted from her.

"The chopper's landed,'' the officer reported from his position at the window, "and the paramedics are on their way up here with the stretcher.''

It took only a few minutes for the medics to strap Burk

on the stretcher, carry him to the helicopter and slide him in. Kate asked the officer to watch for Burk's wallet and her purse when they searched the crash sight and to keep them safe until they could be claimed.

Both she and Burk thanked the officer, and she got in front with the pilot while the medics stayed in back with the patient.

Within half an hour they landed on a helipad at a hospital in Eugene and were taken to the emergency room. It was busy, but there was none of the chaotic confusion that was portrayed on medical dramas on TV.

Kate had never been in an emergency room before, and she found it fascinating in a formidable sort of way. An orderly wheeled Burk's gurney into a curtained cubicle, then told Kate to follow him, and started to walk away.

"Where are we going?" she asked, and eyed Burk anxiously.

"To another cubicle," the orderly answered. "You need to be examined, too, don't you?"

She was sure there was nothing wrong with her, but since she was there she might as well let them check her. It would probably be necessary for an insurance claim. "Yes, all right, but give me a few minutes first."

The orderly shrugged. "I'll be back," he said, and walked away.

She went over to the gurney and looked down at Burk. He was pale, and there were lines of fatigue around his mouth. All the activity had been hard on him, and again fear rose in her. His was not a minor injury, and he needed rest and freedom from stress. She was glad he was finally in a hospital where he could get a medical evaluation and treatment.

He reached for her hand and brought it to his mouth. Gently he kissed her palm then held it to his cheek. "Don't go away and leave me," he said softly.

Her heart turned over, and she leaned down and kissed

his forehead. "I'm not going to leave you until there are members of your family around to take charge," she assured him. "Do you want me to call your parents? Or maybe your...your girlfriend?" She had trouble forcing that last word out.

His brooding gaze roamed over her face. "No girlfriends. I'll call Dad myself after I know how serious my injuries are. Promise you won't skip out on me?"

It bothered her that he was so insistent that she stay with him. Did he think she'd just walk away and leave him with no one to see that he was well taken care of?

Well, maybe he did. He had no way of knowing what she was really like. He'd known her only about twenty-four hours, and most of that time he was only marginally conscious or asleep.

She tried for a smile. "You'll have to beat me off with a stick to get rid of me," she teased.

Just then a man wearing blue scrubs and a name tag with Gordon Westover, M.D. printed on it came in, followed by the orderly. "Mr. Sinclair, I'm Dr. Westover," he said. "I'm going to examine you now. If the young lady will step out to the waiting room—"

"No!" Burk's tone was firm and decisive. "She's been taking care of me ever since the accident about this time yesterday, and I want her here now."

Kate saw the doctor frown. She pulled her hand away from Burk's and straightened up. "I'm Katherine Brown, Dr. Westover," she said. "I was in the accident, too, and I think this attendant has come to escort me to an examining room."

She indicated the orderly who nodded, then she turned to Burk. "I'll be back as soon as they're through with me," she assured him. "Don't worry, if you're in X ray or somewhere, I'll find you."

It was two hours later before Kate caught up with Burk again. Her own examination had revealed nothing but a few scratches and bruises, but Burk had been shifted from one area to another for various tests. She had been consigned to a waiting room where a volunteer poured coffee and dispensed information about patients in surgery or other treatment rooms as it was phoned in to her.

At first Kate sat quietly and glanced through a magazine, then she started to fidget. What was taking so long? Was his injury even more serious than she'd thought? As her anxiety mounted she took to questioning the poor volunteer, who kept explaining that she wouldn't know anything until a report was phoned in from the attending physician.

But what was taking so long? Had the powers that be forgotten she was waiting? Were they doing emergency surgery on him? Why didn't they at least phone in a progress bulletin now and then?

By the time her call finally came, she was pacing the floor and making everyone else in the room nervous.

The volunteer put down the phone with a look of profound relief and smiled. "Ms. Brown, Mr. Sinclair is back in the emergency room and you may see him now."

Kate tore out of there without even remembering to thank the woman.

Burk was still lying on the gurney when she hurried into the stall. Dr. Westover was with him. Both of them looked upset, and she caught her breath and made an effort to brace herself for bad news as she glanced from one to the other.

"S-sorry," she stammered, knowing she must seem like an overprotective mother, or worse, a woman deeply in love with the patient. Her hair was tousled, her face was flushed, she was in stocking feet and wearing a too-big sweat suit that not only looked as if it had been slept in, but actually had been.

"I...I've been worried," she explained to the room in general. "It took so long."

She looked at the doctor. "Will he be all right?"

Burk reached out and took her hand. He looked exhausted. "We're going home," he said, and squeezed her hand.

Again she looked at the doctor. "You're going to release him?" She found that hard to believe.

"Not exactly," Dr. Westover said tersely. "We've found no sign of a fracture, but the scan shows a contusion—that is, a bruising of the brain tissue—and a subdural hematoma, which is a blood clot inside the skull. He needs to be in a hospital where he can be closely watched for a few days, but he insists on going to Portland."

"Now wait a minute," Burk protested. "You're making it sound worse than it is. I've agreed to go to the hospital as soon as I get back home."

The doctor glowered. "An agreement isn't enough. I'll release you from this hospital only if arrangements are made before you leave to check you into one in Portland, and for an ambulance to meet your plane and transport you there immediately. I won't be responsible for you otherwise."

Chapter Four

Burk slept through most of the flight to Portland on the ambulance plane while Kate sat beside him and held his hand. They were on the last leg of the journey home that they'd started separately but would complete together after a twenty-four-hour delay.

The kicker was in that twenty-four hours. Kate was positive that interval had made a lasting impression that could cause her much regret and not a little grief.

How could she have become so attached to a man she'd never met until yesterday and who had turned out to be her sworn enemy, although he didn't know that yet?

She shuddered and stroked a lock of brown hair off his forehead. The area around his eyes was now swollen and a deep dark maroon in color, and his head injury was every bit as bad as she'd feared it was. Before they left the hospital he'd called his parents and talked to them. However, at the same time she'd called her grandmother to alert her to what had happened, so Kate didn't know what reaction Burk had gotten from his family.

In about fifteen more minutes they'd land at Portland International Airport, where he'd be met by an ambulance and taken to a hospital. She'd go with him to see that his admittance was assured and went smoothly, then she'd take a cab to her grandmother's house. There would be no reason for them to see each other again. Their insurance adjusters would take care of her claim against him.

She knew all this. She even accepted it, so why did she feel as if she were about to lose someone dear to her? She liked Buddy—*Burk*—but they were just two strangers whose paths happened to cross, albeit violently, for a few hours. It wasn't as if they were lovers, or even friends. They'd simply touched each other's lives for a brief period, and now it was time to stop fantasizing and move on.

Burk stifled a groan when the small airplane pitched and rolled as it prepared to land. Every jerky movement seemed magnified and made his head throb and his stomach lurch. God, but he'd be glad when he finally got home again! If it hadn't been for Katie and her steadying presence, the past few hours since their rescue would have been unbearable.

He hadn't known how rough a helicopter ride could be, nor had he fully realized just how much his energy had been depleted until they started shifting him around at the hospital and poking and probing his already-aching body. If they thought they were going to put him through all that again in a hospital in Portland, they were in for a rude awakening. He'd sign himself out, take Katie and go home to his condominium.

He didn't need anyone but her anyway. With her soothing voice and gentle touch she kept the pain demons that tormented him at bay. He could relax with her and sleep.

Last night he'd been restless and uncomfortable. Too

keyed-up to sleep, but too debilitated and dizzy to get up. Then she'd come to him, like an angel with a lamp. And when she climbed into bed and snuggled into his arms, the tension drained out of him and he slept straight through until morning.

Ah, yes, morning. That had been a different situation altogether. He'd wakened to find himself curled around her back with one hand cupping her magnificent breast and one leg caught between both of hers. She was relaxed in sleep, and her warm neck was damp against his face where it was nuzzled against her.

She'd been soft, and cuddly, and the faint musky aroma of woman tweaked his nose and sent his hormones into a fit of frenzy. He hadn't gotten that aroused that quickly since he was a teenager!

Resisting that hormonal command was the hardest thing he'd ever done, and he'd almost tripped and fallen in his rush to get out of the bed and out of the room before he gave in to it.

When they got around to making love, he wanted her fully awake and participating!

The plane bucked again, bringing him out of his erotic musing. He squeezed Kate's hand and wished he had the strength to tell her how much she meant to him, but he couldn't even open his eyes. The nurse had given him a shot just before they put him in the plane, but it hadn't done much to ease his discomfort. It just made him sick and too woozy to complain.

The descent brought on another onslaught of pain to his head, and the bump when the wheels touched the tarmac not only ripped a groan from him, but also every swear word he'd ever learned.

Kate murmured words of reassurance to Burk and disentangled her hand from his as the pilot and the paramedics from the waiting ambulance guided the stretcher out of the plane. Once on the ground, they quickly wheeled it across the tarmac to the emergency vehicle, where they were met by a large group of people. They all crowded around the stretcher, and it was apparent they were members of Burk's family.

One older man, a good-looking guy in his late fifties or early sixties, walked out to meet the stretcher as it came toward him. He introduced himself to the pilot as Robert Sinclair, father of the patient, and immediately took charge.

None of them paid any attention to Kate, who had been elbowed out of the way until she was bringing up the rear. They had the stretcher in the ambulance and Mr. Sinclair was about to hop in, too, when Kate reached it.

"Mr. Sinclair," she called. "Wait. Please. I need to talk to you—"

He turned around and glared at her distastefully. Not that she blamed him. She must look really grungy.

"Not now," he said angrily. "Can't you see that we're on our way to the hospital?

He climbed into the ambulance and closed the back doors as the vehicle's engine roared to life and took off, siren blaring, leaving Kate standing there alone and obviously unwanted. Well, that wasn't so surprising. Burk had his family gathered around him now. He didn't need her anymore.

It would have been thoughtful of him, though, if he'd asked if she had transportation home and said goodbye instead of leaving her there without a ride and no way to get one. She'd told Grandma she'd be returning to Portland sometime that night but she didn't know when.

She hadn't remembered at the time that she had no purse, and therefore no money for a cab, or even a quarter for a public telephone! She'd made the colossal mistake of relying on Burk Sinclair to see to it that she got home safely.

Despair and anger warred in her for dominance, and anger won. What kind of a man would con a woman with sweet words and tender gestures to get her to take care of him when he was alone and in need, then just abandon her in an airport without a word of thanks or even a hurried goodbye when his family came to his rescue?

That ought to teach her not to trust sexy, good-looking men. No wonder his wife had divorced him and run off with their daughter! At least now Kate could stop feeling guilty about her part in that abduction. He was probably a rotten father!

She strode into the terminal and found a bank of public telephones. She placed a collect call to her grandmother, who answered on the third ring.

"Grandma, I'm stranded at the airport with no money and no way to get home," she wailed on hearing Emily Kelly's familiar voice. "If I catch a cab, do you have enough cash to pay the fare when I get there?"

"Kathy, what's happened?" Emily asked anxiously, using the name Kate had been called as a child.

"I'll tell you when I get home," she said, too distraught to go into it now.

"All right, dear," Emily said. "I cashed a check today so don't worry. Just get here as quickly as you can."

The first two cabbies she hailed noticed that she looked like a homeless street person and had neither a purse nor luggage. They refused to take her unless she paid cash up front, but the third one wasn't as observant and took her without question.

It was a long ride from the airport to her grandmother's house and the driver's attention was focused on a radio talk show, so Kate settled back and tried to relax and get her revved-up emotions under control. She didn't want to upset Grandma any more than she had already.

Her grandmother had suffered a mild stroke shortly after her seventy-second birthday in February, and Kate had rushed home to be with her. Thank God it hadn't seriously damaged her, but it did slow her up and left her absent-minded at times. A fiercely independent woman, she had vetoed any suggestion to relocate, either to a senior citizen's apartment in Portland, or to live with Kate in Colorado. Finally, Kate had reluctantly given in and returned to Denver, leaving Grandma to live alone as she insisted on doing. There was really nothing else she could do. Grandma's health was good, and absentmindedness wasn't unusual in a person her age.

However, after a while she started forgetting to lock the doors at night, and she sometimes forgot to take her medicine. It was then that her best friends and longtime next-door neighbors, Laura and John Kirkpatrick, had started checking on her each morning and night.

The second time her car was involved in a fender bender because she got confused and ran a red light, Kate knew it was unsafe for the elderly woman to live alone any longer. She wasn't going to dislodge her from her house, however. Instead, Kate had started making arrangements to move back to Portland and once more share her grandmother's home, but this time Kate would take care of Grandma.

The generous and loving lady had taken Kate in and raised her when she had nobody else; now it was time to reciprocate. It was not only Kate's obligation but her pleasure.

She'd left Portland in the first place only because of Burk Sinclair. How absolutely bizarre that he should be the first person she ran into, both literally and figuratively, when she came back!

A glance out the window of the cab told her that they were about halfway to their destination. She loved Portland. It was home. Denver was okay, but she'd always felt like a visitor there. Portland was where her roots were.

She was fortunate to find a job here that was comparable to the one she'd held in Denver. She was a technical writer and she'd been working with classified material for the federal government. The fact that she already had security clearance and an outstanding performance rating had given her an edge when she applied for the position of manager of classified files with one of the big electronics companies that had a branch in Portland. She was due to start work next Monday.

A few minutes later, the taxi pulled up to the curb in front of the Kelly home, and Grandma, who had obviously been watching for them, came out with her purse and paid the tab. Twenty-five dollars plus a five-dollar tip, Kate noticed, and made a mental note to pay her back as soon as she could get to a bank and arrange for a transfer of money from her account in Denver.

Once inside the house, the two women hugged. They were about the same size, and there was a definite family resemblance. Their facial features were similar, with wide cheekbones and chins that sloped to a gently rounded point. Emily's hair was black, short and sprinkled with white, but Kate's was honey-colored as her mother's had been and she wore it long or loosely piled on top of her head. Tonight it resembled a rat's nest, but she was looking forward to a long leisurely bath, shampoo and blow dry that would make it, and her, once more soft and manageable.

"Kathy, honey, you look awful," Emily said as she held her granddaughter away so she could examine her. "For heaven's sake, you're not even wearing shoes. Where have you been? You said something about an accident? Are you hurt? I was expecting you yesterday."

"I know, Grandma," Kate acknowledged. "But there was no phone where we were. I'll tell you all about it, but first you promised you'd make me some of your homemade chicken vegetable soup. Did you? I haven't had a real meal since yesterday morning before I left Bend. I think I need nourishment."

"Of course I made the soup," Emily said and started toward the kitchen. "It was ready yesterday, but when you didn't come I put it in the refrigerator. I'll heat it while you talk. Now sit down at the table and tell me what happened."

Between bites of delicious thick hot soup and home-baked bread, Kate gave her grandmother a detailed account of almost everything that had happened to her during the past two days. She left out the part about her and Burk showering and sleeping together. Grandma was an up-to-date woman, but she wasn't quite *that* open-minded.

"So there I was," Kate concluded an hour later, "stranded in the airport in my stocking feet with no luggage, no purse and no money. I even had trouble getting a cabbie to take me as a passenger. I don't know what I'd have done if you hadn't had enough cash to pay my fare when I got here."

Emily frowned. "That was despicable of Burk Sinclair not to make sure you got home safely after all you'd done for him."

Kate shook her head. "I felt that way at first, too, but when I'd had a chance to cool down, I realized that he probably didn't even know I'd been left behind. It looked like the whole blasted Sinclair family had turned out to meet him, and his dad took charge the minute they got the stretcher off the plane. Don't forget, Burk has a serious head injury and he's not functioning on all six cylinders yet."

"That may be," Emily fumed, "but that doesn't excuse his father. Burk must have told Robert on the phone that you were with him. Even though Robert doesn't know you, he should have realized who you were when you tried to speak with him."

Kate had cooled down her outrage over the situation and was too tired to heat it up again. "Mr. Sinclair was badly upset," she explained. "His only thought was to get Burk to the hospital as fast as possible. I wanted that, too, so I didn't protest as hard as I should have. I just hope Buddy—Burk—will be all right."

"Yes, well..." Emily grumbled, then changed the subject. "What about your clothes? And all the other stuff you were bringing with you? You must have had the back of the car jammed with all the last-minute things you were moving from Denver. Was it all a loss?"

Kate sighed. "I have no idea, but the car was cracked wide open with the motorcycle embedded in it, and I'm pretty sure that anything in there that wasn't broken was destroyed by the downpour of rain. Burk has assured me that it will all be covered by his insurance, but it will probably take a long time to settle the claim."

She looked down at the baggy, too large sweat suit she was wearing. "Meanwhile, except for the out-of-season clothes I sent with the things I shipped, the outfit I have on is all I have to wear."

Emily grunted. "Well, we're both the same size so I can loan you one of my nighties and robes tonight, and I've got plenty of slacks and tops you can wear until we go shopping."

She put her hands on the table and pushed herself up to stand. "You look worn-out. Why don't you take a nice relaxing bath and go to bed? Are you sure the doctor in Eugene said you were all right?"

Kate smiled as a fuzzy feeling of warmth flooded through her. It was nice to have someone to look after her for a change.

"He said I could expect stiff and sore muscles for a while," she said as she tried to stand, then groaned when she discovered that he'd known what he was talking about. "But otherwise I'm in great shape."

Kate's first thought on waking the following morning was of Burk. Had he gotten through the night all right? Did he miss her? Or was he happily reunited with the woman he'd been speeding home to keep a date with when he ran his motorcycle into Kate's car?

She tried to push the questions out of her mind by telling herself she'd wait until after lunch and then call the hospital to inquire about his condition.

When she climbed out of bed, she found that her muscles had tightened up again, and she hobbled around the room like an old woman in the throes of arthritis. She didn't want her grandmother to see her like this so she went across the hall to the bathroom and turned the shower on full force and as hot as she could stand it, then got in and let the massage spray work its magic.

By the time the water cooled off, she was able to move around almost pain-free.

In the kitchen she hugged Emily, assured her she felt great and promptly broke her resolve to wait until later to inquire about Burk by going to the phone and ringing up the hospital.

"Good morning," she said, "I'd like some information on one of your patients."

"The patient's name?" said the crisp voice at the other end.

"Burk Sinclair. He was admitted last evening."

There was a short pause. "Are you a member of the family?"

Kate was caught off guard. "No. I...I'm a friend."

"Your name?"

Kate frowned. Why was this so difficult? She'd called hospitals before to inquire about patients who were friends of hers and never gotten this runaround.

"My name is Katherine Brown. Kate."

Another pause. "I'm sorry but I have no information on that patient," the voice finally told her.

No information? What did that mean? She knew this was the hospital they were supposed to take Burk to. "What do you mean by no information? He's registered there, isn't he? Has he been released already?"

"I'm sorry," the voice repeated, "but I can give you no

information. I suggest you contact a member of his family."

"But I—" A click at the other end told Kate that the phone had been disconnected.

A stab of fear gripped her. What was going on? Were Burk's injuries worse than they'd originally thought? Had he been transferred to a different hospital? Dear God, surely he wasn't—" No, she wasn't even going to consider that.

She dropped the phone in the cradle and went back to the kitchen. Her grandmother took one look at her and frowned. "Kathy, what's the matter? You're white as a sheet."

"I...I just called the hospital to ask about Burk and they said he wasn't there." She heard the panic in her tone but couldn't control it. "Grandma, I know he's there. I was standing at the desk when the hospital at Eugene made the arrangements to transfer him. You don't think something awful has happened and they don't want to tell me, do you?"

Emily poured coffee in two thick mugs. "Tell me exactly what was said."

Kate thought back and repeated the conversation.

When she finished Emily nodded. "Then the person didn't say Burk wasn't there, just that they had no information about him?"

Kate nodded. "Yes, that's right, but doesn't that mean—"

Emily handed her a mug and they both sat down at the table. "You don't need to worry. If you remember I worked as a volunteer auxiliary member at the information desk at one of the hospitals when you were in high school. When a patient didn't want it known that he was in the hospital, or what his condition was, a 'No Info.' notation was put on his admittance card. That meant that we were to tell anyone who inquired about him that we had 'no information' on that patient."

She patted Kate's clenched fist where it lay on the table. "It's no big deal, honey. It just means they're not admitting that the patient is there. It was almost routinely done for people in the public eye such as politicians, or celebrities, or business leaders. Burk fits in that last category. His father may have given the instructions without Burk even knowing about it."

Kate felt relieved but still not pleased. She suspected that during one of the pauses in their conversation the woman on the other end of the line was consulting a list of family and friends who could be given information about him. She sure should have been included on it! After all, she'd probably saved his life.

Meanwhile, at the hospital, Burk fumed with anger and impatience and was venting it all on Robert Sinclair.

"Dammit, Dad, what do you mean you haven't been able to find Katie? She lives here in Portland. All you have to do is look her name up in the phone book. That will give you her address and number."

Robert sighed wearily and stopped pacing the floor to stand beside the bed. "Hell, son, have you any idea how many Browns there are listed in the telephone book? Your mother and I have contacted every one of them, even woke some of them up, but none knew a Katherine Brown that fitted your description and specifications."

"Well, you're going to continue searching until you find her, or by hell I'm going to check out of here and do it myself," he threatened.

"Oh, don't be so damn stubborn," his father admonished. "There's not a thing you could do that we haven't already done. Are you sure she lives here? I checked with the highway patrol and they said she gave them a Denver address as her residence."

"Denver!" Burk thundered. "She never even mentioned

Denver to me. She said she lived in Portland...." He paused. "At least I think she did."

"Well, did she or didn't she?" Robert asked impatiently. "No wonder we can't find her in the Portland phone book."

Burk stomach muscles clenched with frustration and fear. "How in hell should I know? I thought she did. At least she didn't deny it or protest when I insisted that she come home with me." He grimaced. "My stupid brain was only functioning part of the time. Did you contact the Denver address?"

"Yes, of course I did," Robert rasped. "I called and got an operator who said that number had been disconnected. Look, I gather this Katie is a grown woman. She can take care of herself. Why don't you just relax and wait? She's bound to contact your insurance company pretty quick. When she does, she'll give them her current address and phone number, and they've promised to call us immediately."

"Yeah, sure," Burk groaned bitterly. "Just relax and don't worry about her being stranded somewhere with no money and no clothes. If you weren't such a control freak and refused to listen to her last night, she'd have told you who she was and what she wanted and this would never have happened."

"Control freak!" Rob hooted and threw up his hands. "Look who's calling who a control freak." He glanced across the bed at his wife, who until now hadn't been able to get a word in edgewise. "I give up! You do something with him, Jennifer. I'm going out for a smoke."

He turned and stomped out of the room.

Jennifer Sinclair squeezed her son's hand. "You really must calm down, Burk. You're not supposed to be upset. The doctor says he's going to sedate you if you don't stop raging at everybody and relax."

"No, he won't," Burk said angrily. "I won't let him,

and I'll rage at Dad until he finds Katie and apologizes to her. After all she's done for me, he dismissed her at the airport as if she were beneath notice, and left her with no money or any form of identification. If she doesn't live here, she didn't even have a home to go to, or change to make a telephone call for help."

He sank into the pillow, exhausted from the emotional scene, and sick at the thought of sweet, patient, caring Katie being treated so shabbily by his father, who couldn't be bothered to even ask who she was.

"Burk, it was a mistake," his mother insisted. "We're all terribly sorry about it, but try to see it from your dad's point of view. You'd promised Tina you'd be back from the mountains Sunday in plenty of time to take her to the opening of the new touring Broadway play that night. When you neither showed up nor called, she was understandably worried. We all were—"

"She had no business worrying you about it," he muttered. "The tickets were reserved at the box office. She could have gone by herself."

"That's very unkind of you, son," Jennifer chastised. "She called us to ask if we knew where you were. Eventually we contacted Diane and Douglas, too. We were all extremely upset by the time you called from Eugene, twenty-four hours after you were expected home, to tell us you were in the hospital. That made us even more anxious."

She looked away. "Don't be so hard on your father, Burk. He was terrified. We all were. Don't be mad at him for loving you."

Burk sighed. He knew she was right. He should be grateful for his close-knit family, and he was, but dammit, they'd turned Kate away and now he couldn't find her!

Before he could respond, the door opened and a nurse walked in, carrying a syringe. "Good morning, Mr. Sinclair. I have something here to relax you a little—"

"Take it away," he interrupted. "I don't want to be sedated. I've got to be able to think clearly."

"But Mr. Sinclair—" the nurse started to say when Jennifer broke in, her tone low but determined.

"Burk, this temper tantrum of yours is getting us nowhere. You're certainly not thinking clearly now, so for heaven's sake let the nurse give you the shot. As your dad said, it's only a matter of time until Ms. Brown files a claim with your insurance company, and they've promised to let us know the minute she does. Then we'll call her, apologize and offer whatever kind of help she may need."

Burk's head was killing him, and the nausea was getting worse. Maybe his mother was right. A couple of hours' sleep might clear his bruised brain and help him to see the big picture.

"Okay," he agreed reluctantly, "but I want to know the minute you hear from the insurance company."

Later that morning Kate and Emily went shopping, but first they stopped at the bank where Kate arranged to have her money transferred from her bank in Denver. They ran into a problem when she could produce no identification, but her grandmother had an account at the same bank and she identified Kate.

She cashed a check and paid her grandmother back for the cab fare, but when she started replacing her wardrobe, there were so many items she needed that her grandmother insisted Kate charge them to her account.

They had a late lunch at their favorite restaurant in the mall and then went home. It was a satisfying day as far as getting things done, but Kate was never able to rid herself of the nagging worry about Burk.

After all, she had a right to inquire about him. He'd been her patient for two days. She'd been responsible for him. If he was doing well now, she could take some of the credit, and if he was doing poorly she'd have to take a good share of the blame. Maybe in her ignorance of first aid and other medical procedures, she'd done the wrong thing and made his condition worse!

As soon as she got her new clothes hung up and put away she found the phone book and looked up "Sinclair" under the *S*'s. Maybe she could get in touch with some of the family at home.

There were only a few Sinclairs and she dialed them all, whether the first name or initial corresponded or not. None of them belonged to Burk's family.

Her only other option was to try the business number. It was in the Yellow Pages under Computers By Sinclair. She dialed and asked to speak to the office of Mr. Burk Sinclair and was put through without comment.

Tina Harper shoved a file folder of papers into her expensive leather briefcase, careful not to break one of her long red fingernails, then closed the lid and locked it. Burk had asked her to bring the folder to him. As she reached in the bottom drawer of her desk for her purse, the phone rang.

Oh, damn! She didn't have time to talk to anyone now. She wanted to get back to the hospital and Burk before the traffic got bad. She was tempted to not answer the call, but then it might be him wanting something else from his office.

She picked up the phone and the receptionist in the outer office spoke. "Ms. Harper, I have a phone call for Mr. Burk. Do you want to take it? She says her name is Katherine Brown."

Shock jolted Tina. Katherine Brown. Kate? Was this the Kate that Burk had been raising hell over ever since he got to the hospital? "I'll take it," she instructed tersely.

"This is Tina Harper, Burk Sinclair's assistant," she said when the other woman came on the line. "Mr. Sinclair isn't in. May I help you?"

There was a hesitation at the other end, but finally the woman answered her. "My name is Katherine Brown. Mr. Sinclair and I were involved in an accident up in the mountains over the weekend, and I'm trying to find out how he is. The hospital says they have no information on him. Can you give me his home phone number?"

So she was the woman Burk had been so upset over. Tina felt a strong twist of jealousy. She'd never seen Burk so worked up over a young woman before. Just what was she to him? They couldn't have gotten too chummy. They'd known each other only a couple of days, and apparently he was pretty woozy most of that time. So why was he pitching fits over her now?

"I'm sorry, but they have an unlisted number and I can't give it out," Tina answered in her coolly professional tone.

She could, but she wasn't going to. It was best to break this twosome up before it went any further. Tina was sure Burk was on the brink of asking her to marry him, and she wasn't going to let his gratitude to this intruder sidetrack him.

"The family thanks you for your interest, however," she concluded, "and I can tell you that Mr. Sinclair's condition is not serious and he'll be released from the hospital in the next day or two."

There was a pause on the other end before Ms. Brown spoke again. "Oh. Well, I'm glad of that. I wonder, could you give him a message for me?"

Oh, brother. Why didn't she just take the brush-off and hang up?

"I'll try," Tina said noncommittally.

"Please tell Burk I phoned, and ask him to call me at this number." She rattled off the number, then said goodbye and hung up.

A tight little smile drew up the corners of Tina's cherry red mouth as she put the phone back in its cradle.

She'd said she'd try to deliver the message. She didn't promise to do it.

Chapter Five

Kate was still sitting on the edge of the bed in her room staring at the phone on the night table when her grandmother came looking for her.

"Kathy, which would you rather have for dinner—pork chops or fresh salmon steaks?"

Kate made an effort to rise above her disappointment. "What? Oh, salmon, please. The only kind of fish we got in Denver was frozen, and it never tastes as good as fresh."

"What's the matter, dear?" Emily inquired. "You look so...so down."

Kate looked up at her and forced a smile. "It's nothing, really, Grandma. I'm just concerned that I've been unable to find out anything about Burk. The hospital won't give me any information, his family all have unlisted telephone numbers and when I called his number at work just now, his assistant answered and would only say that he was doing well and would be going home soon. The same pap they give to any stranger who might call."

"Did you tell her who you are?" Emily asked.

Kate frowned. "Sure. I told her I was the other person involved in the accident, but all she said was that the family thanks me for my interest. Interest, hell! I'm worried about him. I should think that common courtesy would dictate that I be given a report on his condition. After all, his motorcycle smashed into my car! Doesn't that entitle me to a little consideration?"

Emily sat down beside her. "Of course it does, honey, but that doesn't mean you're going to get it. Maybe they're afraid you'll sue them, and prefer to let their attorneys or insurance representatives talk to you. Speaking of which, have you reported the accident to your insurance company yet?"

Kate shook her head. "No, I haven't. I've had so many other things on my mind that I just haven't gotten around to it. I don't want to do it right now, though. I told Burk's assistant to ask him to call me at this number, and I don't want to tie up the phone until he does.

"That is, *if* he does," she finished with a touch of bitterness.

Burk didn't call that day, or the next, and by Thursday Kate's dismay had changed to full-blown rage. It was clear that he had no intention of calling. He wanted no more contact with her. He'd probably reported the accident to his insurance company and told them to handle it.

Well, fine! She was through playing the role of sweet, long-suffering maiden. If he wanted to avoid her, she'd make it easy for him. She'd sic her insurance company on him and not pull any punches. Many of the articles she'd been bringing to Portland with her in the car were family heirlooms that were irreplaceable.

If he was going to act as if she was just a minor irritant, she'd make sure he found out she could be a major one.

She reached for the phone and dialed the number she wanted in Denver.

When she reached Lester Ewing, her agent, he greeted her with an angry growl. "Where are you? Are you all right? Why didn't you report your accident sooner? When we tried to contact you, we were told your phone number is out of service."

Kate was stunned. How did he know about the accident when so far all she'd done was say hello and identify herself?

"A man named Burk Sinclair in Portland reported it to his insurance company and they got in touch with us," he told her. "How do you expect us to negotiate a claim we don't even know about?"

"Oh, dear," Kate murmured, feeling like an idiot. "I'm sorry. I was in the process of moving to Portland when the accident occurred. I hadn't sent out change-of-address cards yet, and I've had so much on my mind since then that I just didn't get around to calling you earlier."

"Are you all right?" Ewing asked, somewhat subdued.

Kate swallowed. "Yes, I'm fine, but my car and all my possessions in the back seat and trunk were probably totaled."

"Well, I'm glad you weren't injured," he admitted. "Oh, and you'd better call the highway patrol right away. They've been trying to find you, too. Why did you give them your address here in Denver instead of the one in Portland?"

"But I didn't," Kate said.

"Apparently you did, and they're not happy about it," Ewing told her.

"Oh, darn," she muttered. "My mind was in such a muddle by the time help finally arrived that I must have automatically given them the address I've been using for the past five years instead of the new one. I'll call them as soon as I finish talking to you."

"Okay." Ewing sounded somewhat chastened. "Now, tell me exactly what happened from the time you got in the car and left Bend on Sunday until today. But first give me your new address and phone number."

She did, then told him about the accident and what had happened since, leaving out only the more intimate and personal portions.

"Sounds like there's no doubt about Sinclair's liability," he assured her. "Since you're living in Portland now, I'm going to transfer your account to our office there and let them handle it. It'll be quicker and easier all the way around if you're represented by a local agent."

When she finished talking to Ewing, she called the highway patrol, apologized for inconveniencing them and gave them her correct address and phone number, then put the phone down with a sigh. Now it was up to the two insurance companies to hammer out a settlement. She hoped she wasn't going to have to fight the whole Sinclair corporation to get what was coming to her.

Early the following morning Kate received a call from the local branch of her insurance company, asking her to come to the office to get acquainted and to go over her accident report with them in person. She agreed and drove her grandma's elderly sedan to get there. Emily had always kept it in mint condition and refused to trade it in for a newer one. Even now that she was no longer allowed to drive, she wouldn't get rid of it, but kept it in the garage. Thank heaven the battery was still charged.

Kate's new agent, Tyrone Gentry, was a nice-looking man in his early forties who welcomed her and sympathized with her about her loss. The first thing she asked for in a settlement was a rental car, explaining that she couldn't rely on her grandmother's and she had to get back and forth to work, starting Monday. Gentry called Burk's agent and arranged for her to pick one up that afternoon.

Kate got back home in time to have lunch with Emily before taking her to keep her standing Friday appointment at her neighborhood hair-styling salon. Emily insisted that she'd walk back home, saying that she needed the exercise. So Kate left the car at the nearby garage to have it tuned up, arranged for it to be delivered back to the house, then walked home, too.

Kate had just finished stacking the dirty dishes in the dishwasher and was heading toward the bedroom to change out of her leaf green suit and lime silk blouse and into something more comfortable, when the doorbell rang.

She changed directions and opened the door to confront a middle-aged man impeccably dressed in a navy blue suit, white shirt and maroon paisley tie, an outfit that must have cost more than she made in a month. Obviously he wasn't here to sell her something, but by his scowling expression she was equally sure he wasn't going to tell her she'd won the sweepstakes.

He seemed to be as surprised by her as she was by him, and for a minute neither of them spoke.

Finally she broke the silence. "Yes? May I help you?"

"Ms. Katherine Brown?" he asked.

"Yes, I'm Katherine Brown," she admitted.

He came right to the point. "I'm Robert Sinclair, Burk Sinclair's father," he said gruffly. "May I come in?"

Kate blinked. Burk's father! What was he doing here? Had something awful happened to Burk?

She quickly unlocked the screen door. "Please do," she said anxiously, and pushed it open. "How is Burk? Is something wrong?"

She backed up to let him into the small entryway, and her heart pounded wildly.

"Burk's fine, as if you cared," he said, "but I need to talk to you."

She felt weak with relief but it was short-lived. If Burk

was all right, then what was bugging his dad? This was no social call. He was downright hostile.

He was also one intimidating man. Big, taller than Burk and considerably heavier, but his clothes fit as if they'd been tailored to his measurements, which of course they had been.

His dark brown hair was receding but it accentuated his broad forehead rather than detracted from it, and his brown eyes gazed at her with a look of authority that never wavered. He didn't look at all like the frantic man in casual clothes who had met the plane on Monday and whisked Burk away from her.

"Would—would you like to come into the living room and sit down?" she stammered.

"Yes, thank you," he said, and even his voice rumbled with authority.

She led the way and indicated the big lounge chair for him. He stood until she seated herself on the sofa, then sat also.

"My son tells me I owe you an apology," he said without really looking at her. She got the impression that apologizing didn't come easy for him.

"I didn't realize you were with Burk the other night at the airport," he continued rather stiffly before she could say anything. "Burk seems to think you had no money with you for cab fare. I'm sorry if you were inconvenienced."

Inconvenienced! She was a lot more than inconvenienced, and he didn't sound very sorry. She wasn't going to let him off that easy.

"He's right. I didn't," she said coldly. "And if you and Burk knew that, why did it take you four days to contact me and make sure I'd gotten home all right?"

Robert glared at her. "Because we couldn't find you, that's why! Burk didn't know your address or phone number. My staff and I called every blasted Brown in the phone book, but none of them knew you, and the address you gave the highway patrol was in Denver, Colorado. It wasn't until about an hour ago when Burk's insurance company finally heard from yours and contacted him with this address that we knew where you were.''

It hadn't occurred to Kate that Burk didn't know her address here in Portland, but now that she thought about it, they hadn't exchanged that information. He'd apparently been getting the same runaround she had.

''I'm sorry about that,'' she said. ''The phone here is listed under Emily Kelly, my grandmother's name, but—''

''It seems to me you've got more than that to be sorry about if we're going to be assigning blame here,'' he retorted. ''The least you could have done is call the hospital and ask how Burk is. You knew how serious his head injury was.''

Kate took a deep breath to defend herself, but he continued speaking without giving her a chance. ''Burk was going crazy with worry over you, and you were so busy sulking about being overlooked in the midst of the chaos at the airport that you couldn't even bother to inquire about his condition.''

Kate could almost feel her blood pressure jump. ''Now just a darn minute.'' She sprang off the sofa. ''I've done everything I could to contact the high-and-mighty Sinclair clan, but you've built a wall around yourselves that is impenetrable. I called the hospital and was told they had no information about Burk. They wouldn't even tell me if he was a patient there or not. Next, I tried calling all the Sinclairs in the phone book, but, in case you've forgotten, none of your family is listed.''

By now she was pacing the floor. ''As a last resort I called Burk's office and talked to his assistant. I told her who I was, explained the situation and asked for your telephone number. She said it was unlisted and she couldn't give it out, so I gave her my grandmother's number and told her to ask Burk to call me there. That was Tuesday, and I still haven't heard from him, so don't tell me he was worried."

Robert stared at her. "You talked to Tina?"

Kate shrugged. "She said her name was Tina Harper and she was Burk's assistant."

Robert looked puzzled. "She is, but she never said anything about talking to you. Are you sure she knew who you were?"

"I made sure she knew exactly who I was and what I was talking about," she said testily. "I can quote the message I asked her to deliver. It was 'Please tell Burk I phoned, and ask him to call me at this number,' then I gave her the number and hung up."

Robert shook his head. "There must have been a mix-up somewhere. Neither Burk nor I ever got the message. I'll check and see what happened, but for now, Burk has given me strict instructions to bring you to the hospital."

Concern overrode her anger and she sat back down. "Burk's still in the hospital? Then his injury was even worse than we thought?"

"Not really," Robert said. "But he won't settle down and get the rest he needs to let it heal. He's been sure you'd disappeared and something had happened to you, and he's making life miserable for himself and everyone around him. Hell, he hasn't spoken a civil word to me since he discovered I didn't bring you to the hospital with us."

Kate had a hard time believing that. It didn't sound like the lovable Burk Sinclair she'd cared for at the cabin. He'd been so patient and appreciative of everything she'd tried to do for him. Still, she couldn't believe he'd be that upset about misplacing her. Maybe he felt guilty.

"I want to see him as soon as possible, but I don't have a car right now," she explained. "Your insurance company made arrangements for me to pick up a rental later this afternoon, so I'll have to wait until then to go to the hospital—"

"No way," Robert said and stood. "I'm not going back there without you. Burk would blow a gasket before I got a chance to explain. You can ride with me, and when you're ready to leave I'll take you to the rental company to get your car. Okay?"

Kate knew it was the only solution, and besides, she was too eager to see Burk, to wait any longer. "Okay," she said, softening her tone. "Just let me get my purse."

At the hospital, Robert escorted Kate up to the fourth floor and stopped in front of the closed door of room 420.

"Burk was in intensive care until they moved him to this private room yesterday," he told her. "I can see that you two have a lot of misunderstandings to work out, so you go on in alone. I'll run a couple of errands and be back in an hour to take you to get your car."

She smiled, but before she could say anything, he'd turned and was halfway down the hall.

Robert Sinclair was a hard man to understand, but she suspected that now she owed him an apology. She already regretted her harsh words. It was obvious that his anxiety over his son's injury, and his guilt and regret at dismissing her so abruptly the other night at the airport, had overridden his patience and understanding.

She hesitated for a moment in front of the door. Now that she'd finally broken through the protective security that surrounded Burk's privacy, she was hit by a wave of shyness. Should she knock, or was it okay to just push the door open and go in?

It seemed a little silly to worry about such a small nicety when just a few days ago they'd showered and slept together, but that had been for survival. It didn't give her the right to assume the intimacy they'd shared would continue. Probably the only reason he wanted to see her now was to apologize for inadvertently abandoning her at the airport and thank her for taking care of him after the accident.

Her shyness won and she rapped lightly, but there was no answer. So she pushed the door open and stepped inside. Her eyes were immediately drawn to the bed. It was empty. Her gaze shifted and caught Burk standing by the window, but he wasn't alone. There was an attractive woman with him. In the few seconds before they looked up and saw her Kate studied the slender figure dressed in a tailored gray suit. She had dark auburn hair, short and straight that curved inward slightly at her jawline, and she was startlingly attractive. She had her hand on his arm and was talking to him. Neither of them had yet looked in her direction.

"Dammit, darling, stop pacing the floor and go back to bed," she said anxiously. "You'll never get out of this hospital if you don't follow the doctor's orders and rest."

Darling! The endearment hit Kate with a resounding sting. This must be the woman Burk was dating. She sure wasn't his mother!

Burk shifted his glance to reply and caught sight of Kate. There was no recognition in his eyes.

"Yes?" he said, and waited for her to state her business.

Her heart sank. He didn't know her!

It took her a second to realize that it really wasn't so surprising that he didn't. He'd never seen her when she wasn't soaking wet and covered with mud, nude except for skimpy underwear or dressed in a baggy sweat suit with her hair dirty and hanging in unsightly strings around her face. He hadn't seen her clean and fixed up before!

"I...I'm Kate," she said inanely. "Katherine Brown."

"Katie!" His face lit up as he hurried across the room and grabbed her in a bruising hug. "I didn't recognize you," he said, and held her away from him to look at her. "Damn, you clean up good!"

The tension was broken and Kate laughed. "So do you, Mr. Hell's Angel," she teased, but she meant every word of it. She'd never seen him dressed up, but today he was well-groomed and wearing navy blue silk pajamas with a matching robe. He looked sexy enough to light her fire!

He pulled her back into his embrace again. "Oh, God, I've been so worried about you!" he groaned, and she could feel his heart thumping in his chest, as she was sure he could feel hers.

"No more than I've worried about you," she murmured anxiously. He smelled so good. Clean and fresh like expensive shaving lotion.

They just stood there holding each other until the sound of a throat being cleared reminded them they weren't alone. Burk seemed reluctant to release her, but he slowly turned so they were standing side by side. He kept one of his arms around her waist as he faced the woman.

She not only didn't look happy, but Kate was sure it was fear she saw in the green eyes that met hers briefly before they looked away.

"Sorry, Tina," Burk said casually. "I'd like you to meet Katherine Brown, the Katie I've been looking for who rescued me from almost certain death when my motorcycle hit her car."

His gaze met Kate's again and clung for a moment until he spoke. "Katie, this is my assistant, Tina Harper. She keeps my business on an even keel."

Kate tried not to show her surprise. So this was the woman she'd talked to on Tuesday. Was she his main squeeze as well as his business assistant?

Apparently so, because this time it was anger that stared icily out of those expressive eyes as the two women shook hands so briefly that they hardly touched.

Now Kate knew why she'd seen fear in her eyes before. Tina had deliberately not given Burk her message, and she hadn't expected Kate to show up in person to question why!

"How do you do, Tina," Kate said coolly. "I believe we talked on the phone once."

Burk looked startled, and Tina immediately shook her head.

"What's this?" Burk asked Tina.

"She's mistaken," Tina said imperiously. "It must have been someone else she talked to."

Burk glanced from Kate to Tina and then back to Kate. "When do you think you talked to Tina?"

Kate's ire rose. "It was Tuesday. I told her where I was and the phone number and asked her to have you call me."

Tina shook her head stubbornly. "That's not true! She must have talked to someone else and thought it was me."

"Someone using your name and title?" Kate shot back. She wasn't inclined to protect this woman who had caused both Burk and her so much anxiety by simply not delivering her message.

"That's absurd," Tina said angrily. "No one in our office would do such a thing. You must have misunderstood whoever answered the phone."

Kate could hardly believe that Burk's assistant would stand there and lie so blatantly. Well, she wasn't going to let her get away with it unchallenged.

"You no doubt have your reasons for lying, but my hearing is excellent, and I know what you said."

"Now, hold on, ladies," Burk ordered. "Calm down and let's sort this out. Kate, are you sure you were talking to my office?"

"I am," she said resentfully. "They wouldn't give me any information about you at the hospital, and your home phone is unlisted, so I finally called the office and asked to speak with you. Instead, the operator put me through to Ms. Harper who said you weren't in but she'd take a message. Apparently she never delivered it!"

"That's not true!" Tina grated. "I always deliver messages meant for you, Burk. You know that."

He looked uncertain. "Yes, I do. Katie, are you sure it was Tina you talked to?"

Kate was sure, but she knew it would be hard to prove. "Obviously I didn't see her," she admitted, "but she identified herself as Tina Harper and said she was your assistant. I don't know how much more proof I need."

Tina shot a nasty glance at Kate. "Well, I don't enjoy being accused of something unprofessional that I didn't do." She looked at Burk. "If I'd received the message, I'd have delivered it to you immediately."

He nodded. "I know you would have, Tina," he assured her, which Kate took to mean he didn't believe *her.*

She drew in her breath in an effort to lessen the pain. Now that she knew he was going to be all right, she wasn't going to stand here and indulge in a cat fight with his girlfriend. After all, she—Kate—was the interloper.

"I can see that I'm wasting my time," she said, and held out her hand to him. "Goodbye, Burk. I'm glad you are recovering well from your injury. Take care of yourself."

He just stared at her. She turned and started out the door, but he caught up with her in one step and turned her around, then took her in his arms. "Hold on a minute there. Where do you think you're going?"

She tried to push away, but he just tightened the embrace. "Since neither you nor your dad believe me, I'm going home."

"Like hell you are," he muttered. "I've finally found you, and I'm not going to let you get away again. We need to talk."

He looked up and met Tina's gaze. "Will you excuse us, please, Tina?"

Kate had her back to the other woman so she couldn't see her, but she heard the disbelief in her tone. "But the papers—"

"I'll go over the papers later and sign them, then give them to Dad to take back to you at the office," he told her.

"Well, of course. If that's what you want," Tina said

huffily, and Kate heard the click of high heels going toward the door, then the door opening and shutting behind her.

Burk caressed her back and rubbed his cheek in her hair. "Have you any idea what I've been going through since I arrived here and found that you'd been left behind?"

"Your dad told me," she said, then told him about the problems she'd had finding him. "I really did call the office and talk to Ms. Harper, or at least someone who identified herself by that name," Kate concluded.

"All right," he said huskily. "I'll sort it out when I get back to work. Now tell me everything that's happened since we were separated. How did you get home from the airport? Where do you live? Where do you work?"

"I'll tell you, but first you have to get back into bed. I heard Ms. Harper say you're not supposed to be up and walking around."

"I'll lie down if you'll lie down with me," he murmured into her hair.

That idea was altogether too appealing. "You know I can't do that, Burk. The first nurse who came in would kick me right out of the hospital."

"I suppose," he said on a sigh, "but I haven't slept worth a damn since the night you crawled into bed with me. I've missed you and worried about you so."

His words made prickles run up and down her spine. "I've missed you and worried about you, too, so please get back into bed so your poor bruised brain can heal and you can go home."

She pulled away from him and started picking at the knot in his robe belt. He stood quietly and let her unknot the sash and slide the robe off his shoulders. "I like having you undress me," he said with a teasing smile. "Feel free to continue."

She was sorely tempted to do just that, but resisted the temptation. "That's enough for now," she teased back.

"But don't forget, I'm not unfamiliar with your nude body."

"No, ma'am, I haven't forgotten," he said as she led him back to the bed. "Nor have I forgotten what yours looks like. How could I? I see it every time I close my eyes."

This conversation was getting altogether too intimate. She helped him back into bed, then pulled the covers over him.

"Okay," he said as he took her hand and pulled her down to sit on the bed beside him. "Now I'm lying down, so tell me what's been going on with you since you were left standing at the airport alone and with no money."

She started at the beginning and gave him a step-by-step account of her activities since arriving in Portland, including a repeat of her efforts to find him.

"I swear that I did talk to your assistant," she said in conclusion. "When you didn't call back, I assumed you didn't want to continue our...our friendship...."

He squeezed her hand and brought it to his mouth to kiss the palm. "I'm looking forward to it's being a lot more than just a friendship," he murmured, and put her hand to his cheek.

Robert returned shortly after that and finally managed to pry Kate away from Burk after she promised she'd come back that evening. As they drove toward the car-rental agency, Robert questioned her.

"Did you really give Tina a message for Burk that she didn't deliver?"

Kate was getting tired of defending herself when she hadn't done anything wrong, and she told Burk's dad so. "Why would I lie about a thing like that, Mr. Sinclair?" she asked angrily. "I'd never met the woman until I walked into Burk's room an hour ago."

"Call me Rob," he instructed her. "Most people do. You know, she could say the same of you."

"That's true, but with one big difference. I'd never even heard of her before, but she's been hearing about me for several days, and getting the brunt of Burk's bad temper because of me. I gather he's been giving everybody a bad time?"

"That's for sure," Rob muttered.

"Is she the woman Burk was rushing home to keep a date with the day of the accident?" Kate couldn't resist asking.

Rob nodded. "Yeah. He'd gone up to the mountains to have some time alone to catch up on his paperwork, but he promised her he'd be back Sunday night to take her to the theater. The storm delayed him so he decided to start out anyway."

"Are they...are they living together?" Kate stammered. She knew it was none of her business, but she had to ask.

"No, they're not," Rob answered dryly. "And that's all I'm going to say on the subject. Besides, here we are at the car rental agency. I'll come in with you and see that you get a good one."

A short while later Kate was driving away in a red sports car, a considerable upgrade from what she'd expected, but Burk's dad had insisted.

Chapter Six

That evening after she had filled her grandmother in on all the events that had transpired while Emily was at the beauty shop, Kate went back to the hospital as she'd promised Burk she would. They'd hoped to have time alone together, but instead she walked in on a family gathering.

Again an attack of shyness left her standing uncertainly just inside the door. The room was filled with people surrounding the bed where Burk was lying propped up and holding court. He saw her immediately and smiled as he reached out to her. "Katie, I've been watching for you. Come here. Sit down." He beckoned, then patted the side of the bed.

Feeling the stain of embarrassment creeping into her face as all eyes turned to look at her, she hung back. "May—maybe I should come back tomorrow," she said apologetically. "I—I don't want to intrude...."

His smile disappeared and was replaced by a frown. "That's ridiculous. You could never be an intrusion."

Again he patted the bed. "Come on over here and sit beside me. I want to introduce you to my family."

There didn't seem to be any hope of getting away from the scrutiny of all these strangers, so she decided to pull herself together and make the best of it. She only wished she hadn't changed from the suit she'd worn when she was here earlier and into the more casual forest green slacks and matching long-sleeved shirt. The outfit was neat and new, but the other women were dressed as if they had come from their offices, in business suits and high heels.

Taking a deep breath for courage, she smiled and walked over to sit down on the side of the bed.

Burk took her hand and glanced around the room. "Kate, I'd like you to meet some of the members of the Sinclair family."

His gaze settled on the attractive middle-aged woman sitting in a chair next to the bed on the other side. Her coloring was a lot like Kate's, dark blond hair and brown eyes, but while Kate's complexion was creamy, this woman's was more of a honey beige.

"This is my mother, Jennifer."

Kate was surprised. The woman didn't look old enough to have a son Burk's age.

Jennifer smiled and nodded. "It's an honor to meet you," she said in a warmly cultivated tone. "We owe you a great deal more than we can ever repay." Her voice broke slightly.

"Not at all, Mrs. Sinclair," Kate insisted. "I'm just thankful I was able to rise to the challenge."

Burk squeezed Kate's hand and moved his gaze to another, younger woman on the same side of the room who was standing next to a little girl approximately ten years old. "This is my sister, Diane, and her daughter, Ashleigh. Diane is vice president of our company."

Burk's sister looked more like her father than her mother.

She was tall, probably close to six feet, and big boned but well proportioned. She wore her clothes beautifully.

"I'm glad you finally surfaced," she said, "and I speak for the whole family when I say we're so sorry for the mix-up at the airport."

"Thank you," Kate said smoothly, "but it really wasn't anybody's fault. There was a miscommunication on both sides."

She looked at the child. "I'm very glad to meet you, Ashleigh."

The little girl looked like most young girls, her features not yet defined enough to distinguish her from all the others in her age group. She had a sweet shy smile and she blushed endearingly as she answered. "Thank you for taking care of Uncle Burk."

Kate grinned. "How could I not?" she asked. "Your uncle Burk is a pretty special person."

Burk squeezed her hand again as Ashleigh nodded gravely. "Yes. I love him."

Kate felt tears gathering behind her eyes, and she noticed that Burk was having trouble controlling his emotions. "Ashleigh's my favorite niece," he declared somewhat unsteadily.

The child laughed gleefully. "I'm his only niece," she told Kate, and everybody chuckled.

"You just wait until my brain heals and I can think faster," Burk threatened happily. "Then I'll get you."

Ashleigh didn't look a bit worried as she continued to giggle.

"Okay, let's get serious here," Burk said as he deftly changed the subject by singling out a young man, younger woman, and two small boys who were on her side of the bed. The woman was sitting on a chair with the youngest boy on her lap, and the man and the older boy were standing beside her.

"This good-lookin' guy is my younger brother, Douglas,

with his wife, Maria Elena, and their sons, Roberto and Dougie, named after their grandfather and their father.''

Burk wasn't exaggerating about his handsome brother. Douglas looked a lot like his mother with medium blond hair and a smaller build than his dad, Burk or Diane. His pretty young wife was Hispanic, with black hair, flashing black eyes and an olive-tone complexion. The little boys, probably three and five or thereabouts, were darker than their dad but lighter than their mother, and both were adorable.

Douglas leaned over and shook Kate's hand. He had a firm grip, and a big smile. "It's almost impossible for us to find words strong enough to tell you how much we appreciate your courage and generosity in getting Burk to the cabin and out of the storm. It's difficult to adequately express our gratitude.''

Kate tried to blink back the tears that welled in her eyes, but they spilled over anyway. "Please," she said desperately, "you're making me cry. I only did what had to be done. Actually, neither one of us had any business being out in that storm. It's a wonder we weren't both killed.''

She grabbed a tissue from the bedside table and dabbed at her cheeks.

"Well, thank the good Lord you weren't," Burk's mother said fervently. "Burk was just telling us he's being released to come home tomorrow.''

She looked directly at her son. "You will come home to us where Lottie and I can take care of you until you're stronger, won't you?''

Kate assumed that Lottie was the housekeeper.

Burk smiled but shook his head. "I don't need any more taking care of, Mom." His tone brooked no argument. "I haven't even been able to go to the bathroom for the past week without someone standing by in case I fall over. I need some space. I'll be just fine at the condo.''

"Oh, but a head injury such as yours can be dangerous

even after you're feeling well enough to be up and around,'' Jennifer said anxiously. ''I wouldn't have a moment's peace if I knew you were all alone in that condominium with no one to know in case you had a relapse....''

Burk took his mother's hand. ''Come on, Mom, be realistic,'' he said gently. ''The doctor wouldn't release me from the hospital if he thought there was the slightest chance of such a thing happening.''

''I'd worry all the same,'' she insisted.

Burk sighed. ''I don't want to upset you unduly, but I need to be in my own place.''

He closed his eyes for a minute, then opened them to look at Kate while still addressing his mother. ''Maybe I can talk Kate into spending the next couple of days with me before she has to go to work. I'll never find another nurse as competent as she.''

Kate blinked as he continued. ''How about it, honey? I have three bedrooms, in case you're afraid I'm planning a seduction.''

Her heart speeded up even as her good sense screamed warnings. Then she was brought back to reality with a jolt as she remembered why such an arrangement was impossible.

''I...I'm sorry, Burk, I'd like to help you out, but I can't. I came to Portland to be with my grandmother who's in her early seventies and suffering the aftereffects of a small stroke. There was no serious damage, but she is forgetful at times, and I don't want to leave her alone overnight again until I've had more of a chance to evaluate how well she functions.''

There were murmurs of sympathy for Emily from the others in the room, but Burk came up with an immediate solution. ''Bring her with you. I'd be happy to have her for a guest. She can have her own room with a television and a semiprivate bathroom that she'd share with you.''

The proposition was tempting. Almost irresistibly so, but

Kate wasn't going to fool herself. If she spent a night at Burk's condo, it would be in his bed. The magnetism between them was too strong to resist. It was like nothing she'd ever experienced, and it frightened her.

Even if it weren't for their troubled history, it would be a big mistake to fall into bed with a man she'd known less than a week. But the fact that she had a secret that would enrage him if he found out about it made the very idea insane.

There was definitely no future for the two of them, and that was a given!

Diane's voice gradually intruded into Kate's thoughts. "Now really, Burk, don't put the poor girl on the spot. She's already been severely inconvenienced by you, and there's no need for you to impose on her further...."

Kate snapped to attention. She didn't appreciate Diane's rather curt defense. Kate couldn't let him think that was her reason for refusing to help him, and she interrupted without giving it further thought.

"Diane. No. Please. Burk has never been an inconvenience to me. I'm just thankful I was able to help and didn't do him any damage. I'm not a nurse. I've never even been sick except for mild childhood illnesses, but if he really wants me to stay with him for a couple of days until he's feeling stronger I'll be happy to do it."

She looked at him, and he was smiling. "That is, if you're sure you don't mind my bringing Grandma along."

"Bring anyone you want," he said happily, and Kate knew she'd just jumped off the edge of a pit and had no idea where she would land.

Later, when she got home, she told her grandmother what she'd agreed to and how it had happened. "I just couldn't let Burk believe that I thought he was taking advantage of me," she said uncertainly.

"I can understand that," Emily told her. "And now that you've agreed to do it, you must carry through. I'm perfectly capable of staying here alone at night. I did it all the time you were making arrangements to move back to Portland after my stroke, but I agree that I should stay at Burk's home with you tomorrow. It wouldn't look right for you two to spend the night alone together in his apartment.''

Kate swallowed a gasp of astonishment. Grandma was going to Burk's in the role of chaperon, not guest. She hadn't yet caught on to the fact that a steady dating relationship these days almost always included sex, and few people thought of it one way or the other. Grandma was afraid people would talk if Kate spent the night alone with him!

A warm feeling of affection for the older woman crept over her. Grandma tried hard to keep up with the rapidly changing morals of the times, but she was usually a beat behind. Well, that wasn't surprising. Even the baby boomers had difficulty following the New Age customs.

''I knew I could count on you,'' Kate said affectionately as she looked at her watch. ''I told Burk we'd pick him up at the hospital at ten o'clock in the morning. Is that okay with you?''

Emily looked startled. ''Oh, no, I'm not going to spend the whole weekend with you two, just tomorrow night. I have plenty to do here to keep me busy. You can come get me after dinner.''

After a brief discussion they finally agreed that Kate would pick Emily up in time to have dinner with them, and Kate called Burk to tell him of the change in plans.

Burk was up and dressed by seven o'clock the following morning, then was faced with a three-hour delay before Kate arrived to take him home.

Home. He and Katie were finally going to be alone together at his condominium where nobody could intrude on them without his permission. He'd been euphoric when she'd called last night to tell him that her grandmother would only be spending the night with them. That meant they'd have two full days of uninterrupted time for...

For what? He'd promised he wouldn't seduce her, but even as he denied that intention, his thoughts had betrayed him. Now that he was feeling well and energetic again, it was impossible to control his lusty fantasizing.

That shouldn't be a problem. After all, he was a thirty-six-year-old male with a full complement of testosterone and he'd always been able to take these perfectly normal urges in stride. But not with Ms. Katherine Brown. They'd flared up as soon as he was conscious enough to be fully aware of her, and they'd increased every time he'd gotten near her since then.

Even that wouldn't alarm him if it were just sex he wanted, but that was only the tip of the iceberg. There were stronger, deeper feelings that scared the hell out of him. He didn't believe in love at first sight. He didn't even *want* to believe in it!

His experience with Fleur should have taught him the folly of marrying in haste. Their marriage had been a mistake from the start, and their divorce had been a disaster. If he was even halfway smart, he'd call Kate right now, tell her he wouldn't need her caretaking after all and break off the relationship without a backward glance.

Sure he would, but his smarts had evaporated in direct proportion to the rise of his libido!

Kate woke that same morning after a restless night of both longing and regret. She'd taken the forbidden leap; now she had to chart out a path for her future.

Burk was dressed and waiting for her when she arrived. Looking great in tan cotton slacks, a tan shirt and a brown cardigan, he caught her in his arms as soon as she walked in the door.

"There's my sweetheart," he murmured as he held her close.

She loved the feel of him, the sound of his voice, even the way he smelled. It was a citrus fragrance with a faint undertone of musk. Her restless tongue twitched with the urge to taste the side of his throat where her mouth was resting, but she quickly decided that wasn't the best way to discourage him from wanting to make love with her anytime soon.

"Are…are you ready to leave?" she murmured.

"Ready and eager," he assured her. "I'm all signed out. All I have to do is say goodbye."

It wasn't quite that simple. He was given some prescriptions to have filled, and then was outraged when the nurse insisted that he be taken out of the hospital and to the car in a wheelchair.

"I'm not going to be pushed around in a wheelchair," he fumed. "There's nothing wrong with my legs—it's my head that was bashed in. I'm as capable of walking as you are."

The nurse had obviously heard that speech before from men who thought it a weakness to ride in a wheelchair, and she let him rage on until he came to a stop.

"I'm sure you're in great shape, Mr. Sinclair," she assured him, "but it's hospital policy. If you want to leave us, you'll have to get in this contraption and let us push you to your car."

He muttered a few obscenities under his breath but finally did as the nurse told him, and Kate went on ahead to bring the car around to the front door.

Burk's condo turned out to be on the twentieth floor of a modern high-rise glass-and-steel building in the McCleary Park area. It had more floor space than her grandmother's house, and was conveniently laid out and artistically furnished.

"Oh, Burk, it's beautiful," she said breathlessly as she stood in the spacious living room with its floor-to-ceiling glass wall, which offered a magnificent view of the Willamette River below and the towering Mount Hood in the distance. "No wonder you were so eager to come home. If I lived here, I don't think I'd ever leave."

Burk came up behind her and put his arms around her. She looked like a wide-eyed innocent as she gazed approvingly around his living quarters, but in his arms she felt like a soft and enticing woman. "If you lived here, I wouldn't ever leave, either," he said huskily, and let his hands roam.

Kate's stomach quivered as he gently stroked it, and she moved back against him in spite of her better judgment. She couldn't help it. The allurement between them was too captivating to ignore.

His heart hammered as he lowered his head to nibble on her exposed throat. She'd pinned her thick blond hair up in a loose knot at the top of her head, except for a few stray tendrils that had escaped their confinement. It gave him unrestricted access to all areas of her neck, and he felt her whole body quiver as he nibbled and licked and kissed.

Slowly he ran his hands up her soft, sensuous, mauve-silk-covered rib cage and stopped just short of the rise of her breasts, then shivered with anticipation as his thumbs continued the exploration until they found her nipples through the blouse.

Kate gasped softly as Burk massaged the sensitive nubs. He paused. "Do you want me to stop?" he whispered against her ear.

"Oh, no, please don't," she murmured tremulously as an involuntary shudder caused her to rub her derriere against his groin.

He groaned and pushed his lower body hard against her bottom, making her fully aware of his throbbing arousal. "Katie, if you don't want this you'd better stop me now. I...I don't think I'll be able to in a few more minutes."

The very thought of not continuing was agony. She

turned in his embrace and put her arms around his neck. "I want you," she whispered, fully aware of the possible consequences but unable to resist.

Without another word he scooped her up and carried her through the living room and down the hall to what was obviously his bedroom, although she was too bemused to notice details. He laid her down on the king-size bed then lowered himself beside her with one leg between her thighs and the upper part of his body propped up with his elbow.

"Kiss me, Katie," he said hoarsely as his mouth covered hers.

She had her wits about her enough to remember that this was their first kiss. And it was everything she'd dreamed it would be—urgent but sweet, hot but restrained.

His tongue probed eagerly and she opened her mouth to him. He cupped her head with his hands and gently caressed it as he thrust and withdrew until she understood what he wanted of her, and her own tongue danced and teased with his in time to his rhythm.

Kate was getting hotter by the minute as their imitation of the real thing became more and more exciting. She tried to turn toward Burk so she could clasp her legs around him, but he held her off.

"Take it easy, sweetheart," he said huskily as he devoured her mouth. "The longer it lasts the better it is."

She wasn't convinced of that. She wanted him now. The throbbing in her most intimate places was driving her crazy.

Kate moaned softly as Burk's hand crept under the elastic band of her slacks and rubbed across the crotch of her panties. She was warm and wet and ready, and he struggled to retain control of his own runaway needs.

A satisfying cry of exhilaration escaped her throat, and he knew he was giving her pleasure. Maybe even almost as much as he was getting from her, and that thought helped him to keep a tight rein on his agonizing urgency.

Again she tried to turn toward him, and it took all the

restraint he could muster to once more hold her away. "Just a minute until we get our clothes off," he murmured raggedly as he withdrew his hand and used it to pull off her slacks and panties.

Kate should have been embarrassed but she wasn't. Her body had no secrets from this man. They'd been nearly nude in each other's presence before, and now all she wanted was that erotic explosion that would send the two of them into paradise and back.

He unfastened her blouse as she clumsily worked at releasing the buttons on his shirt. Her fingers seemed to be all thumbs, and when she reached the waistband of his slacks, she paused with uncertainty. She hadn't had much experience at this, even though she was twenty-eight years old. Most of her friends slept with the men they went out with, but she was too selective to give her body without also giving her heart.

Up to now that hadn't been difficult because she'd known few men who touched her emotions that deeply, and none who invaded her soul the way Burk had.

The fire in Burk's loins made it difficult for him to be patient with Katie's hesitation. Finally he could bear it no longer. "What are you waiting for?" he asked, trying to keep the anxiety out of his tone. "Go ahead and release the zipper."

Before she could answer, a monstrous thought struck him. *What if she didn't want to go all the way?* Cold sweat broke out all over him, and he bit back a groan of pure agony.

"Or are you having second thoughts?" he forced himself to ask. "I'm not going to force myself on you, Katie."

His words drove all the timidity from Kate, and she grabbed the button that held the waistband together. "I'd never have second thoughts about making love with you," she said adamantly.

The closing didn't come apart easily, and as she grappled

with it, the heel of her hand rubbed against the bulge under his fly and he gasped.

Quickly she withdrew her hand. "I—I'm sorry," she stammered as another influx of unwelcome embarrassment washed over her. What was the matter with her anyway? She wasn't all that innocent.

"Don't be sorry," Burk said, and reached for her hand to position it completely over his hard, swollen shaft. Her fingers closed around him, and the exquisite relief of her touch was only overshadowed by the dire necessity of his need to be in her. To bring them both to completion.

Still, this predicament was his own fault. He was the one who had wanted to take it slow. What in hell could he have been thinking of? He knew the explosive effect she had on him.

"Don't ever be sorry. Just do whatever comes naturally," he told her, and hoped he could hold back until she was ready.

He lowered his head and once more took her mouth. The thrill that rippled through her caused her fingers to tighten, and he moaned and bucked into her hand as his own fingers grasped the fleshy part of her hip and kneaded it.

Kate knew the time for foreplay was over, and she quickly pulled down his zipper and released him from the confines of his trousers. He surprised her by rolling away from her and standing up. "Take off your shirt and bra," he said as he swiftly finished undressing.

She sat up and removed the rest of her clothes, then sank back down on the bed and held out her arms to him in welcome. He was every bit as perfect a male specimen as she'd remembered—trim with bulging muscles but not an ounce of fat. And his overabundant virility could never be called into question.

He knelt over her, straddling her legs, and licked one nipple then the other. They both hardened even more than they already were, and her breasts throbbed and tightened with anticipation.

Her hands roamed over his back and she tried to pull him down to her, but he was still intent on her breasts as he took one nipple in his mouth and sucked gently. It sent tongues of fire to her lower regions and made her cry out with burning need.

"Oh, Katie, I love you," he groaned in her ear as he shifted so that he was positioned between her thighs.

She was afraid her heart was going to explode with happiness as she wrapped her legs around his hips and he lowered himself to thrust gently at first then more and more urgently into the raging heat of her welcoming wetness.

It was only seconds before the whole world exploded for both of them.

Chapter Seven

Kate lay curled against Burk, their arms and legs entwined
in the breathless but contented aftermath of lovemaking.
Nothing like this had happened to her before. It was beyond
anything she could ever have imagined!

The only other man she'd been intimate with had been
clumsy and fast, more intent on his own satisfaction than
hers. That affair, her one and only, hadn't lasted very long.

She also had women friends with similar complaints, so
she'd assumed that was just the way it was: pleasurable for
the man, disappointing for the woman.

Boy, had she been wrong!

She turned her head and buried her face in Burk's tautly
muscled chest. This was a man who knew how to pleasure
a woman and would go to any length to do it. It must have
been not only frustrating but actually painful for him to be
patient with her until he was sure she was ready, but he
hadn't uttered a complaint. He'd been kind and gentle, and
he'd even said he loved her.

She could still hear his musical baritone voice saying it. *Oh, Katie, I love you.* The most beautiful words in all the languages of the world. They had filled her with joy and sent her soaring.

She loved him all the more for being so thoughtful, but had he meant it?

Much as she wanted to believe he had, it didn't seem likely. He'd probably just been caught up in the passion of the moment. After all, their union had certainly been explosive, and he may have mistaken lust for love. Or maybe he knew that was what she wanted desperately to hear and decided to make the experience memorable for her.

Either way, she didn't want his thoughtful but empty good intentions. The barrier between them was too impenetrable. If she confessed who she was, he'd hate her for what she'd done to him, and if she didn't, she'd hate herself for her deception.

No relationship could survive under those pressures.

No, there was no hope for them as a couple. So if he didn't mention it again, she wouldn't, either. If he did, she'd let him know that she understood it was just an endearment murmured in the passion of the moment and she wouldn't hold him to it.

But, oh, how she wished it had been wrung from his heart instead of his mind. She'd suspected almost from that first day that she was falling in love with him, but she'd tried to deny it. Love at first sight was a myth. It had no substance. You had to know a person before you could love him.

But now she knew it was possible. Not only possible, but it had happened to her. Love had blossomed in her up there in the mountains in the rain and wind and cold, and in spite of the fact that Burk Sinclair was the one man in all the world who could never return her love if he knew what she'd done to him. There had been no way she could stop it, and now she was going to have to live with the consequences.

She moved her head a fraction of an inch and ringed his large male nipple with her tongue. His arms tightened around her, and she took the nipple in her mouth and laved it. She felt his masculinity rising to the occasion, and she giggled happily.

"How can that happen again so quickly?" she asked, only half teasing. "I thought men needed some recovery time."

He nuzzled the top of her head. "So did I," he murmured as he stroked her bare bottom. "But the things you do to me just by being with me defy the laws of nature. I've longed to make love with you, but I had no idea it would be like this. That it *could* be like this."

A warm surge of happiness stole over her and she looked up at him. "Do you really mean that?" she asked incredulously. "You're in your mid-thirties and you've been married. Surely you must have had a lot of good sex."

She felt him tense and saw surprise flash in his eyes before he blinked and dispelled it. What had she said that took him unawares?

"I have," he said, "but I've never experienced anything as totally consuming as this."

Exuberantly she buried her face in his chest again and relaxed, but when he spoke once more she realized he was still tense.

"Katie, how do you know I've been married?"

Her whole body twitched with astonishment and alarm. "Why, I... That is, you...you told me." Even her voice betrayed her dismay.

"No, I didn't," he said evenly. "You've never asked. I thought it was a little odd, but you apparently weren't interested so I never volunteered the information."

Oh my God. Now she'd really done it! How could she have forgotten to ask such an important question as that?

he remembered that he'd asked if she was married, but it
dn't occur to her to inquire if he was because she knew
: wasn't. Maybe she could twist her prior knowledge into
plausible excuse.

She wasn't sure whether she pushed away from him or
he released her, but they disentangled themselves and lay
de by side without looking at or touching each other. Kate
lt bereft and terrified of again saying the wrong thing.

"D-don't forget, Burk," she said shakily. "I lived in
ortland until a few years ago, and my grandmother always
is. Your family is well-known here. You were in the
:wspapers a lot, and…and around the time I moved to
enver you and your…your ex-wife were involved in a
:ry public and volatile child custody suit."

He didn't move or look at her when he answered. "But
at was over five years ago. How did you know I hadn't
arried again in the meantime?"

Kate felt sick with fear as she searched for a plausible
iswer. Why was he making such a big thing of this? Why
as it so important to him?

Finally she settled on the truth. "Grandma told me.
'hen I mentioned that it was Burk Sinclair who had run
to me, we got to talking about you and I asked her if
ou'd ever remarried. She said no."

For a while he said nothing, which was worse than talk-
g. At least when he talked she knew what he was think-
g. As the silence grew, her guilt slowly turned to anger.
was true she was in the wrong, but he was impugning
:r integrity!

What bothered her was that he was right to do that. Her
:racity at that time five years ago had been seriously
awed!

Finally her patience snapped under the pressure of her
ixed feelings, and she sat up cross-legged in the bed, the
leet over her lap. "Just what is the problem here, Burk?"
:r agitation was thick in her tone. "Why is it so important

to you to find out how I knew you weren't married? Afte
all, it was fairly obvious. You...you don't wear a weddin
ring?'' It came out more like a question than a statement

''That's true,'' he agreed, ''but a lot of married me
don't. Surely you've noticed that.''

Of course she had, starting with her own dad. He was
machinist and it would have been dangerous for him t
wear any kind of ring at work, so he just didn't wear the
at all.

''All right, I'll concede that,'' she agreed. ''But yo
never mentioned a wife, you never expressed concern tha
your wife would worry when she didn't hear from you an
you admitted that you were in such a tearing hurry to ge
home because you had a hot date that night. Was I to infe
that you were cheating on a wife?''

He looked startled, but she didn't wait for an answe
''Dammit, are you accusing me of not caring whether yo
were married or not? Do you honestly think I'd make lov
with another woman's husband?''

That thought inflamed her further. ''That's pretty rotte
and I'm not going to stay around and let you flay me wit
insinuations.''

She jumped off the bed and had rounded it to retriev
her clothes off the floor on his side when he bounded u
and grabbed her around the waist from the back.

''Katie, no! That's not what I meant at all!'' he cried a
she fought to shrug him off.

His hold on her tightened. ''Please, sweetheart, don
fight me! Let me explain.''

She knew she was on shaky ground to take exception t
his questioning. He had a right to suspect her of ulteric
motives. She was the one who was being evasive! Sh
stopped struggling to stand passive in his embrace. He nu
zled her ear and nibbled on the lobe, putting her in seriou
danger of forgiving him anything, no matter how insultin

He took a step backward and sat down on the side of th

ed with her on his lap. "Let's lie down again," he murmured as the tip of his tongue explored the inside of that
same sensitive ear.

She felt the rise of his passion under her bare bottom
and her own liquid response. She ached to curl up with him
again and forget his apparent misgivings, but knew it was
imperative that they settle this misunderstanding, if that's
what it was, before this love affair went any further.

"I—I don't think that's a good idea," she stammered,
and forced herself to break away from his embrace and
stand up.

He sighed and reached for his briefs and slacks while
she got into her underwear. He pulled on his clothes while
she took her robe out of the overnight case she'd brought
with her and put it on. It was a wraparound robin's egg
blue satin that she'd bought at a lingerie party in Denver a
month ago and never worn.

He eyed her as he zipped his zipper. "You're not making
this any easier for me," he groaned. "I can't decide
whether you're more enticing nude and sexy or wrapped in
soft smooth satin that makes my hands itch to explore every
inch before I take it off you."

How could she resist him when he said things like that?
She was probably driven by her own guilty conscience in
her need to forgive him, but she'd never allowed a man to
abuse her, either verbally or physically, and she never
would. If he had such a low opinion of her, then it was
best that she find out now.

It was true she had wronged him in the past. She'd also
paid for it with unceasing remorse and her compunction to
leave her home, loved ones and friends for five years of
exile.

There was nothing to be gained by admitting her past
sins to him and, more important, that wasn't even what he
was quizzing her about now. He thought it didn't matter to

her whether or not he was married. That she'd have a
affair with him anyway!

She couldn't bear to watch the combination of hurt an
desire in his expression, and turned away from him. "I'
not a plaything, Burk." Her voice was raw and throbbing
"I'm sorry if I've given you that impression, but all I'
guilty of is indulging in a little gossip. Grandma told m
you hadn't remarried, and I saw no reason not to believ
her. She's an avid reader of the newspaper, especially th
notices of weddings, births and obituaries."

"Katie, please, just listen to me," he pleaded. "I realiz
that I overreacted, and I'm sorry. The only way I can ex
plain it is to tell you the whole story of my divorce an
custody suit. It won't take long, and it's very important t
me that you know why I'm so touchy on the subject."

Now Kate was the one who was surprised. She'd neithe
expected nor even really wanted him to discuss it with he
Actually it terrified her that he was thinking about it at al
The topic was riddled with land mines. There was alway
the chance that she'd trip up and say or do something, th
way she just had, that would point his suspicions towar
her!

"That—that's really not necessary," she stammered.

"Yes, it is," he said gravely. "I need you to understan
when I go off the deep end once in a while that my ire i
not aimed at you. It's aimed at a phantom news reporte
whom I don't know and can't find."

Kate didn't hear him move until she felt his arms encircl
her waist and pull her gently against him. She couldn't sta
angry with him when she knew what was bothering hir
and the depth of his despair. He was right. She did need t
hear his version of the unfortunate incident.

But first she needed a few minutes to calm her shattere
nerves.

She let herself relax against him. "All right, Burk," sh

said, somewhat wobbly. "But first I want to put my clothes on. Would you mind waiting in the living room for me?"

"Anything you want, love," he murmured, and released her.

As soon as he left she dressed, brushed her disheveled hair and left it swinging loose around her shoulders, then repaired her lipstick. By the time she joined him she felt more in control.

By unspoken mutual consent they sat down in the two big comfortable lounge chairs, his oxblood color leather and hers fawn velour. She didn't want them to sit on the sofa where he'd be close enough to touch her. She knew if he did, she'd melt and nothing would be accomplished between them except to again sate their raging lust for each other.

Kate sort of burrowed into her chair as if it could somehow protect her from the pain the subject of Burk's derailed custody suit always brought her. He on the other hand sat straight, shoulders squared and eyes focused ahead as if to deflect the agonizing memories that he knew were about to overcome him.

"Fleur and I met twelve years ago at the Sorbonne in Paris where she was studying for her degree and I was taking some postgraduate liberal arts courses," he began. "We started going out, and one thing led to another as they sometimes tend to do...."

He paused for a moment then cleared his throat and continued. "Anyway, at the end of the year we married and came back to Oregon to live happily ever after."

He grimaced. "It didn't happen. The glow lasted approximately six months and then she got homesick and started pestering me to move to France. She couldn't seem to understand that I had a growing and successful business here and relocating was out of the question."

Kate could understand the loneliness of being homesick. She'd experienced an acute case of it after she left her home and family here and moved to Denver. It never completely went away, but she'd eventually learned to compromise. To accept the inevitable and get on with her life.

"Did she know when she married you that you intended to live in this country?" Kate asked.

He grunted. "Of course she did. I made that plain. I explained about the family business and my responsibilities to it. Not once did she protest or indicate that she didn't want to leave her country."

He stood and walked over to the fireplace where he stood with his back to her. "It became obvious later that she'd married me only for what I could give her. Her parents had six children and her dad worked at a low-paying job. They were barely able to scrape by. Fleur was exceptionally bright and was going through university on scholarships plus what she could earn, I found out later."

His last words were uttered in a bitter tone that warned her not to ask why. Besides, she already knew.

"I supported her family with a check every month from the time we were married until she disappeared," he continued, "and Fleur grew to like my life-style. She loved the attention she got and the influence that being a part of my family gave her. She enjoyed buying expensive clothes and getting her picture in the papers as a sponsor for various charity functions. She didn't work on the projects, just donated money to them and took credit for being a gracious and generous donor."

"Did she ever go back to France to visit?" Kate asked.

He turned to face her. "Oh, yes," he answered angrily, "twice a year, and each time she was gone for six weeks. That's no way to fix a troubled marriage. I wanted a family but all she wanted was a lot of money and a good time.'"

Kate blinked. "But you had a child."

He nodded, but couldn't hide the lines of pain her reminder brought to his mouth and eyes. "Yes, Monique." It throbbed in his voice, too. "She came as a surprise. Fleu didn't want a baby, but her religion forbade abortion. So did I. It was my child and I wanted it. That fact didn't have any effect on her, so when she talked about having an abortion anyway, I threatened to divorce her and cut her off with no spousal support if she did.''

Kate's eyes widened. ''Could you do that?''

He walked across the room to the glass wall and stood looking out. ''Probably. She was well educated, capable of supporting herself and had no children.''

Kate shivered. How could a man and a woman live together in such a venomous atmosphere? It must have been hell for both of them!

''So she went ahead and had the baby.'' It wasn't a question, since she knew the answer, it was just a statement.

Again Burk turned to look at her, and she thought she saw a tiny smile at the corners of his mouth. ''She not only had Monique but she loved her and was a good mother.''

That really astounded Kate. ''But then why did you get a divorce later?''

His shoulders slumped and he jammed his hands in his pockets. ''We tried to make a go of our marriage for the child's sake, but we were totally incompatible. Although we seldom agreed on anything, the biggest gap was the hassle over where we'd live. After the baby was born, she was even more insistent that we move back to France to be with her family. I was equally determined to raise our little girl here in this country.''

He began pacing slowly back and forth. ''When Monique was six months old Fleur wanted to take her to France to show her off to her parents. I refused to let her. I felt, and still do, that the baby was too young to travel so far to a foreign country, but I paid their fare to come here—her parents and three siblings. By that time Fleur and two of her siblings were married and on their own.''

Kate smiled. ''That was generous of you. I imagine they were thrilled at the opportunity to travel.''

Burk shook his head. "Not really. They didn't speak English so had trouble communicating, and they didn't like the weather here. Too much rain. Also, they'd never been out of France and were eager to get home. They were supposed to stay a month, but left after only two weeks."

Kate could understand and sympathize with his frustration. She could see why the marriage had ultimately ended in divorce.

"When Monique was three years old, Fleur filed for divorce and full-time custody of her," he continued. "I agreed to the divorce and even the excessive financial arrangement she insisted on, but I wanted custody of Monique. I knew Fleur would find a way to take her out of this country and back to France to live, and I wasn't going to allow it. I no longer cared where Fleur lived, but I wanted to raise my daughter. Fleur was equally determined to have custody, and it turned into a mud-slinging brawl that attracted all the news media in the state."

Kate closed her eyes in anguish as her runaway thoughts castigated her. *And in my youthful and misguided eagerness to make a name for myself in journalism I was partially responsible for you losing her altogether.*

She bit her lip and clenched her fists in an effort to ignore the overwhelming desire to confess everything to him and apologize. That would accomplish nothing and do irreparable harm.

Instead she cleared her throat and hoped her voice wouldn't tremble. She knew only too well what happened next, but he'd be suspicious again if she didn't comment. "As I remember, the custody issue was never settled?"

He slammed his fist into his hand in a barely controlled show of violence. Obviously he was still furious and in no mood to forgive what Kate had done.

"Oh, it was settled all right," he rasped. "I won, for all the good it did me."

This she hadn't known, and it startled her. "But I

thought... That is, does she live with you? You've never mentioned her until now.''

He sank back down into his chair and rubbed his hands over his face. "You thought her mother took her and disappeared," he said bitterly. "You're right, she did, and I haven't seen either of them since."

His obvious agony was breaking her heart, but there was nothing she could do about it but sit by and watch him suffer. She might as well help him get to the point and get it over with.

"So what happened?" she asked.

"Fleur and I both had top attorneys, and each was determined to win. They battled toe-to-toe. First hers would score a point, then mine would match it. It was too close to call when I came on some information about Fleur that almost guaranteed me custody. Ordinarily I wouldn't have used it—after all, she was the mother of my daughter—but I was desperate. My lawyer was preparing to present it when some scuzball reporter found out about it and sold it to our local tabloid newspaper as a blind item."

As he spoke, Kate's breath seemed to become trapped halfway between her lungs and her throat, and her heart pounded with guilty panic. Parts of what he said were untrue, or at least incomplete.

It's true she'd come across the material and written the article to sell to the tabloid. The editor had been happy to pay her for it and she'd taken the money, but then started having second thoughts. Belatedly she'd realized it was a sleazy thing to do. It wasn't news, it was gossip, and it could even influence the outcome of the custody battle.

She'd tried to buy the item back, but the editor was only interested in selling papers and making his tattle sheet well-known and popular. He ran the item the following day. Kate could still see it in bold black letters. We've Just Learned That A Well-known Local Businessman, Embroiled In A Custody Battle For His Young Child, Has A Secret Weapon That Should Guarantee His Victory.

Fleur Sinclair and her small daughter disappeared that night, and to the best of Kate's knowledge hadn't been seen or heard from since.

Burk had been nearly out of his mind with rage and grief, and had vowed to destroy both the tabloid and the reporter who compiled the item.

When Burk finished recounting the story to her, he sat on the edge of the chair with his head in his hands, looking totally wrung out. She hated that it had been necessary to put him through reliving that painful time in his life, but there was still one more question she had to ask, even though she knew the answer only too well.

"What was it the item referred to?"

He raised his head and looked at her through haunted eyes. "I'd just learned that when Fleur was at university she supplemented her scholarship money by working as a high-class call girl!"

Chapter Eight

Kate cringed as an echo of Burk's pain slashed through her. What a blow that would have been to his ego and pride! She'd learned in the short time she'd known him that he was a proud man. Also a moral one.

"How...how did you find that out?" she queried.

"I hired a private investigator to try to find something about her that would tip the scales of the custody hearing in my favor." He spoke in a monotone. "I knew nothing about her past before we met. I thought there may have been some indiscretions, but I never expected anything like that. I questioned it, but the investigator had solid proof, including a couple of johns who had indiscreetly bragged about being serviced by the crème de la crème of prostitutes. She was only available by appointment to the rich and famous in the area."

He dropped his head back in his hands, and this time Kate couldn't resist going to him. She sank to the floor beside his chair and nestled her face on his thigh.

"Burk, I'm...I'm so sorry," she said brokenly and caressed his knee with her hand. "Would you really have introduced that in open court?"

He stroked her head. "Only if the judge's decision had gone against me, but as it turned out it wasn't necessary. She recognized herself in the blind item and knew she probably wouldn't stand a chance if I used it. The day the paper came out she panicked, took Monique and bolted."

She felt him tense, and he stopped his stroking. "I'm not going to rest until I find the low-life reporter who sold that article to that scandal sheet." His tone was chilling. "The editor admitted that he'd planned to run the full story as a follow-up in the next issue. I put him out of business, and when I catch up with the reporter I'll make him wish he'd never learned to write!"

Kate shivered. She knew Burk didn't make idle threats. If he ever learned she was that reporter, he'd be as merciless with her as he had been with the editor. Why, oh, why had she been such a scatterbrained idiot?

After a moment he continued. "When it became clear that Fleur had abducted Monique and disappeared, the judge issued a warrant for her arrest and awarded me full and permanent custody of my daughter."

His voice cracked and he took a deep breath. "Not that it did me much good. I've had detectives searching all over the United States and Europe, but it's as if they've vanished off the face of the earth."

She choked back a groan, then rubbed her cheek against his thigh and kissed it. "Couldn't you trace her through her parents?"

He resumed absently stroking his fingers through her hair. "I'm sure she went back to France, but if she did, she hasn't contacted them openly. It's impossible to keep a twenty-four-hour watch on them for five years. I'd have gone broke by now—plus it would probably be considered harassment. They know where she and Monique are but they're not talking."

A wave of anger washed over Kate. "That's pretty ungrateful of them considering you'd been supplementing their income all the time you were married to their daughter."

Burk's fingers stilled. "Would you give up your daughter and granddaughter just because you owed your son-in-law a debt of gratitude?"

"No, of course not!" she sputtered indignantly, then closed her mouth as she understood the message he was sending her.

"Neither would most parents," he pointed out. "Besides, even if we did find Fleur and Monique it's unlikely the French authorities would extradite her to this country. After all, she's a French citizen, and so is Monique. As the child of a French citizen born in the United States she has dual citizenship in both countries. The best I can hope for is to be allowed to visit my little girl in France and know that she is safe and well."

His fist clenched and inadvertently tugged painfully at Kate's hair. "It's the not knowing that drives me crazy," he groaned.

She blinked back tears of remorse and slowly caressed his inner thigh. She couldn't sooth his anguish, but maybe she could take his mind off it for a little while.

Very soon her ministrations had the desired visible effect, and his fingers dug into her scalp. She trailed kisses in the wake of her caresses and murmured, "Would you like to go back into the bedroom and see if we can find a way to relieve your...anxiety?"

He leaned down and kissed her cheek. "I think I could be persuaded," he whispered against her ear, then stood and pulled her up with him. "You can relieve my...umm...anxiety anytime you want to."

* * *

Kate soon found out that he meant what he said, and they spent most of the weekend making love, except for Saturday night when Emily was there. Then they slept in separate rooms. Kate knew they weren't fooling her grandmother, but she also knew Emily would be more comfortable if she wasn't confronted with the indisputable fact that her granddaughter and Burk were sleeping together without benefit of clergy.

Burk didn't repeat his declaration of love, but although Kate was disappointed, she really hadn't expected him to. She told herself to be content with what she had because that was all she was going to get. A temporary fling that could end at any time. She decided that was better than nothing.

She went back to her grandmother's house late Sunday evening and started work Monday morning. Hemingway/ Price was one of the biggest manufacturers of computer software in the country, and she'd been hired by their branch in Portland as Manager of Classified Files. It was pretty much the same kind of work she'd done for the federal government in Denver.

The first day was spent getting acquainted with the people she'd be working with and the job site, but by the end of the week she was off and running. Being in charge of the extensive inventory of classified files was a huge responsibility, but it was also fascinating and she enjoyed it.

Burk's doctor hadn't cleared him to go back to the office yet, but that didn't keep him from working. He just had his secretary come to the house and conducted business from there. Kate stopped by every day after work and scolded him for not resting as much as the doctor told him to, but he just grinned, sent the secretary home and led Kate off to bed where she quickly lost touch with reality while they made erotic and exhilarating love.

Afterward they had dinner delivered from one of the

nearby restaurants, but she left every evening at ten o'clock to spend the nights with her grandmother.

Burk and Kate had planned to spend this weekend together again, but Emily refused to chaperon them this time.

"Burk has a lovely apartment, but it's too fancy for me," she told Kate. "I prefer my own house and my own bed. I'll be just fine. I'm not an invalid, for heaven's sake. You don't have to worry about me."

Kate knew there was no way to change Grandma's mind, and besides, she really was getting along very well.

She joined Burk at his condominium in time for breakfast on Saturday morning. This time he didn't rush her into the bedroom. After all, they had the whole weekend. Instead he cooked and served her eggs Benedict, fresh fruit cup, muffins and both coffee and tomato juice. It all smelled yummy and tasted delicious.

"You didn't tell me you could cook," she said after she swallowed her first bite.

He chuckled. "You didn't ask. To be truthful, I'll have to admit that I bought the muffins, but they taste like homemade when warmed in the microwave."

She bit into one and sighed. "Ohhh, they most certainly do," she said ecstatically. "How come you decided to unveil your talent this morning? Last Saturday I had breakfast before I came over, and on Sunday Grandma fixed it for us here."

He nodded. "I know, and she's an excellent cook, but today we're alone, and I want everything to be special."

There was a huskiness in his tone that caught her attention. "Every day with you is special," she murmured, somewhat embarrassed by her admission. "So what's different about today?"

He reached out and took her hand. "Maybe it won't be, but just humor me, please?"

"Anything you want," she said, looking up at him

through thick lashes and deliberately making her voice provocative.

"Now stop that," he ordered, and squeezed her hand. "You're getting ahead of the script."

She blinked. "The script? You mean you've got the whole day choreographed?"

He grinned. "I guess you could say that. First, breakfast. Then a tour of the city including lunch. Third, a movie—your choice. Fourth, free time for shopping or whatever, and fifth, dinner at the Esplanade restaurant with the panoramic view overlooking the river. Does that suit milady?"

Kate's head was reeling. "Sounds great, but why a tour of the city? I was raised here and so were you."

He took a sip of coffee before answering. "That's true, but I'll bet you've never taken a commercial tour."

She picked up her mug. "No, I haven't."

"And I'll bet you've never taken the time to visit most of our historic or public places," he challenged.

"Right again," she admitted. "Except for when I was in elementary school and we went to some of them on class field trips. I guess it is time I became better acquainted with my hometown."

He looked enormously pleased. "Good. Now eat up. Our tour starts at nine."

Kate had a marvelous time. Like many residents of interesting cities, she'd driven by the landmarks but had never investigated them. She hadn't realized what she'd been missing! Their guide led them on walks through the American Advertising Museum, which chronicled the history of American advertising since 1683; the restored French Renaissance Pittock mansion and its priceless seventeenth-and eighteenth-century antique furnishings; took an abbreviated walk through part of the ten miles of trails among the coniferous flowering trees and shrubs at the Hoyt Arboretum in Washington Park; then wound up almost next door at the Metro Washington Park Zoo, where they not only viewed the animals but also had lunch at the AfriCafé, where they watched the colorful tropical birds in an adjoining aviary.

Kate sighed. "I don't remember when I've enjoyed myself so much," she said with a contented smile as she sipped her coffee. "You really know how to entertain your women."

He picked up her hand and kissed the palm, a gesture that always made prickles run down her spine. "Not women, sweetheart," he said huskily. "You're the only *woman* I want to entertain, and I'm glad you've had a good time this morning. Have you decided what movie you want to see?"

She puckered up her brow. "Gee, I don't know. I haven't seen any lately, but could we steer clear of the ones with a lot of blood and gore? It's been such a calm and peaceful morning that I don't want to taint the mood."

He squeezed her hand. "My sentiments exactly. How about a romance?"

She nodded. "Sounds great, but do they still make them? Seems like everything these days is so violent—even the ones that are supposed to be love stories."

He grinned. "Oh, I think we can find one. I'll pick up a newspaper when I pay the bill, and we can look through the entertainment section on our way back to the tour office."

The movie they chose was the sweet old-fashioned kind, a real tearjerker, and as they walked out of the theater two and a half hours later Kate was sniffling and dabbing at her eyes. Burk put his arm around her and hugged her to his side while they walked to his shiny white sedan in the parking lot.

"Oh, that was just...just great," she murmured on a shaky breath. "It was *so* sad!"

He hugged her closer. "Women!" he said, but his tone

was light. "You don't like good clean violence, which is usually too far-out to be believable, but you'll sob all the way through a motion picture that tears your emotions apart."

She wiped her face with the back of her hand. "Violence is never good or clean," she said huffily. "And anyway, this is different."

He released her to get his keys out of his pocket as they neared the car. "Whatever you say, love," he muttered. "Everyone to their own mayhem."

By the time they got back to the condo Kate had herself under control, and was looking forward to a few hours alone with Burk before they went out to dinner.

"Do you mind if I take a shower?" she asked as he shut and bolted the door.

"Not at all," he said as he came up behind her and put his arms around her waist. "Do you mind if I take one with you?"

She felt the usual surge of desire at his embrace, and his enticing answer. "Please do," she said eagerly.

He let his hand wander over her stomach then stopped at the waistband of her black jeans and unbuttoned the button. She felt him get hard against her bottom and couldn't resist rubbing against him. He quickly unzipped her fly and slipped his hand inside to cup her palpitating femininity.

She reached back between them and fingered the bulge in his own jeans, eliciting a moan from deep in his throat. He fastened his mouth to her neck and sucked gently, sending waves of need to her core at the same time as his fingers stroked the crotch of her panties, leaving her mindless. She writhed her hips in encouragement even though she knew this was happening too fast.

He slid his fingers beneath the silk and entered her. She clenched her teeth to keep from crying out in ecstasy even as she clasped his wrist in protest. "No, Burk, not without you. Slow down."

She wasn't making sense but he'd know what she meant. His fingers stilled and he rubbed his throbbing groin against her buttocks. "It's all right, sweetheart." His voice was raw with unfulfilled urgency. "I like pleasuring you this way. We'll get in bed and come together very soon and it will be great for me, too. Truly it will."

It was torture for her to remove his hand and turn in his embrace. She put her arms around his neck and snuggled against him. "Some other time, I promise," she said shakily, "but for now I want you with me when we climax."

He reached down and scooped her up. "If that's what you want, that's the way it will be," he whispered in her ear as he carried her into the bedroom.

They stripped off their clothes in record time and fell into bed. Seconds later they both soared in rapture.

Kate and Burk must have slept a while afterward because when she surfaced again they were cuddled together in each other's arms and the clock on the bedside table told her it was 5:13.

She loved curling up with Burk. He always made her feel so...so safe, and cared for. He was such a nice man, and she loved him so much that it scared her to think about it. What was going to happen to her when he eventually decided to break off their relationship? Or when he found another woman more to his liking?

She shuddered and he must have felt it because he grunted and opened his eyes. "What's the matter, honey?" he murmured. "Are you cold?"

His arms tightened around her and she burrowed closer. "No, not at all. I guess I just woke with a start. It's after five o'clock and we haven't had our shower yet. When are we due at the restaurant?"

His hand caressed her nude body. "We'll have time for the shower—the reservations are for seven-thirty."

He cupped her bare breast and made it tingle. "We won't if you keep that up," she teased, and nibbled at his throat.

He didn't laugh as she'd expected, but put his fingers under her chin and raised it for a kiss. It was gentle and sweet, and she parted her lips for his invasion. She was addicted to the taste of him, a barely discernible minty flavor, and the smell of his expensive shaving lotion.

His hands once more roamed over her back and derriere, and she felt him harden against her knee, which was positioned between his thighs. He rolled over onto his back, taking her with him so that she was lying on top of him.

"Katie, my darling," he murmured against the corner of her mouth. "Have you any idea how much I love you?"

For a moment the words didn't register. When they finally did she assumed she'd heard wrong.

"How much you what?" she asked, praying he'd said what she thought he'd said, but certain he hadn't.

"How much I love you," he repeated, sending shock up and down her nerve endings.

For a few seconds she couldn't gather her thoughts enough to say anything, and when she finally did speak she sounded a little slow-witted. "You love me?" She wondered if she looked as stupid as she felt.

"Of course I love you." He sounded puzzled, as if he was questioning her intellect, too. "I told you that last weekend. Don't you remember?"

Now he sounded hurt, and she couldn't let him think she'd forget such a momentous occasion. Not remember? It was those three words that had alternately thrilled and tormented her all week!

She kissed him on the mouth then buried her face in the side of his neck. "Oh, Burk, of course I remember, but I didn't think you meant it. I thought you were just carried away with the passion of the moment. You never mentioned it again."

He rolled onto his side, sliding her off him and onto her

back, then propped himself up with his elbow. He looked annoyed. "Katie, I don't make declarations of love unless I mean it. In fact, you're the first woman I've ever said that to since Fleur. I didn't mention it again because you didn't respond, so I thought you didn't want to hear it."

She gasped. "Didn't want to hear it? The truth is I wanted so badly to hear you say it to me that when you did, I was afraid to believe you. That's the only reason I didn't respond. I didn't want you to feel trapped into a relationship you hadn't intended. I figured that if you meant it, you'd say it again, but you didn't, so..."

His scowl cleared and was replaced by a hopeful smile. "Is there any chance that you're trying to tell me that you love me, too?"

She reached up and put her arms around him, pulling him down to lay across her chest. She knew that sometime in the next few hours she was going to have to wrestle with the undeniable fact that a relationship between them could shatter them both, but right now she wasn't prepared to face that.

She pushed away her misgivings and let a blinding burst of happiness flood her whole being with light.

"Burk, darling, I think I fell in love with you the day of the accident when I found you on the muddy ground in the middle of that dreadful storm in the mountains. I know I was in love with you by the time we got to the cabin. I guess that sounds silly but I swear it's the truth."

He nuzzled her bare breast. "It doesn't sound silly, it sounds wonderful." His voice was raspy with emotion. "Apparently we were meant to fall in love. Do you agree?"

He moved his head slightly to nuzzle the other breast, and she ran her fingernails provocatively over his back. She didn't agree with his line of reasoning. They were definitely *not* meant to fall in love, but she couldn't tell him that. Later, maybe, but not now.

"It would seem that way," she hedged as her fingers found and kneaded his trim butt.

He made a little sound of contentment and moved against her, brushing her leg with his tumescent shaft and sending erotic shivers through both of them.

"Then I can't think of any reason why we shouldn't get married. Can you?" he asked gently.

"*Married!*" The word sent bolts of shock accompanied by red lights and blaring sirens ripping through her, and sent her whole body into spasm.

Although she wasn't aware of it, she must have said the word out loud, because Burk rolled away from her and sat up. "Katie, what's wrong? Why does the mention of marriage upset you so? Is the thought of having me for a husband so distasteful to you?"

He sounded both upset and hurt, and again, before she could think, she sat up and put her arms around his shoulders. "No, Burk, of course not! You'd be a wonderful husband. It...it's just that I wasn't expecting a proposal—"

"Why in hell not?" he interrupted. "You must have known as well as I what our...our relationship...was leading up to. You said you love me...."

"I do love you...."

"And I love you. So what's the problem?" He pulled away from her and stood.

Kate's eyes were glued to him. He was magnificent in the buff! Especially when he was angry. His taut muscles rippled, and his stance was that of a warrior on the verge of going into battle.

She swung her legs around and put her feet on the floor, then pulled the sheet over her lap. She'd never seen this side of Burk before. This man was a stranger who made her feel exposed and vulnerable without covering.

"We...we've only known each other a couple of weeks," she said, casting around for words to tell him they couldn't risk marriage without telling him why.

She could see by his expression that he wasn't going to accept that excuse. "If we love each other, what difference does that make?" he thundered.

She tried again. "Well, we…we haven't had time to get to know each other very well."

"So what do you want to know?" he asked impatiently. "You've admitted that you've heard gossip and read news releases about me and my family for years, and I've told you about my troubled marriage and losing my daughter. What more do you need?"

She could see that she was getting nowhere. He wasn't going to let her get away with vacillating answers to his questions.

She pulled the sheet up to cover her breasts, too. "Nothing," she said shakily. "But you hardly know me at all."

His expression softened and so did his voice. "I know that you're warm, and generous, and loving. You've nursed me through a potentially serious head injury, you've never once scolded me or complained because my recklessness caused the accident that totaled your car and inconvenienced you for days, and you're absolutely fabulous in bed." That last was said with a smile. "Good Lord, woman, what more do I need to know about you?"

She couldn't help smiling, too, even though she knew it was imperative that she make him understand how impossible it was for them to marry. If she said yes, she'd also have to tell him she was the reporter who had been responsible for him losing his child, and then it would be all over. Nothing she could ever say or do would wipe out that one fatal mistake!

"Don't you think we should get better acquainted before we take any vows? What if we get married and then you find out you don't really like me very well after all?"

This time he grinned. "Honey, I'm not a teenager, and neither are you. We both know the difference between lust and love. And what's all this nonsense about I might not like you? Nothing can change my feelings for you. It's more likely that you would be disenchanted with me. I can be a real bastard at times, but I'm willing to try to change if that happens because I love you too much to lose you.''

Kate sat there with her heart in her throat and tears in her eyes. How could she be sensible when he was so romantic? Would it really be so bad if they got married? Just being his wife would be all the happiness she could ever want, and she'd do her best to make him happy and content. If, in the course of time, her secret became known, he could divorce her without guilt since she'd deliberately concealed the truth from him.

Surely she couldn't be expected to live the rest of her life afraid to take the next step for fear of discovery. She wouldn't know if her world was going to fall apart unless she started living in it.

It was folly to sit around waiting for the other shoe to drop. The man she loved wanted her to be his wife. And she wanted him to be her husband. So why was she hesitating?

The cold chill of integrity swept over her and made her shiver. Because she couldn't marry him without telling him the whole truth. That's why she hesitated. He had every right to know who she was and what she'd done to him. It was wrong for her to start a life with him under the burden of so vital a secret! If she wanted to accept his proposal, she had to confide in him first.

''Katie?'' Burk's voice was laced with uncertainty. ''If you don't want to marry me, just say so.''

''It—it's not that, darling,'' she assured him. ''But there's…there's something I need to tell you before I give you an answer.''

Burk grinned and cupped her head with his hands. ''Is this a confession of past sins?'' he asked.

''Well, sort of,'' she said slowly.

''Have you murdered somebody?''

She blinked in astonishment. "No, of—of course not," she sputtered.

"Did you embezzle millions of dollars from your last employer?"

She shook her head, trying to dislodge his restraining hand. "Don't be silly, of course I didn't. You're not taking me seriously—"

The grin disappeared as quickly as it had appeared. "Oh, but I am, love. Now I have just one more question. Would you be marrying me for my money?"

"Oh, Burk, you know I wouldn't. If I marry you it will be because I love you with all my heart, but—"

He released her head. "Then I don't want to hear whatever it is you feel you must confess."

Kate was stunned. "But you need to hear it. It's important!"

He shook his head. "No, I don't, sweetheart. Whatever you may have done in the past isn't important. I certainly haven't lived the life of a monk. The only thing I want from you is your promise that you'll love me forever."

Kate was flabbergasted. "Burk, you don't even know what I'm trying to tell you. How do you know it's not important?"

He reached out and took her in his arms and drew her close. "Because the past doesn't matter. We're both old enough to have made a few mistakes, but I'm not going to tell you mine, and I don't want to hear yours. We'll start fresh and new and concentrate on making each other happy in the present, not rehashing mistakes from the past. Okay?"

Kate snuggled into his embrace. What he said made sense. No one was guaranteed a long and happy life. If she married him and eventually he left her, she'd be devastated, but she'd be equally so if she didn't marry him and sent him away on the slim chance that he might find out her secret and leave her anyway.

At least if they were together they'd be happy while it lasted. If she turned down his proposal they'd still have all of the pain and none of the joy.

With a sense of relief at having the decision taken out of her hands, Kate put her arms around his neck and snuggled close.

"Burk, my darling, I've never doubted my love for you. If you feel the same about me, I'll be happy and honored to be your wife," she murmured huskily, and raised her face for his kiss.

Half an hour later, still naked and glistening with sweat, he disentangled himself from Kate and got out of bed. After rummaging around in one of his dresser drawers, he found what he was looking for and brought it back to hand it to her.

It was a velvet jeweler's box. Carefully she opened it and stared. Inside was a large square-cut diamond set in a gold engagement ring with a matching gold wedding band.

"You had this all planned," she said in wonder. His proposal hadn't been a spur-of-the-moment decision but a well-thought-out one. "This is why you said today was special."

He sat down on the edge of the bed, then took the diamond from the box and reached for her hand. "I didn't know if you'd agree to marry me," he said, and there was a touch of awe in his voice, too. "But I never doubted that if you did it would be the most memorable day of my life."

He slid the ring on her finger, and they never did make it to the restaurant that night.

Chapter Nine

The following three weeks went by in a glow of happiness. The next day when Kate and Burk announced to her grandmother and his family their intention to be married within a month, the relatives were all a little concerned about the short time the couple had known each other, but each side welcomed the other and seemed genuinely delighted.

Burk's parents gave them an impromptu engagement announcement party, which included not only the entire Sinclair clan but friends of both families, too numerous to mention, and all of the people Kate now worked closely with. It was a gala evening at the country club, and her head whirled with the effort to put names to faces and remember them.

The party and the announcement were written up the next day in the newspaper. Burk was the perfect fiancé, and she'd never been so excited!

The wedding date was a problem. Burk insisted that it

take place within a month, but not even the Sinclairs could arrange for a church and wedding clothes that quickly, so when there was a cancellation at the Protestant cathedral two weekends past his deadline, he reluctantly agreed to wait.

"I want you to belong to me body and soul," he said as he held her close and attempted to explain why he was so impatient. "I know that's a politically incorrect way of putting it, but it's how I feel. It sounds like I want to rule you, and that's not it at all, but I can't shake this dark feeling that if I don't bind you to me with vows now, I could lose you."

A cold shudder of apprehension froze Kate. My God, did he suspect she was keeping something from him? Or was he reading her mind? Either way it would be disastrous.

"Wh-why would you think a thing like that?" she stammered.

He hugged her closer. "I haven't the foggiest notion. It's silly and totally unsubstantiated, but it won't go away. The longer we delay the wedding, the stronger it gets."

He rested his chin on the top of her head. "It probably has something to do with my losing Monique so unexpectedly and so completely. My daughter was the dearest thing in my life, and when she disappeared it nearly destroyed me. I've never felt that deeply about anyone before or since until you came along. Now I have nightmares about you disappearing the way she did, and it scares the sh—the hell out of me. I'd never survive a loss like that a second time."

He wasn't the only one who was scared! He couldn't possibly know how close he was to the truth. He wouldn't lose her, but he'd most assuredly send her away!

There was one way to put an end to their fears. "Darling, I have no burning desire for a big fancy wedding. I'm perfectly willing to cancel all those plans and marry you tomorrow with just a minister and our immediate families present."

He trailed kisses in her hair. "Is it any wonder I love you so much? You're so sweet and thoughtful, but I wouldn't deprive you of the fairy-tale wedding I gather all women dream about. After all, you're only going to get married once, and I don't want you to have any regrets. It's going to be all you've ever hoped for."

"Marrying you is all I ever hoped for," she assured him, "and I don't care how the deed is accomplished. I'll come to you barefoot with wild flowers in my hair or wearing a jewel-encrusted satin wedding gown and tiara. It doesn't matter to me just so long as you say 'I do' when that all-important question is asked."

"You can count on that, my love," he murmured huskily, "but we can't embarrass our families by calling off the fancy wedding at this late date. After all, the invitations have gone out and the caterer contracted for."

Confessing to Kate what he considered his unreasonable fear seemed to loosen its hold on Burk, and as the big day grew closer they both relaxed and enjoyed the rounds of showers and other prenuptial parties. It really was going to be a fairy-tale wedding, and Kate managed to shove aside her misgivings as her happiness grew and expanded.

But that was before Evel Jensen accosted her.

Two and a half weeks before the wedding Kate was floating on air. Burk's mother and Kate's grandmother were taking care of all the wedding and reception arrangements so Kate had all the fun and none of the stress. All she had to do was show up wherever and whenever she was told to.

On this Wednesday morning she was busy at her desk checking a file that had just been returned to her to make sure all the classified information was there when Mr. Jensen, a production line technician, came in. She knew him fairly well because he was the friendly type who always spoke to her when they happened to meet, and a couple of times he had joined the group she was with at a table during lunch in the cafeteria.

He was a tall, slender man in his late forties or early fifties, with thinning brown hair and large tortoiseshell glasses. He told her he was married and had two sons in college. She didn't particularly like him, but neither did she dislike him.

"Good morning, Kate," he said cheerfully. "You're looking especially pretty this morning."

His line of patter wasn't original, but neither was it annoying.

"Thank you, Mr. Jensen," she said and smiled. She called him "Mr." because he was her senior both in age and in the advancement climb to the top, and he'd never asked her to call him Evel. She didn't blame him. It was such an odd name to give a child. The only other time she'd heard it was when Evel Knievel, the motorcycle stuntman, was in the news.

"What can I do for you?" she asked.

"I need the Project 2000 file," he said pleasantly, using the code name for their newest and most secret project.

Kate's mind went immediately on alert. She'd been working here only for a few weeks, but one of the first things she'd done was familiarize herself with the names of all the people with security clearance who had access to the files under her charge, and she was sure he wasn't one of them.

She brought up the information on her computer screen and found that she was right. "I'm sorry, Mr. Jensen, but you don't have the security clearance to see that file." She kept her tone even and with a touch of regret. She'd get nowhere by antagonizing him.

He looked perturbed. "Oh. I thought I did."

He was lying. He had to be, because anyone who was

given security clearance had to submit to an extensive back-ground check and couldn't possibly not know what it was for. She decided to call his bluff.

"If you'd like, I can call Security and ask if your name was left off by mistake."

His reaction was smooth but immediate. "No. No, don't do that. I must have misunderstood. Sorry to have bothered you."

He turned and walked out of her office.

Now what was that all about? Was he really trying to access files he had no business seeing? Or was it an honest error? That seemed unlikely, but it could happen. Should she report the incident to the director of security? If she did it would be a black mark against Jensen until he was cleared of suspicion. She hated to do that. After all, he was probably innocent of any wrongdoing, but the black mark could do a lot of damage to his career even if it was erased later.

She decided not to take any action right away but keep close track of him. If he tried anything like this again, then she'd turn him in without a qualm.

Kate didn't see Jensen again for the rest of the week, and she'd decided the incident was just a fluke and had relaxed her vigilance when he came to her office the fol-lowing Monday. This time he was neither smiling nor friendly.

"Kate, I need to talk to you but not here, and I know you don't live alone."

She blinked. "No, I don't," she said firmly, "and I also don't date married men."

"I'm not asking you for a date," he growled. "This is strictly business, but it can't be conducted here or at your place. I promise it will be worth your while to listen to me."

Dammit, why did some men have to be so obnoxious?

She opened her mouth to retort, but he didn't give her a chance.

"Don't tell me you can't use some extra money," he wheedled. "It must have been expensive changing jobs and moving here from Denver to be near your grandma, Emily Kelly, after her stroke."

Kate's mouth snapped shut. How did this man know so much about her? And about Grandma? Kate had met him only after she started working here, and until today they hadn't exchanged more than a few words.

Of course a new employee was always the subject of gossip for a short time after she started working, but Jensen even knew her grandmother's full name and that she'd suffered a stroke. That wasn't a fact Kate had shared with anybody here at work, although he could have been introduced to Grandma at the engagement party.

The flaw in that thinking was that Evel Jensen hadn't been invited to the party. He didn't work in her area and she didn't know him well enough to invite him.

Could he have somehow seen her personnel file? He was in no position legally to have access to it!

She decided she'd better play along and see what he was up to. "I imagine everyone can use extra money," she said casually, "but if you're offering me overtime, I—"

"Not overtime," he interrupted. "And it won't take more than an hour or so. Come on, Kathy, at least listen to what I have to say."

Kathy! No one but her grandmother still called her Kathy! He must have been in touch with Grandma. Had he somehow wormed his way into her confidence and learned all these small but personal things about both of them?

Was he subtly threatening Kate? Letting her know he knew her vulnerable areas and could apply pressure if she didn't go along with whatever it was he wanted? Or was she just getting paranoid? A condition that wasn't uncommon to people in her occupation.

If it was the former, he didn't know her as well as he thought he did. She'd fight the bastard and make him wish he'd never picked on her! This time she was going to report him.

She stood up and glared at him. "Now get this straight, I'm not going anywhere with you, so stop wasting my time. I want you out of my office, right now, and if you don't go willingly I'll call Security and have you thrown out."

He glowered right back at her. "Oh, I don't think you will," he said heatedly. "Not if you want to marry Burk Sinclair next week."

Burk! Her nerve ends came to immediate attention and a wave of fear swept through her. What did he know about Burk and her?

"I—I don't know what you mean." Her voice was barely above a whisper and a dead giveaway of the panic that was strangling her.

A glance at his expression told her that he actually enjoyed tormenting her. "Sure you do," he purred. "And just what do you think he'd do if I was forced to tell him you were the reporter who sold that story to the tabloid you were working for, about his ex-wife's...ummm...extracurricular activities during her college days. Give it some quick thought, baby, because I'm not leavin' here until you make up your mind."

Her legs gave way, and she dropped back down in her chair. He knew all about her part in Burk's losing his daughter! How had he found out when even Burk's investigators hadn't been able to trace her to it? He had her locked in a vise, and if she had any hope of marrying Burk, she'd better go along.

All he wanted was to talk to her somewhere privately. She was probably overreacting.

"All right," she said reluctantly. "I'll go with you. Where do you want to meet me?"

"In the parking lot right after work," he said quickly.

"You'll ride with me. I'll bring you back here to your car when we're finished."

A stab of fear jolted her, and her intuition screamed warnings. *Don't go! You'll be alone with him with no way to escape! Tell him no and run, don't walk, to the nearest security officer for protection!*

It took a couple of deep breaths and a lot of self-discipline for her to speak in a normal tone. "I'd rather take my own car. I'll follow you."

A look of impatience flashed across his face before he managed to subdue it. "There's too much traffic at that time of day. If we got separated you'd never find it. I'll wait for you by your car when the shift's over and walk you over to mine."

She knotted her fists in her lap so he wouldn't see that her hands were shaking. He apparently knew which car of all those in the parking lot was hers. That could only mean he'd been watching her, spying on her.

"I'm sorry," she said firmly, "but I'm not going anywhere with you in your car when you won't even tell me where we're headed. I'll go in my own car or I won't go at all."

"Oh, all right," he said angrily and reached for a notepad and pen on her desk. "I'll write down the address for you, but you'd better not stand me up."

"Am I supposed to take that as a threat?" she snapped.

"Let's just call it an urgent suggestion." He scribbled something on the pad, then turned and left.

The rest of the day was a total loss for Kate as far as getting any work done. Her mind was in turmoil. She wasn't familiar with the address Jensen had given her, but a search of the city map showed her that it was in a new upscale area of large and expensive homes. She'd called his lead foreman to get his home address from the emergency list to see if the building belonged to him, but he'd listed only a post office box number. She should report this conversation to security. Right now!

But would they believe her? She had no proof of any wrongdoing, and it wasn't against the law to have a P.O. box. It was just her word against his, and he was a longtime and valued employee at Hemingway/Price, whereas she'd been with them less than a month.

What did he want to talk to her about? Did it have anything to do with the Project 2000 file? That seemed to be most likely, considering his suspicious attempt to get it last week.

But he must know she couldn't let him borrow it. It was highly classified, top secret, and if she let him see it without authorization she could be sent to prison!

As it drew closer and closer to quitting time, her nerves were raw and her stomach lurched. She should go to the director of security and tell him what was happening, then let him handle it. But if she did, she could kiss goodbye her plans for marrying Burk, and she couldn't stand to even think of that. Not when there was still a slim chance that what Evel wanted of her wasn't all that bad.

She left her clerk in charge and went into the women's lounge, a small room off the ladies' rest room outfitted with a couch and a couple of soft chairs. She breathed a sigh of relief when she saw that no one was in there, then stretched out on the couch. She needed a quiet place to pull her thoughts together.

She'd already agreed to go with Jensen so she'd follow through. After all, he'd agreed to her taking her own car, and the house they were going to was in the quarter of a million-dollar-and-up range.

Also, she wasn't altogether unprotected. She'd had classes in self-defense and handgun safety in Denver as part of the training for her job there. She even owned a gun, a Beretta, and had a permit to carry it. She kept it locked in the glove compartment of her car and hadn't fired it since she finished her training more than five years ago. It was about the only thing in her totaled car that hadn't been damaged.

Fortunately it was raining today and she'd worn her loose-fitting raincoat with the big pockets. When she got into the new vehicle that Burk's insurance had bought her, she could slip the gun into one of the pockets.

The very thought made her weak in the knees. She hated weapons of any sort, but especially guns. She kept hers loaded for security reasons, but she doubted that she had the guts to aim it at someone and pull the trigger.

An hour later at the end of the shift she put on her raincoat, rummaged through her purse for her key ring, then hurried out to her car. It was no longer raining, but the sky was overcast and it was darker than it should have been on the late afternoon of an early summer day.

Her knees shook as she walked across the parking lot. Her rank wasn't high enough to entitle her to her own marked parking space so she had to park wherever she could find an empty one. Today she'd been a little later than usual so she'd had to park farther away from the building.

Once in the car she gingerly unlocked the glove compartment and took out the weapon. It was small and black but she couldn't remember the size of it. She did remember how it felt in her hands when she aimed it and pulled the trigger, and it was not pleasant.

It would fit in her purse, but if Jensen decided to search her that would be the first place he'd look. It would be better to go with her first inclination and put it in the pocket of her raincoat. He'd search there, too, but she could get at it quicker than in her purse.

As she drove out of the parking lot she had a strong urge to go around the block then come back and tell her story to Security, but she took a deep breath and squared her shoulders. She couldn't let Jensen ruin her plans to marry Burk. Not yet. Not until she knew what he wanted of her.

Jensen had been right about the place being hard to find. Even with the map she drove past a couple of streets she should have turned on and had to find her way back and start over. She finally spotted the right one, however, and drove up to a big two-story house on a sprawling lot. If this was his home he sure hadn't bought it on just his salary!

She shut off the engine and was getting out of the car when Evel came out the front door. He was scowling. "Where have you been? I was starting to think you weren't coming," he grumbled when they met halfway up the driveway.

He sounded as if he'd expected her to come bounding out of the plant the minute the clock struck five and then break all speed limits getting here.

"I had to finish the project I was working on before I could leave," she snapped as they walked to the front door. "Then I got lost trying to find this place."

"I told you you'd have a hard time," he boasted triumphantly as he opened the door and ushered her inside.

The house was beautifully furnished and decorated, but he didn't give her a chance to browse. Instead he took her arm and led her quickly through the living room and into a small office. This room was clean but cluttered and messy in contrast to the entryway and living room, which were immaculate.

"You have a beautiful home," she said.

"It belongs to a friend. I'm just looking after it for him while he's gone for a few days," he mumbled hurriedly. "Do you want to take off your coat?"

"No!" She almost shouted the word before she realized she was overreacting. The last thing she wanted was to let the gun get away from her, but she had to be careful not to arouse his suspicion.

"That is, I'd just as soon leave it on. I won't be here very long."

He nodded and motioned her to a chair in front of the desk then seated himself behind it.

Kate was almost certain he was lying about not owning the house. More than likely it was his home but he didn't want her to know it.

She didn't know what his wife's occupation was, but unless she was a highly successful doctor, or lawyer, or CEO of a company, even their two salaries combined couldn't pay for this place as well as put two sons through college. Not to mention the Mercedes he drove. If he was getting rich by selling the company's secrets it would also explain why he had a post office box listed at work instead of a too-affluent home address.

She was so immersed in her thoughts that she almost jumped when he spoke again. "Let me have that notepaper I wrote this address on." It was more of a command than a request.

She reached down beside her chair and took the paper from the outside pocket of her purse then handed it across the desk to him. He took it and tore it into small pieces then dropped them in the wastebasket.

Kate had expected that he'd do something like that so she'd written the address down on a separate sheet of paper earlier and locked it in the security file at work. She did feel that it would be prudent to protest, however.

"Why did you do that?" she cried.

"I don't want you to bother my friend who owns the house," he said irritably.

"Oh, don't be ridiculous," she fumed, and not acting this time. "What's with all the dramatics anyway? Why don't you just tell me what you want of me?"

He glared at her. "That's what I'm going to do if you'll just shut up and let me. I need to borrow the Project 2000 file for about an hour. I promise you nobody will ever know it was gone, and there's an easy twenty-five thou in it for you.''

Kate felt the blood drain from her face, and it seemed to her that her heart stopped beating for a few seconds. So that *was* it! She'd suspected it would be, but still it shocked her. She couldn't even imagine sabotaging the company she worked for.

It took her a while to start breathing again so she could talk. "I can't do that. It's dishonorable as well as illegal, and I couldn't live with myself if I let you see it.''

She could hear a chuckle in his tone. "Sure it is, lovey. So's growin' pot and hirin' illegal aliens, but they're both big business in this country. The trick is not to get caught.''

Kate couldn't believe what she was hearing. Evel Jensen was offering her twenty-five thousand dollars to let him copy one of her top-secret files!

She might as well try to find out why. "What are you going to do with that information?''

"That's none of your business," he growled.

"The hell it's not!" she retorted. "I'm responsible for that file. I'll wind up in prison right along with you if you get caught.''

He frowned at her. "I already told you, I don't get caught. What's with you anyway? The risk is minimal and the profit is almost as much as you make in a year by working eight hours a day five days a week.''

Kate was dumbfounded. This man was serious. He actually saw nothing wrong with stealing the secrets of the company he worked for and no doubt selling them to another one as long as he didn't get caught!

"Evel," she said, deliberately using his first name. He no longer deserved the respect she'd been according him by calling him Mr. Jensen. "Haven't you ever heard of loyalty? Or honor? Or morality? How can you sell out the company you've been working for all those years?''

He snorted. "Easy. I've worked my butt off for Hemingway/Price for over twenty years, and what have they ever done for me? Not a damn thing. They've passed me over every time a supervisory position came up. I'm stuck in this nowhere job, and no matter how much I protest, the promotion always goes to someone who's not half as qualified as I am. Who can blame me for pickin' up some extra cash when the opportunity presents itself?"

"I can," Kate snapped. "Doesn't the very fact you've been passed over so often tell you anything? If you were good supervisory material you'd have been promoted. It's probably your attitude that's holding you back."

"Attitude, hell!" he said with a sneer. "Listen to little miss goody two-shoes here. What do you know about discrimination? You with your honey blond hair, those big brown eyes that would melt an iceberg and hooters out to here that no man could resist. You got it made, baby."

Kate winced at his crudeness and feared he was indeed capable of violence. She'd better soft-pedal this conversation a little.

"Have you taken your complaint to the union?" she asked.

He muttered an obscene oath. "You better believe I have. They won't do anything. They're afraid to act for fear of losing their own jobs."

He was obviously paranoid, she thought as he continued to ramble about his problems with the union. Probably the only way she could get away from him would be to agree to let him copy the file and then report him to the head of security as soon as she got back to the plant.

"Evel," she said, breaking into his monologue, "if I loan you the file this time, will you promise not to ever ask me to do such a thing again?"

He looked surprised. "What's with you? You're the first person who hasn't jumped at the chance to make such easy money. Oh, but I forgot, you're marrying a millionaire in a few days."

He paused for a moment. "Or are you?" he reminded her.

She didn't need reminding, and she shivered at the menace in his tone. He was so sure of her that he actually admitted culpability. "You've approached people with this type of offer before?"

"Hell, yes," he answered. "And I've never been turned down. The lure of cold hard cash, plus a little extra incentive, is potent."

"What do you mean by 'extra incentive'?" she asked.

"Never mind," he said coldly. "Are you in or not?"

She hated even the pretense of industrial sabotage, but it was the only way she could get the proof she needed if she decided to turn him in to the authorities.

She hesitated for a few seconds. "All right, count me in, but just this once, understand?"

His smile was as evil as his name. "Oh, I think you'll cooperate no matter how often I ask you to."

A wave of foreboding rocked her. There was something he wasn't telling her, but what? She had enough on him already to send him to prison if she decided to turn him in, and it could be substantiated with a little undercover work once the plant security and the local police investigated her charge.

"I'm warning you," she said with as much bravado as she could muster. "If you come to me again for a look at a confidential file, I'll turn you in to Security."

His sinister smile spread. "I'm sure you would. In fact you already suspect that you can't do anything criminal, even if it means losing Mr. Money Bags Sinclair. It's written all over you. You're not a very good actress, sweetie pie."

Kate could only stare at him as amazement and fear rocked her. He'd suspected that she couldn't go along with his scheme, and yet he'd not only laid it out for her but he'd confessed that he'd recruited others to give him access to the files in the past. He was either stupid or brilliant, and she wouldn't bet on stupid.

She finally found her voice. "If you think that, then why did you bother to ask me to loan you the file?"

What was he planning to do with her? They were in this house alone, she was certain of that. No one knew she'd arranged to meet him after she left work. He could kill her and nobody would ever suspect him!

"I just wanted to see how you'd react," he said. "You pure, innocent, righteous girls are so sickeningly incorruptible. I like it when I can tempt one of you, but you weren't tempted. I can tell by your expression and body language that you'll have to be persuaded by something other than lust or greed."

What was he talking about? If he killed her then he couldn't "persuade" her. So what else did he have in mind?

"If—if you think I'm going to turn you in, then why are you telling me all this?"

His smile was gone. "Because you won't go to the police."

He said it so calmly that for a minute she didn't understand the implication. When she did she was puzzled. "What makes you think I won't?"

"I know you won't," he reiterated. "Because you're too fond of Burk Sinclair. I seem to have overestimated your desire to marry him, but you're a tenderhearted little cuss. I'm bettin' that you won't stand by and watch him get his face rearranged. My organization has boys who are expert with a knife. He won't be nearly so handsome when they get through with him."

Chapter Ten

No, not Burk! Evel Jensen was threatening to hurt Burk! Kate grabbed the arms of the chair as a wave of dizziness swept over her. She couldn't allow that. It was all her fault. If she'd done her job and reported Jensen to Security the first time he asked for the file, he'd have been dealt with and none of this would ever have happened.

Or even further back, if she'd told Burk that she was the reporter responsible for the publication of the item that lost him his little daughter, he'd never have gotten mixed up with her in the first place.

"Hey, babe, you're not going to pass out on me, are you?" Evel's anxious voice helped her to regain her balance. No way was she going to faint at his feet.

"You wouldn't!" Her voice shook. "You couldn't do a thing like that to Burk."

He shrugged. "You're right, I couldn't. I'm not tough enough, but we have men who can and will. I'd hoped you could be scared into giving me the file by threatening to stop your wedding, but you'd better understand that we always get what we want. I hope you won't push us on to the third step. You really don't want to know what that is."

She shuddered. No, she didn't. She probably would have sacrificed her hopes of a long and happy life with Burk in order to save her integrity, but she wasn't going to let them do dreadful things to him.

She lowered her head, unable to look at Jensen. She'd never seen a real live monster before. "I'll do whatever you want." She had to stop and clear her throat. "Just stay away from Burk."

The monster actually smiled. "That's my girl. I knew you'd come around. And since you're being so cooperative I won't even tell him your little secret. You can get married and he'll never know."

That dreadful time five years ago when Fleur Sinclair read the blind item Kate had been responsible for and disappeared with Burk's small daughter replayed itself over and over again in Kate's mind as she gripped the chair harder to keep herself from slumping to the floor.

Evel had found out about that, but how? How had he discovered in just a few short weeks what Burk with all his private detectives hadn't been able to find out in years of searching?

"How—how did you know?" she stammered.

He chuckled. "It wasn't difficult once I started looking for your sins. Few people live to be twenty-eight years old without something in their past they don't want made public."

"You even know how old I am." It was more of a statement than a question. He was showing off. Letting her know how deeply he'd pried into her personal life. Well, it had paid off. He had her right where he wanted her now.

"Sweetie, I know everything about you. When I set out to investigate a person, I do a thorough job of it. It was just a matter of digging.'' He was actually bragging about it.

"But Burk had professionals looking for me,'' she said, "and they were never able to find out who I was.''

Evel laughed. "That's because he didn't know who he was looking for. I was investigating *you*, and your history led me right to the Sinclair debacle, whereas he was investigating the *incident*, plus he was looking for a man, and there was nothing to tie you to it from that angle.''

"You really are a bastard,'' she muttered.

"Tsk, tsk, such language,'' he said. "Actually I'm being quite generous. If you supply me with the files I want, when I want them, I won't say a word to him. I don't know him. There's no reason for me to contact him as long as you behave yourself and give me what I ask for. Of course if you double-cross me…''

He let the sentence trail off but his meaning was clear. If she contacted Security or the police he wouldn't hesitate to set his goons on Burk as well as telling him everything he knew about her!

She covered her face with her hands. She had no options. No choice. She had to give Jensen free access to the confidential files.

She rubbed her face, then dropped her hands and looked at him. For the first time she realized it had started raining again; she could hear it coming down hard on the roof. Evel sat relaxed in his leather upholstered desk chair.

"Don't take it so hard, doll,'' he said jovially. "If it's the Sinclair fortune you're after, you can still have it plus what you can make workin' with me. If you play along with me, he'll never know it was you who lost him his kid.''

"I don't expect you to understand,'' she said. "I love Burk deeply, but I've always been an honorable woman. Even when I sold that article to the tabloid I realized the next day that it could do a lot of damage and tried to buy it back. I can't conceive of sabotaging the company I work for. At this stage that file is worth millions to Hemingway/Price and they trust me to protect it."

"Yeah, well, that's their problem, not mine," he said with a sneer. "And it's not yours, either, so start thinkin' of yourself. You know too much already. And there's always pretty boy Sinclair. I guarantee he won't be so pretty when the guys I work for get through with him if you should make it necessary."

Kate's stomach roiled and she was afraid she was going to be sick. It was no longer just a case of losing Burk, which was bad enough. Now she was afraid for his life.

"I'll let you borrow the file," she said, "but only because you haven't left me any choice. Frankly, I hope you roast in hell."

"I expect I'll do that with or without you," he said, "but why are you so upset with me? Your wedding will go off as planned, and you'll make lots of money that you won't even have to pay taxes on. Our payrolls are handled under the table, so to speak."

Kate wasn't listening. Her mind was on Burk and their coming marriage. God help her, but she was relieved that Jensen had made it impossible for her to refuse his demand. Now they could go through with the wedding, Burk would never know her secret and maybe she could learn to live with her guilt at betraying her employer since it was impossible not to.

Evel recaptured her attention by raising his voice. "Hey, Kate, are you with me? Listen up, because I'm only going through this with you once. Your files are only available during the day shift, aren't they?"

Kate nodded. "Yes. I lock them up when I leave the building."

"And if anyone on swing shift needs to see them, they have to make arrangements ahead of time with you, right?"

He was right, which meant he'd done this before since

only people with security clearance knew of those arrangements, and he didn't have that clearance. He was testing her to see if she'd tell him the truth.

"Right," she said curtly.

"Has anyone requested them for tomorrow night?"

She hesitated. If she lied and said yes it would buy her time, probably until Monday since the plant wasn't open on weekends. But what good would that do? It was no longer a case of just protecting her secret from Burk. Now it was possibly his life that was at stake. She couldn't take the risk. She had to go through with this.

"If you lie to me, I'll find out, and you're not going to be happy with the consequences," Jensen snarled. "Now answer my question."

"No, no one," she snapped, and knew it was her first step into criminal activity.

"Okay then here's what we'll do..."

By the time Jensen had finished detailing his nefarious plan, Kate's head was spinning. But all she could think about was protecting Burk.

He pushed back his chair and stood up. "Now, if you have no questions you're free to leave. When you drive away, just forget this address, and don't keep me waiting tomorrow. I don't have a lot of patience, but I do have Burk Sinclair's unlisted home phone number."

Kate walked to her car on shaking legs, carrying the address Jensen had instructed her to bring the file to. She started the engine, but she quickly realized that her whole body was trembling so hard that it affected her ability to guide the car.

Pulling over to the curb, she put the car in Park and slumped forward. Her hands gripped the steering wheel and her face was supported by her arms as the magnitude of what she'd agreed to do rolled over her with suffocating heaviness.

She couldn't go through with it! No way could she turn

that highly secret file over to an industrial saboteur to be copied and sold to the highest bidder. It would mean that another company would put on the market, at the same time as her company did, the revolutionary computer software that Hemingway/Price had spent years developing. Possibly even before, if they didn't take the time to work out the bugs the way Hemingway/Price did.

It would cost her company millions of dollars in lost revenues, and she wouldn't, couldn't, be a part of that!

She let loose of the steering wheel and leaned back against the seat. But how could she not? She loved Burk so much, and he'd never forgive her if Evel Jensen told him what she'd done. She'd lose him forever, but even more important, she had to protect him from being disfigured!

She couldn't put him at risk.

A cry of anger and frustration was torn from her throat. Burk was a strong man, but he was no match for whatever it was Jensen had in mind to do to him if...

Kate sat up and pounded on the steering wheel with her fists. Dammit! She couldn't take chances with his life! He was still recovering from the head injury.

She straightened up and shifted back into Drive. Thank God Burk had flown to San Francisco this morning on an overnight business trip. He wouldn't be home until tomorrow evening, which meant his condo would be empty until then. She had a key and she was going to take Grandma and spend the night there where it was secured, and nobody would know where they were. She had a lot of thinking to do and far too little time to do it.

Kate hadn't told her grandmother the whole story, and Emily had objected to leaving her own home and bed, but Kate had been adamant so she finally gave in and grudgingly packed her overnight bag. By ten o'clock she was in bed at the condo and sleeping peacefully while Kate paced the floor, trying to find a way to expose Evel Jensen's crooked scheme while at the same time protecting the man she loved most in all the world and hopefully keeping her past mistake a secret.

It was an impossible situation and the more she pondered it the more tangled it became. Finally at 4:00 a.m. and after two pots of coffee, she came to a decision, the only one that, being her, she could come to.

She dialed Clifford Oakley, Director of Security at Hemingway/Price, at home, told him someone was trying to get hold of the Project 2000 file, and asked him to meet her at the plant in exactly one hour. Next she showered, dressed and wrote a note to her grandmother, who thankfully was still asleep, telling her there was an emergency situation at work and for her to stay in Burk's condo and not open the door for anyone until either she or Burk came home.

Burk had taken his car to the airport and left it in the long-term parking lot so Kate had parked in his space in the basement of the building.

She arrived at the plant a few minutes early, but the security officer on duty wouldn't let her in without authorization. Cliff wasn't long in coming, and he escorted her to his office in a separate small building just inside the front gate of the cyclone security fence that surrounded the grounds.

He was a middle-aged man, probably fifteen or twenty pounds overweight, with a belly that even his uniform jacket couldn't hide. He was fit, though, with muscles that rippled and an air of authority. Kate understood that he'd once been a police officer.

"Okay, Ms. Brown," he said after he'd plugged in the coffeepot and seated Kate on the leather couch then sat down beside her. "What's this all about? It better be good. Four o'clock in the morning is an ungodly time to be tumbled out of bed."

Kate could attest to that last statement. She hadn't gotten

to bed at all. "I'd like for you to call me Kate, Mr. Oakley, because I think we're going to be very well acquainted before this day is over."

He frowned. "All right, Kate it is. I'm Cliff. Now, what's the problem?"

She started with the first time Evel Jensen came to her office and requested the Project 2000 file, and continued with the events in sequence until she finished with his threat to do harm to Burk if she didn't show up with the file after work this evening.

It took a long time. There were several starts and stops when he interrupted to ask questions or she got something out of sequence and had to backtrack, but after he'd gone through several cups of coffee, she finally came to the end.

Cliff scowled at her. "You realize, of course, that it's just your word against Jensen's. Dammit all, Kate, why didn't you come to me the first time he approached you? I'd have started an investigation on him immediately."

"I told you—"

"I know," he said, brushing aside an answer he already knew. "Your reasons are understandable, but when you're working with classified information you assume everyone who acts suspicious is guilty until proven innocent. Sorry, but that's the way it has to be. Now you know the results of disregarding that rule. We're out of time and will have to take drastic action. It could be dangerous. Are you willing to cooperate?"

Kate nodded. "I'll do anything you tell me to. Just protect Burk."

Nothing could be as bad as the mental torture she'd been through for the past twenty-four hours. She'd even become resigned to losing Burk, but she wasn't going to let Evel Jensen corrupt her or harm Burk!

Cliff drummed his fingers on the desk. "All right, here's what we're going to do. I want you to do exactly what you've agreed to. Put in a full day at work and when the shift's over slip the file in your briefcase and leave. I'll make sure the guards don't search you. Meanwhile I'll contact the police and make arrangements to cover you every step of the way—''

That alarmed Kate. "If you bring in uniformed officers Jensen will be suspicious."

"They won't be in uniform," he assured her. "They won't even come to the plant. They'll stake out the address he's given you, and I'll assign our own men to watch you while you're here.

"What you'll have to do is follow his directions to the letter. Go to the house, give him the file and wait for him to come back. You won't see the police officers, but I guarantee you they'll be there. Don't look around for them or do anything you wouldn't have done if you hadn't contacted us. Jensen will probably have somebody watching you while he's gone."

Kate shivered. How had she gotten herself into this mess? She'd just been minding her own business and looking forward to her wedding day. Hers and Burk's. The pain that slashed through her when she thought of Burk was almost unbearable. There would never be a wedding for her now. Burk wouldn't want her, and she couldn't imagine spending her life with any other man.

"Kate. Are you listening to me?"

Cliff's voice shook her out of her waking nightmare, and she blinked. "I—I'm sorry. What were you saying?"

His expression softened. "I know you're scared. Anybody would be, but we'll be there to protect you."

He'd misunderstood her distraction, but it brought to mind something she did want to ask him. "I have a gun. A Beretta. Shall I bring it?"

Cliff blanched. "Oh, Lord, no! We don't want any gunfire. Do you have a permit to carry it?"

"Yes, but until yesterday all I did was leave it locked in

the glove compartment of my car. Yesterday I took it out and put it in the pocket of my raincoat before I met Evel."

She could see by his infuriated expression that she was going to get an angry lecture.

"You're lucky you weren't killed, woman," he raged. "If he'd searched you, you very probably would have been. Don't even have it in your car when you meet him this afternoon. In fact, take my advice and get rid of it altogether."

Kate sighed. "Yeah, I guess you're right."

"I know I'm right," he said firmly. "Now, to get back to Jensen... When he returns to the house, if everything goes the way he's indicated, he'll give you the money and the file. After you accept them that's when we'll make ourselves known. If he should pull a gun, get the hell out of there, understand?"

"Perfectly," she assured him. "But what about my grandmother? My fiancé, Burk Sinclair, is out of town on business, so Grandma and I stayed at his condo last night. I left her there asleep, but if something should go wrong and Jensen finds out about this, he might decide to show me he meant what he said about revenge against Burk and go there. Jensen has a quick and vicious temper, and he wouldn't hesitate to...to do something to Grandma if...if Burk wasn't available...."

Sobs of panic made her voice break and she couldn't go on.

"Don't worry," Cliff said. "I know the layout of the building where Mr. Sinclair lives. It has a good security system, but I'll also assign a female officer to be there with your grandmother. As soon as I do, you'd better call your grandma, tell her what's happened and let her know someone is coming. She'll be watched until this situation is resolved."

Burk looked at his watch as he deplaned at Portland International Airport carrying his one carry-on piece of luggage. It was only a little after noon. He'd managed to get all his business taken care of and still cut nearly three hours off his agenda. He was back in time to stop by his office to brief his dad on the results of his trip before taking Katie out to dinner this evening.

He couldn't believe how much he'd missed her in just two days and one night. That one night had been pure torture! How was it possible for a woman to insinuate herself into a man's heart and soul in such a short time? He couldn't sleep without her. For that matter he couldn't sleep *with* her for very long, either, but when he had her in bed with him, the waking time was spectacular. All he had to do was touch her and his body thought he was sixteen again instead of thirty-six.

He strode through the terminal and, seeing no shuttle buses available outside, decided to walk to the long-term parking lot. He was in a hurry. He wanted to get to the office and call her, hear her slightly husky voice that promised all sorts of delights.

He also wanted to tell her how much he'd missed her, and how he looked forward to dinner at a candlelit restaurant where he could feed her, from a round toothpick, cold shrimp marinaded in cocktail sauce, and hold her glass while she sipped champagne with bubbles that made her slightly upturned nose twitch.

It took Burk about forty-five minutes to get to his office, but the coast was clear once he did. He didn't bump into anyone he'd have to talk to, and even his secretary was away from her desk, so he closed the door, headed for the telephone and punched out Kate's number at work.

She answered on the first ring, and his heart pounded at the throb of her sexy tone as she murmured, "Classified Files, Kate Brown speaking."

He lowered his voice to a husky baritone. "Good afternoon, Kate Brown. This is Burk Sinclair calling to tell you I love you."

He heard her gasp. "Burk! Where are you! You *are* calling from San Francisco, aren't you?"

She sounded more upset than happy to hear from him. "No," he said, "I'm right here in Portland in my office. I managed to catch an earlier flight home."

"Oh, Burk." It was a moan instead of the squeal of delight he'd counted on. "Why did you do that? I mean...that's great, but—"

"But what?" he interrupted as his anticipation turned to concern. "Katie, is something wrong?"

"Yes! Uh, no! That is I... I'm running late and am going to have to cancel our dinner date. Why don't you...um... stay there and catch up on your work, then have dinner downtown before you go home?"

Her sentences were choppy, fragmented, and all of Burk's sharp instincts snapped to attention. Something was very wrong. His unflappable Kate was on the verge of hysteria. She hadn't once lost her cool when she'd nursed him through a dangerous head injury while they'd been stranded in the mountains by a vicious rainstorm, but now her tone as well as her garbled conversation indicated a loss of control.

"Kate, what in hell are you talking about?" he growled. "If you don't tell me what's the matter, I'm coming out there to find out for myself."

"No!" she cried before he'd even finished his sentence. "Don't do that. I mean it. Hang up and wait beside the phone. I'll call you back in a few minutes. Don't, I repeat, *do not* come out here."

The line went dead.

Burk paced the floor in front of his desk, waiting for the phone to ring. What could have happened to upset her so? God almighty, was she in some kind of danger? If anything happened to her... He didn't dare think about that or he'd disregard her frantic warning and go find out for himself.

Finally, after the longest twenty minutes he'd ever spent, the phone rang and he snatched it from its cradle and barked, "Kate!"

"No, Burk, it's Jason Galloway," said the voice at the other end.

Police Chief Jason Galloway? They were good friends, but he didn't have time to chat—

Jason continued. "The director of security at Hemingway/Price tells me you're about to mess up an important sting—"

"What in hell is going on?" Burk demanded. "Is this call about Katie? If you're using her as a decoy—"

"Oh, for Pete's sake, will you shut up and let me talk!" Jason interrupted. "I can't discuss this on the phone. It's crucial that you not go to the plant, but if you'll haul your butt down here to the station I'll tell you all I can about what's going down."

"I'll be there in five minutes—ten max," Burk sputtered and slammed down the phone.

Once Kate had contacted Cliff and told him about her problem with Burk, Cliff had assured her he'd handle it. She hoped he had because she hadn't heard anything more from either of them. She wished someone would let her know what was going on. Now her nerves were getting tighter and tighter as the minutes ticked by. A glance at her watch told her it was four-thirty. In another half hour she'd have to put into action the crime story Evel Jensen had conceived, and the director of plant security and the chief of police had approved. Was she a good enough actress to play the starring role?

She had no idea how Cliff and the police had persuaded Burk not to intrude on their little sting, as she believed it was called, but they must have because Burk had neither shown up nor called back.

By the time the quitting whistle blew, Kate was in a real dither. It was now or never. There were no rehearsals. She had to play the most important role in her life cold, and if she didn't give an award-winning performance the first time, the broken lives littering the stage would be real. She wouldn't get a second chance to do it right.

She sat at her desk mindlessly going through papers she'd picked at random until she was sure no one else would be coming in or leaving. Then she picked up her briefcase and went back to the locked cabinet that contained the Project 2000 file, unlocked it, removed the folder and slid it into the case, then relocked the cabinet and put the key in her purse.

Now she was committed. If Jensen caught on to the sting too soon, he could deny everything, and Kate would be left holding the bag, plus the top secret file.

She wasn't stopped at the gate, but the walk through the parking lot to her car seemed interminable. There were too many people around for her to tell if anybody was following her.

Once she got to the car, she tossed the briefcase on the passenger seat beside her. She had no way of protecting herself since she'd followed Cliff's stern order and left her gun at Burk's place. She just hoped Cliff had contacted the police and all the officers had been assigned their roles and knew what they were doing.

This time she didn't have any trouble locating the address. It was on the east side of town, and the little white house with the For Sale sign was easily recognizable. As near as she could tell she was still alone. There had been cars both behind and in front of her all the way, but none that stayed long enough to be escorting her.

Her sweaty palms gripped the steering wheel. Why had she ever agreed to this? It wasn't part of her job. All she was required to do was report Evel's attempted blackmail and let law enforcement take it from there. Nowhere was it written down that she had to be a target for a madman!

She parked her car in front of the house, but there were no other vehicles around. Wasn't Evel here yet? And after he had made such a big thing about her being a few minutes late when they met yesterday.

She sat there for a short while, but then decided to get out and see if there was anybody in the house. It wasn't like him to be late. Had there been a change in plans? Is that why there weren't any cars around? Had Evel discovered that she was working with the police?

Chapter Eleven

As Kate climbed the two steps to the covered porch with her briefcase clutched in her hand, her trembling knees nearly gave way, and she was thankful for the wrought-iron handrail. At the door she paused, then rang the bell. There was no answering call of "I'm coming," or even the sound of footsteps from inside.

She waited a few seconds, then tried again. Still no answer. Damn, why would Jensen arrange to meet her here and then not show up? A glance at her watch told her she'd had plenty of time to get here from the plant, which meant he had, too. Maybe he'd been held up by unexpected mandatory overtime, or an emergency.

Or maybe he'd spotted the undercover police. Oh, God, no, anything but that! It did seem unlikely, though. She hadn't even seen them and she knew they were here.

Or were they? Maybe they hadn't even been notified. Or had been and didn't think it was worth their time to investigate. She should have known better than to trust Cliff, but on the other hand he'd assured her everything was in place when she'd talked to him about Burk just a few hours ago. Still, that didn't mean something couldn't have gone wrong.

She saw that her hands were trembling as she once more reached out to punch the doorbell. That irritated her, and she squared her shoulders and made up her mind. All this dithering wasn't getting her anywhere. She'd try once more then leave. If Jensen didn't like it, that was his problem. He was the one who wasn't following the script.

She jammed her finger on the button, and at the same time banged on the door with her other fist. To her surprise the door opened a few inches. She pushed it farther and looked around inside but there was no one in sight. The door had been only partially latched.

She pushed it clear open and went in. The place was not only unoccupied but unfurnished. There was worn carpeting on the floor and closed metal blinds at the windows, but other than that the living and dining rooms were bare.

She closed the door behind her and called out, "Evel. Evel, are you here?"

There was no answer. Quietly she crept through those two rooms and turned left into the kitchen. There was a stove, refrigerator, built-in dishwasher and faded linoleum on the floor but no food or dishes in the cupboards.

What was going on here? She hadn't been stewing all day and working herself up to a nervous breakdown just to tour an unfurnished house for sale that she wouldn't live in if someone gave it to her. She called out again, but still no response.

Retracing her steps, she went back to the living room and through an open archway on the opposite wall. She found herself in a short hallway with a bedroom at each end and a bathroom in the middle, none of them furnished, and all with bare wooden floors. Entering the back room she opened the closet door only to find it bare of anything but clothes hangers.

She took a step back and bumped into something big and solid that wrapped one steely hard arm around her waist and clamped the other burly hand over her mouth and nose, cutting off her air.

Terrified, she tried to scream but could only make moaning noises in her throat. She couldn't breathe and struggled to get away from him but he only held her tighter.

"Be quiet," said Evel's voice. "I don't want to have to hurt you."

"Air," she gasped, and tried to shake his hand away from her nose.

It came out garbled, but he must have understood because he lowered his hand enough that she could get some oxygen.

"Will you promise not to scream if I let you go?" he muttered.

"Yes," she struggled to say, and again it must have been satisfactory because he dropped his arms to his sides while she leaned against the wall and gulped deep mouthfuls of air.

"Turn around, take a few steps back and put your palms on the wall," he commanded. "I'm gonna pat you down."

She glared at him. "Like hell you are," she said angrily, and started to move away from the wall.

In a quick movement he grabbed her by the upper arm and whirled her around. "Like I said, I don't want to hurt you, but I will if I have to. You could be wired. Now put your hands against the wall and spread your legs."

She shuddered but decided she'd better do as he said, although just the thought of his big rough hands exploring her body made her want to throw up.

He started under her arms, which also gave him access to her breasts. He seemed inclined to linger there, squeezing and pinching while she squirmed, until she could stand it no longer. Taking advantage of his preoccupation, she doubled up her fist and swung around to sock him with all her strength. The blow landed on his jaw and staggered him.

He roared with rage and slapped her across the face so hard that he knocked her down.

"You friggin' witch," he bellowed. "I was bein' a gentleman, but if you want to struggle, we'll struggle. It's more fun that way anyhow. Especially with a gal built like you."

Dropping down on the floor beside where she sat, crumpled in a heap with her hand to her stinging cheek, he tumbled her onto her back and began mauling her with his hands. She tried to get away but was no match for him. She was thankful she'd worn slacks to work today. It saved her from the indignity of enduring his hands on her panties and her bare flesh under a skirt.

When he was through groping her, she was thoroughly humiliated, but he knew beyond a doubt that she wasn't wearing a transmitter. He had to know because his slimy hands had covered every inch of her.

"You can get up now," he said as he let her go and stood. "That would have been a hell of a lot easier if you hadn't fought me. What did you do with the file?"

"Sure it would have been," she said sarcastically as she rolled over to get up. "So why didn't you meet me at the front door instead of scaring me half to death?" She was still shaking with indignation. "It would have been a whole lot easier if you'd just answered the doorbell in the first place instead of staging that scene out of a third-rate suspense movie."

"Because I had to make sure you were alone," he said gruffly. "I don't trust you, lady, and with good reason. If you thought you could get away with it, you'd turn me in to the cops in a minute."

He walked over to the window and looked out between the shutters of the blinds. "Unfortunately, the broad next door is a stay-at-home mother with a couple of little kids and a habit of sticking her nose into other people's business. She's the neighborhood gossip with ears that can pick up the human voice from two blocks away. If you'd screamed, she'd have had 911 on the phone in a minute.''

Kate couldn't resist letting him know exactly what she thought of him. "You're right not to trust me. People like you are despicable, and I'd love to see you locked up in prison.''

He chuckled and seemed amused rather than insulted. "I'll bet you would.''

He reached out and ran his finger down her cheek. "Do you know you've got the most beautiful eyes? They actually spit fire when you're mad.''

Angrily she shook her head and stepped back, dislodging his caress. "Keep your hands off me!''

His amused expression vanished. "You're a little wildcat, too. Someday I'm gonna tame you, but for now just give me that file.''

She picked up her briefcase from the floor, where it had landed when she dropped it as Evel grabbed her. She had an almost irresistible desire to throw it at him and run, but she knew she'd never get away with it. Also, it would destroy the police's carefully set-up plan to trap him. That is, if they were carrying out their part, or if they were even around.

"The file's in here," she said, and handed it to him.

He took the case, opened it, pulled out the folder and leafed through the papers in it.

"It's all there," she volunteered. "I'm not so stupid as to try to hold out on you.''

"For your sake I hope not," he grumbled before closing it and stuffing it back into the case. "I'll warn you again—don't step outside this house until I get back. You've got all the comforts of home here. All except furniture, but you can sit on the floor. Hope you brought along a good book.''

She wasn't going to let him intimidate her, no matter how scared she was. "How can you go anyplace without transportation?" she taunted, hoping he'd offer some bit of information that might be useful. "The only car parked on the street is mine."

His face split in a nasty grin. "You don't give me enough credit, doll. Did you really think I was gonna park my car in the driveway? That would be pretty dumb if you'd tattled on me. I make it a point never to broadcast my whereabouts in a situation like this. Someone's picking me up."

He turned and walked to the front door and opened it, then turned again to face her. "Remember, don't even so much as stick your head outside the front or back doors. If you do you're gonna be very, very, sorry."

His tone was even more frightening than his words.

"How will you know whether or not I leave the house?" she called as he stepped out onto the porch.

"Oh, I'll know all right—believe it."

He shut the door behind him, and Kate hurried to the window to look out the side of the closed metal blinds. Jensen was getting into a nondescript gray vehicle stopped in the middle of the road with the motor running. It sped off before he had the door shut.

Now what? she asked herself. How was she going to survive for up to two hours all by herself in this empty house, wondering whether or not she was covered by police protection? Surely Cliff could have gotten a message to her some way to let her know what was going on. Whether or not his hastily conceived plan was being implemented.

And what about Burk? He must have talked to Cliff, but she hadn't heard a word from him. Was that a good sign or a bad one? She'd told him not to come to her office, but he could have phoned again just to reassure her that everything was going as planned.

Kate was too charged with nervous energy to sit quietly

on the floor so she searched every nook and cranny of the house. She didn't know what she was looking for, but knew she'd recognize it if or when she saw it. It didn't take long since the rooms were small and empty, and she was just finishing the last one, the bathroom, when she heard a souped-up car speed by and then the crash of metal against metal.

A male voice yelled as she ran across the living room and pulled up the blind. The driver of the vehicle had apparently lost control of it and jumped the curb, then plowed into the van parked in the driveway of a house across the street and up one.

A couple of angry men came flying out the door, and Kate was trying to see if the driver had been hurt when a familiar voice behind her spoke. "Katie, lower the blind again, quickly."

It was Burk! She'd know his voice anywhere.

Acting purely on reflex she let loose of the blind, sending it crashing down, then turned and ran into his arms.

"Burk! Oh, Burk! Oh, Burk!" Her relief was so great that she couldn't think or reason. All she could do was cling to him and moan his name over and over.

"Everything's all right, sweetheart," he murmured into her ear as he folded her tightly in his embrace. "You're safe. Harry and I are here, and there are more officers in the garage as well as at the house next door. You're not alone, although it must have seemed as if you were."

Harry? Who was Harry? She raised her face which had been buried in Burk's shoulder and saw a short, slender man standing beside them. He looked fairly young, maybe thirty, and had a boyish smile that he flashed at her. "Hi, I'm Harry Reece, Portland P.D.," he said.

Kate smiled, too. "I'm Kate Brown. I guess you know all about me."

"Pretty much," he admitted. "Hey, why don't I just go back to the garage and play cards with the other guys? We got the layout of this place last night so we'll know where we're going and what we're doing if there should be any trouble.''

He backed up a few steps. ''Nice to meet you, Kate. Wish it could have been under different circumstances. See ya, Burk.''

He turned and walked back into the kitchen where there was a door to the attached garage.

''I'll owe you one, pal,'' Burk called after the retreating figure.

Even before Harry was out of sight, Burk lowered his head and captured Kate's lips with his own. It was a tender kiss rather than a passionate one, and for a while they just stood there exploring each other's mouths and letting the relief they felt flow through them.

She'd never been so glad to see anybody in her whole life! It not only meant he was safe and knew what was going on, but that the police were watching over her and she wasn't alone.

She could feel his heart hammering the same way hers was, and after a minute he raised his head and searched her face anxiously.

''Let me look at you, Katie,'' he said shakily. ''Did that son of a bitch hurt you? We could only hear what was going on. They don't have cameras planted in the bedrooms and bathroom.''

She saw the fury in his brown eyes and tried to reassure him. ''Not really, darling. He just slapped me and did a rather rough body search.''

''*Just* slapped you and searched you!'' His tone was low and dangerous. ''Did he—''

''No, Burk,'' she broke in hastily. ''He didn't rape me or even attempt to.''

Burk was rigid with anger. ''I'll kill the bastard if he violated you in any way.''

Kate felt she had been violated by the man's intimate search, but she wasn't going to tell Burk that.

"He didn't," she insisted. "If you were listening to a receiver, you must know that there wasn't time for that."

He pulled her closer again. "I heard, but it wouldn't take long if the man was already aroused. That creep sounded like the type who gets his jollies by being rough with women."

"He probably is," Kate agreed, "but I started it. I slugged him in the jaw."

Burk's eyes widened. "You did? So that's what set him off. You never should have provoked him, sweetheart. The man's dangerous. When he started raging and I heard that slap, it took both of the guys I was with to hold me back and keep me from coming over here after him. They're not very pleased with either you or me and our responses."

She chuckled. "I'm surprised they let you come with them."

"They weren't going to," he said, "but the chief of police, Jason Galloway, is a friend of mine. I threatened all sorts of mayhem until he decided it was easier to put up with me than to deal with me if he refused."

"It's nice to have friends in high places," she muttered thoughtfully as her arms tightened around his neck.

"Yes, it is," he agreed. "But they couldn't have kept me away no matter who I had to do battle with."

He pulled her even closer so that their bodies were melded together, and spoke softly into her ear. "We both know the house is bugged so we don't have much privacy, but I have to say this. I don't think you understand even yet how much I love you, Katie. You're my life. Now that I've found you I can't live without you. The very thought of that man touching you, hurting you, nearly drives me crazy."

For a moment, reality returned to dim the beauty of his declaration. Would he still feel that way when Evel returned and revealed her secret in a fit of rage for Kate betraying him?

She forced the question out of her mind. This might be the last hour or two she and Burk would spend together. She was determined to make the best of it. To pretend that he loved her as much as she loved him. So much that nothing could shatter it.

"I love you too, Burk," she said softly. "So deeply that I couldn't bear it if anything happened to you, so don't stir things up. Let the police handle this. They're professionals and know what they're doing. I promise to keep my temper under control if you will. I just want to get this thing over with so we can get on with plans for our wedding."

Or cancel them, as the case may be.

"You can't possibly know how much I want that, too," he assured her. "Then we can live together. I missed you so while I was gone. It seemed like forever instead of just two days and a night."

He rubbed his face in her hair. "The night was the worst. All the nights we don't spend together are bad. I can't sleep. I keep reaching for you and you aren't there."

"Oh, Burk," she said tremulously as her eyes filled with tears. "Promise me you'll always feel that way."

She knew it was a futile pledge she was asking of him, but she needed to hear him say it.

"Of course I will," he said as he raised his head to look at her, then frowned. "Katie, sweetheart, why are you crying? Did I say something to upset you?"

"Oh, no!" she quickly reassured him. "Quite the contrary. I just love you so much, and am so happy to know you feel the same way about me."

"Surely you've never doubted it," he said gently, and wiped the tears from her cheeks with his thumbs. "Come on. Let's go in the bedroom and sit on the floor. We can't be seen there and it may be a while yet before Jensen comes back."

They sat on the floor in the front bedroom with their backs braced against the wall and their arms around each other. Kate snuggled into his embrace, savoring every minute of their time together.

"Burk," she said anxiously, "how do the police know this house isn't bugged? Maybe Evel has people listening to us, too."

"That were prepared for that," he said, "and sent a man over early this morning to look. He found nothing, and that's when our side put in both transmitters and cameras. The place has been under surveillance ever since."

"You might have let me know what was going on," she grumbled. "When I saw no cars or people around, I was afraid the police had abandoned me."

He hugged her. "I'm sorry, honey, but don't forget, I just got in on this a few hours ago. One of the things I had to promise if they let me come along was that I wouldn't contact you in any way. When I protested, Jason threatened to charge me with being a public nuisance and lock me up in one of his jail cells until the sting was over."

Kate laughed. "I'll bet he would have, too."

Burk wasn't quite so amused. "You'd better believe it," he muttered.

"Where are the police staked out?" Kate asked.

"The house next door. The one Jensen said was owned by the neighborhood gossip. I don't know about that, but she couldn't have been more cooperative with the officers. She let them relocate her family for the whole day in order to take over her house."

Kate was amazed that Burk and a contingent of police officers could have been observing her from just a few yards away and she neither saw nor heard any sign of them.

"Evel implied that he had people watching the house," she told Burk. "Do you know where they are?"

"Yeah, there's two of them and they're staked out in the house across the street where a van just ran into their car."

That jolted Kate's memory and she started to get up. "Oh, good heavens, the accident. I forgot all about it...."

Burk pulled her back down beside him. "It's all over. No one was hurt and the car's driver is fully covered by insurance, which will take care of the damage to the van."

"But how can you know that?" she asked doubtfully. "It just happened and you haven't even been outside."

He grinned. "The van's driver was one of our officers. The accident was staged to distract the men in the house so we could run across the two backyards and into your garage without being noticed."

A knock on the hall wall distracted them and Harry came into view. "Sorry to interrupt," he said with a grin, "but I have to give Kate some instructions."

He lowered himself to the floor, sitting cross-legged in front of them. "You've been briefed, Burk, but Kate has to know how we want this handled."

He looked straight at her as he talked. "There are two officers in the garage and two more at the house next door, listening to and watching what's going on. When Jensen comes back, Burk and I will hide in the back bedroom closet. Jensen thinks the house has been under continuous surveillance by his men so it's unlikely that he'll bother to search again. He'll be in a hurry to get away from here with his copy of the file."

Harry shifted his gaze around the room then back to her. "What we want you to do, Kate, is try to get him to stand in the dining room just across from the kitchen door with his back to it. A closed door might make him nervous so we'll leave it open, but the two guys who are in the garage now will be in there watching and listening.

"When he hands you back your briefcase, open it and make sure the original files are in it. Talk about it. Tell him what you're doing. We need that on tape as evidence. I don't know whether he'll have put the money in there or in a separate container, but open it and count the money out loud. Burk and I will be watching and listening from behind the wall in the hall.''

Kate's mind was so crammed with instructions that she wasn't sure she could remember them all as Harry continued. ''When you're finished counting the money, that's when we'll step in and arrest him. If he should draw any kind of a weapon, run for the nearest exit and get out of there. *Is that understood?''*

Kate nodded. ''Perfectly. I'm not inclined to stick around and get caught in the cross fire.''

Harry stood up. ''After listening to your conversation with Jensen earlier, I'm not so sure I believe you,'' he observed, ''but don't try anything like that again. Be submissive. We need him to think everything is going smoothly and he's going to get away with this. Otherwise the whole thing could blow up in our faces.''

He left to go back to the garage and Kate and Burk resumed their cuddling. As the minutes ticked by, she became more and more nervous. What was taking so long? Had there been a glitch somewhere? Maybe Jensen had never intended to return. Maybe he was going to keep the original file as well as the money intended for her and swear that he knew nothing about either!

Finally she became too jumpy to sit on the floor any longer with Burk and got to her feet. He stood, too, and appeared to be as nervous as she was.

''I know it's hard on you, love,'' he said, ''but try to calm down. That's a lot easier said than done, but you need to keep your wits about you when Jensen gets here.''

He plowed his hand through his hair. ''Damn! I just wish I could do this for you....''

Just then Harry rushed into the room. ''Jensen just drove up. Everyone to their places,'' he ordered softly, and grabbed Burk by the arm. Burk grabbed Kate with his other hand and they all three ran down the hall and into the back bedroom.

"Get her out of here," Harry commanded as he opened the closet door.

Burk wrapped one arm around Kate and kissed her, hard and fast, then released her. "Be careful, sweetheart," he said as Harry pulled him into the closet and shut the door.

Kate heard footsteps on the porch and took a deep breath as the door opened and Evel walked into the living room. She walked through the archway just as he closed the door behind him. He was carrying her briefcase.

"Well, well, if it isn't Sleeping Beauty," he taunted. "You been sleepin' on the floor in one of the bedrooms?"

She must look disheveled from all that making out with Burk. "Trying to," she said grumpily, and it wasn't acting. Just looking at him made her sick. "You could have at least supplied me with a sleeping bag. Where's my file?"

She walked to the invisible line that separated the living room from the dining room and stood against the wall so that he had to turn his back to the kitchen in order to face her.

"I've got it right here all safe and sound," he said, and patted the briefcase. "Your money's in there, too. Buy yourself a fancy wedding gown. The festivities will go on as planned."

Her stomach muscles cramped. She didn't want him talking about the wedding. He might say something to give away the secret she and he knew about.

"Not so fast," she said as calmly as she could. "I want to check it first."

Setting the briefcase on the floor, she squatted down and opened it, then pulled the thick file folder out and opened it. The case also contained a large brown manila envelope.

"It's all there, dammit," he grumbled. "I don't need the originals—I've got copies."

She paid no attention but began checking out each page aloud, quickly but audibly.

When she finished, she took out the manila envelope and opened it.

Evel muttered a rude oath. "It's all there—twenty-five one-hundred-dollar bills in stacks of ten. You can see it, you don't have to count it. I've got an appointment to keep."

She looked up at him. "I'm sure you have, but I don't trust you any more than you trust me. If you're going to make me break the law, I'm going to make sure I get paid for it."

She continued counting, one stack at a time until she'd computed every bill. Jensen was fuming and didn't hear one of the policemen from the kitchen sneaking up behind him.

"Thank you, Evel Jensen, you bastard," she said loud and clear as she stood up, making sure her voice would be caught on tape. "Every cent of the twenty-five thousand dollars you promised to pay me to let you copy the confidential Project 2000 file is here. I hope you spend the rest of your natural life in prison."

"And I hope I never have to work with you again," he said with a sneer just before the officer behind him stuck the muzzle of his gun none too gently in Evel's back.

"Evel Jensen, you're under arrest," he said.

In a second Evel's expression changed from impatience to shock. He whirled around and swung at the officer, but the second one who seemed to come out of nowhere grabbed him and wrestled him to the floor then yanked his arms behind him and cuffed him.

At the same time the room seemed to fill with people as Harry and Burk ran in from the other side of the house. Burk grabbed Kate in his arms and held her to him.

The first officer still covered Evel with his pistol as he droned on. "You have the right to remain silent. Anything you say can and will be used against you in a court of law...."

He continued to read the prisoner his rights under the Miranda decision while Evel lay on the floor, seemingly stunned, with the gun pointed at his head.

When the first officer had finished, the two of them hauled Evel to his feet. He shook his head as if to clear it, then glared at Kate, sparks of pure hatred shooting from his eyes.

The string of obscenities he directed at Kate was cut off when Burk lunged at him. For a short time it took three officers to hold him back as he struggled to get at Jensen.

"Cut it out, Burk," one of them commanded harshly. "Don't hit him while he's cuffed. We don't want to give him any reason to cry police brutality. I'd like nothing better than to remove the restraints and let you have a crack at him, but we'll need a clean collar for a maximum sentence."

Kate knew what was coming and closed her eyes as she crossed her arms over her roiling stomach. Maybe if she couldn't see Evel's vengeful expression it wouldn't happen.

Burk stopped scuffling and glowered at Jensen. "Keep your filthy mouth shut or I'll—"

"You'll what, Mr. High and Mighty Sinclair?" he snarled, his tone heavy with sarcasm. "You'll take a swing at me and put these officers at risk of an internal affairs investigation? Or maybe you'll bring all of your considerable influence to bear to have me convicted of a crime that has nothing to do with you? I don't think you're going to bother with either when you find out who your bride-to-be really is."

Burk's fists clenched again. "Get him the hell out of here." he growled.

The two policemen each clutched one of Jensen's arms and tried to lead him toward the door, but he dug in his feet and refused to cooperate.

"You don't want to hear what I have to say?" he taunted. "Well, then, I have no choice but to go to the newspapers. You poor sucker. I was tryin' to give you a break so the whole town wouldn't know, but it makes no difference to me one way or the other.''

Dead silence followed, and after a few seconds Kate opened her eyes. Everyone seemed to be waiting for Burk to speak, but he appeared to be immobilized—whether with indecision or inability she didn't know.

She'd just opened her mouth to put an end to this agonizing suspense and tell Burk herself the secret Jensen was tormenting them both with, when he beat her to it.

''Your pure and innocent fiancée here is the reporter you've been looking for all these years. The one who broke the story of your ex-wife's, uh, shall we say 'cottage industry' during her college days and scared her into absconding with your little daughter.''

Chapter Twelve

Kate felt Burk's body tense, and his fingers dug painfully into the fleshy part of her arm where he held her beside him. She glanced at him and saw disbelief mixed with rage.

"You lying lowlife." His tone was low and guttural. "If you so much as breathe a vicious rumor like that outside this room, I'll take you apart. I didn't even know Kate when that happened."

A look of assurance spread across Jensen's face. "No, but she knew you. She told you that, didn't she? Did she also tell you she was working for that now-defunct tabloid at the time? That she studied journalism in college and was a real eager-beaver reporter?"

He was throwing out questions so fast that Burk didn't have a chance to assimilate them, but each one hit Kate like a blow. Evel was out for revenge, and he'd do or say anything to get it, no matter how many lives he had to ruin in the process.

"You want to know how she got the story?" he asked,

then continued on before Burk could answer. "She was covering the trial and had gone to your building to try to get an interview with you when she overheard two of your most trusted employees talking about it. She stayed out of sight and taped the conversation. Most of those tabloid papers required taped interviews so she had her miniature recorder with her."

He looked at Kate, and she could see that he was enjoying this. "How about it, babe? You're looking a little peaked. Have I got it right? Don't hesitate to correct me if I'm wrong."

She was as frozen with horror as Burk was, and made no effort to answer. After all, what could she say? Evel's facts were right on—she couldn't deny that—but he was slanting them to make it look as if she hadn't cared how much suffering she inflicted on Burk and his family as long as she got her sensational story published.

That wasn't true. She'd been irresponsible but she'd never meant to be malicious!

Kate looked around and saw that everyone in the room was looking at her, even Burk. They were all waiting for her answer.

Burk's face was totally colorless, and his eyes bored into her while his fingers continued to clutch painfully at her arm.

"Come on, Kate, tell him it's not true. You are going to deny it, aren't you?" Burk's voice had a dry cracking sound as if it hadn't been used in a long time.

She couldn't do that. There had already been too many half-truths and cover-ups. If there was ever to be a chance for the two of them to have a life together it had to start out with a clean slate.

She took a deep breath and looked at him. "No, Burk, I'm not. I can't."

She saw the mixture of shock and pain in his eyes as he

dropped his hand from her arm. "Are you saying that you *are* the reporter who gave that information to the tabloid?"

She nodded and looked away, no longer able to meet his gaze. "Yes, I am, but I'd like to explain—"

"Don't bother," he said grimly, then turned and walked out of the house, taking her broken heart with him.

There was a smile of pure triumph on Evel's face. "Sorry about that, sweetie, but you can't say I didn't warn you."

Burk was vaguely aware that he'd been driving the car for a long time, but he was too filled with anguish to sort out where he was or why. Maybe if he just cruised the streets, this nightmare would eventually end and he'd wake up. He had to. He couldn't live all the rest of his life with the agony that slashed and tore at him. Soon there had to be a stopping point.

Later—he had no idea how much later—the motor of the car sputtered and died, leaving him stranded on a dark and lonely two-lane road. The only illumination came from the crescent-shaped moon and the headlights of his car.

He suddenly felt very tired. Wiped out, actually, and there was nothing he could do about getting help in the middle of the night when he didn't even know where he was. There was no sign of houses or business buildings along the road.

He had a cellular phone for the car, but for some reason he'd left it somewhere. He couldn't remember where or why, and he didn't want to. All he wanted was to go to sleep. Maybe in the morning he'd be more alert.

It took all of his energy to get out of the front seat and into the back where he collapsed in exhaustion.

The sun was shining brightly when Burk woke up, and it took him several minutes to remember why he was sleeping in his car in the middle of a deserted countryside instead of in his own bed with Katie in his arms.

Then it hit him with the force of a ramrod. He wouldn't be sleeping with Kate anymore! The agony that tore through him took his breath away, and he clutched the back of the front seat to keep from crying out in his pain.

There would be no more self-pity. He didn't remember any of what happened after her confession except that he'd left the house and walked around the block where his car was parked. After that it was all a blank, and he hated that

He'd lost control only once before, and that was when he found out that his wife had taken his little daughter and disappeared. He'd sworn then that it would never happen again. He was a strong man, one whom people looked to for support, not one who went whimpering to others for comfort.

He'd let down his guard with Katherine Brown, and she had turned out to be just as deceitful as Fleur. Well, thank God he'd found out about it before they were married. He wouldn't have to go through the public scrutiny of a divorce this time.

He reached for the door and discovered that it wasn't even latched, let alone locked. Boy, he really had been out of it last night!

When he stepped out, his head spun and his legs turned to rubber. He stumbled and would have fallen if the car hadn't been there to prop him up. Dammit, he felt like he was coming to after a three-day binge, but he knew from the taste in his mouth that he hadn't had a drop to drink.

He leaned against the car and looked around. Nothing was familiar. If he remembered right, he'd run out of gas just before he collapsed last night. Obviously the only thing he could do was start walking until he came to someone who could tell him where he was and where he could get in touch with a service station.

He straightened away from the auto and put one foot in

front of the other. He was shaky, but after a few more steps he'd be okay.

Katherine Brown ruined his life once; he wasn't going to let her do it again.

For a week Kate tried to contact Burk, but when she called him at home she got his answering machine and when she called him at work his secretary told her crisply that he wasn't in. When she tried to contact other members of his family she also got an answering machine. Her messages to please call her were ignored. She'd even written him a letter pouring her heart out to him, but so far she'd had no answer.

Obviously he wasn't going to listen to her explanation. Not that it mattered. There was nothing she could say, no excuse that she could offer him for the damage she'd done earlier or for not telling him the truth when they first met.

Had he been in love with her? Apparently not. He'd said he was, but could love be such a fragile emotion that he could slip in and out of it at his convenience?

She couldn't think of anything he could do that would make her stop loving him.

At work she was a true heroine. By the following Monday a write-up of the arrest of Evel Jensen and her part in it had been in all the news media and she was lauded for her bravery. There was nothing about Evel's curious conversation with Burk. Apparently, nobody picked up on what they were talking about, and just put it down to malice on Evel's part.

But now time was running short, and what about the scheduled wedding? It was unlikely that Burk intended to go through with it, but none of his family would talk to her to tell her if the guests had been notified. She couldn't just let everybody show up at the church except the bride and groom!

Her dilemma was resolved on Friday, a week and two days before the ceremony. Both she and her grandmother received printed notices resembling the invitations that had gone out several weeks ago, but with a very different message.

We regret to inform you that the wedding of Burk Sinclair and Katherine Brown, which was to have taken place on Sunday, June 3 at Trinity Cathedral, has been canceled. All nuptial gifts will be returned.

The formal declaration was the last blow to her self-esteem. Burk could have at least told her in person that he no longer intended to marry her!

She'd been bearing up pretty well until now, but the deliberate cruelty of that announcement shattered her tenuous composure and wrung sobs from deep within her soul.

Her grandmother held her but made no attempt to stop her crying. "Go ahead, my dear," she said gently, "get it all out. You've been far too calm. You can't start to heal until you give vent to your feelings."

Kate couldn't have stopped if she'd wanted to, and she wailed in Emily's comforting arms. For a long time the anguish poured out, but eventually she got herself under control again and mopped at her face with tissues from a box that had magically appeared on the sofa beside her.

"I...I guess Burk's family has everything pretty well under control." She sniffled and blew her nose.

"I would say so, yes," Emily said with barely suppressed hostility. "I never would have believed that Burk could be so merciless. He should have at least talked to you and told you in person that the marriage was off."

Another sob shook Kate. "Don't blame Burk, Grandma He has good reason to be furious with me. I'm the one in the wrong. I knew he'd never marry me if he found out who I was. Still, it's going to be hard to face my friends at work on Monday.''

The day that would have been their wedding was the hardest one to get through. Kate woke up with a headache and then lost her breakfast. It wasn't the first time in the past two weeks that she'd done that, but she attributed it to stress. God knows she'd been under plenty of that. The icky feeling never lasted long and by lunchtime it was gone, so she hadn't paid much attention.

Today, however, she could hardly drag herself out of bed and pull on her robe. It must be that intestinal flu that had been going around. Several people at work had called in sick with it. She'd have to tell Grandma she couldn't take her to church today.

She stumbled into the dining room, where Emily took one look at her and gasped. "Kathy, you look awful. Are you sick?''

Kate nodded and dropped down into one of the straight-back chairs. "Yeah, I think it's a touch of intestinal flu."

"There's no such thing as a 'touch' of intestinal flu," Emily said. "It's nasty stuff and you've either got it or you haven't. You get right back upstairs and go to bed. I'll bring you some milk of magnesia. It should quiet your stomach down.''

It did but only slightly, and when Kate wasn't any better the following day, Emily insisted on making an appointment for Kate to see the doctor.

Later that afternoon she was ushered into the office of Dr. Lyons, who had been their family physician ever since Kate could remember. A few minutes later he walked in and picked up her chart.

"So what's the problem, Kate?'' he asked after they got the preliminary hello's out of the way and she was lying on the examination table.

"My stomach's got something against food," she groaned. "It won't keep anything down."

"I see," he murmured and poked her several places in the belly with his fingers. "How long has this been going on?"

"About a week," she admitted, "but it's gotten worse the past couple of days."

"Mmm-hmm. And how are you otherwise? When was your last period?"

Kate searched her mind but couldn't remember. "Gee, I don't know. It must have been a couple of weeks— No. It's longer than that. Darn, now that I think of it, it has to have been a couple of months. I've been under a lot of stress with the accident and the Evel Jensen thing. It's probably messed up my natural cycle."

The doctor positioned himself at the bottom of the table. "Okay, I'll take a look and see what's going on."

Twenty minutes later Kate was dressed and waiting in the doctor's office. He opened the door and came in, then closed it behind him, sat down across the desk from her and beamed.

"Well, Kate, I'm happy to tell you that you're one of the healthiest patients I have."

The beam dimmed and his expression became serious. "You're also approximately two months pregnant."

Chapter Thirteen

Kate was stunned! Pregnant? Well, of course she was! Any other woman would have recognized the symptoms weeks ago, so how had she missed them?

She hadn't missed them; she'd ignored them. Blinded first by the glory of her love affair with Burk; then by the anguish she experienced when it was shattered; to say nothing of the terror she'd been put through by Evel Jensen in between the two events, she hadn't paid any attention to the message her body had been trying to send her.

She was pregnant with Burk Sinclair's child!

"Kate! Kate, are you all right?" She blinked and looked up to see Dr. Lyons standing over her with his hand on her shoulder.

They made eye contact and he let out a swoosh of breath. "Dammit, Kate, I was afraid you wouldn't be very happy about the pregnancy what with your wedding being called off and all, but you do have options, you know."

What did he mean, options? She didn't need options.

She pulled herself together and shook her head. "No, you don't understand. I'm just shocked. We'd been using protection."

The doctor patted her shoulder and went back around the desk to sit down. "Contraceptive failure happens," he assured her. "Unfortunately, only abstinence is one hundred percent effective. I don't deliver babies anymore, but I can recommend a good obstetrician...."

By the time she left his office she had an appointment with a specialist and a prescription for something to quiet her stomach down. She also had the astounding certainty that she was carrying Burk's child!

Back home, Grandma met her at the door, anxious to know what the doctor had said.

A tiny smile lifted the corners of Kate's mouth and she put her hand to her stomach. "He said you're going to be a great-grandmother."

Grandma didn't look nearly as shocked as Kate had been when she heard the news. "Oh, Kate, I was afraid of that," she admitted. "What are you going to do?"

Kate frowned. "What do you mean, what am I going to do? I'm going to continue throwing up every morning for a while and then buy some maternity clothes."

Emily surveyed her closely. "Do you want the baby?"

Kate pondered for a moment. "It doesn't much matter whether I want it or not, it's already growing inside me. If you mean did I get pregnant intentionally, the answer is no. I wouldn't deliberately have a child to raise as a single parent. I believe babies should be part of a family with both a mother and a father, but since I wasn't given a choice I have to admit that I rather like the idea."

"And what about Burk? Are you going to tell him?"

Kate hesitated. "How can I tell him when he won't even talk to me?"

Emily shook her head sadly. "I don't know, dear. That's strictly your decision and I wouldn't presume to advise you.

I'm just sorry that such a happy event as the bearing of a child should be clouded by quarrels and doubt.''

''Burk and I didn't quarrel, Grandma,'' Kate reminded her. ''He simply walked out of the room and off the face of the earth without a word. One thing I do know, this is not the news he wants to hear from me. He'd probably either deny the baby is his or accuse me of getting pregnant on purpose to trap him.''

Shock registered in Emily's expression. ''Kathy! Do you really believe that? Surely Burk wouldn't shirk his obligation to his own son or daughter!''

For some reason Emily's quick defense of Burk angered Kate. ''Let's get one thing straight, Grandma. Burk has no obligation to either me or my baby. I'll try again to get in touch with him and talk to him about this turn of events, but I'm not going to plead. I will not tell him about his impending fatherhood through a third party or a machine. If I can't relay the information to him myself, face-to-face, then I'll assume he doesn't want to know.''

She stopped to take a breath. ''Either way, I'm not going to accept support from him, nor will I share custody.''

The following day Kate started trying to reach Burk but with the same negative results. He was never available and all her messages went unanswered. Once more she wrote him a letter, this time insisting it was urgent that she speak with him, but again it also went unanswered.

Finally, even Grandma agreed that Kate had done all she could, and they settled down to planning for the little one and enjoying the prospect of having an infant to love and raise. She didn't tell anyone else she was pregnant, and, because the antinausea medication didn't do much good and she still couldn't keep her breakfasts down, she was slowly losing weight instead of gaining it, so by her fourth month she still wasn't showing.

* * *

August was an unusually warm and dry month this year with temperatures in the high sixties and little rain. Several men had asked Kate for dates since her aborted wedding plans had become so public, but she hadn't felt well enough either physically or emotionally to accept.

Now, though, she had an invitation from a man she couldn't turn down. His name was Peter Vernon and he was the son of the family who lived next door. He was only a year older than she and she thought of him as the brother she'd never had. They'd grown up together until he went away to Stanford University and law school in California. After he earned his law degree he accepted a position with the district attorney's office in Sacramento so it was seldom that he was able to get away to visit his parents.

Now was one of those times. He was spending a short vacation at home and he wanted her to go to the Mount Hood Jazz Festival with him. She accepted eagerly. She wasn't enthusiastic about dating anyone, but this wasn't a date. It was a day spent with her dear friend, and besides, it was time she started getting out once in a while.

For one thing, when her pregnancy became obvious she probably wouldn't get any more dates, but more importantly she wasn't going to sit at home any longer and grieve over her loss of Burk. He'd made it plain that he didn't want anything to do with her, and his rejection tore at her heart, but she was determined not to let depression cripple her. Now that she was going to be a mother, she needed all the vivacity and stamina she could generate.

The festival was held on the campus of the Mount Hood Community College and featured jazz musicians from all over the country. It had started off that morning with a renown spiritual singer and her choir, then had progressed all day with jazz groups belting stimulating rhythm through the air both indoors and out.

Kate was having a marvelous time, but by late afternoon she was exhausted. Her obstetrician had warned her that the growing fetus plus her continuing nausea would sap her strength and she must not get overly tired, but she didn't usually get this much exercise so she hadn't noticed any problem before.

Pete didn't have any idea she was pregnant so he'd been rushing her from one building to another with little chance to sit down and relax until now her legs ached and her feet were swollen and on fire. It was also warmer than usual and sweat had broken out on her forehead.

They were walking hand in hand down the road, and she'd just turned to look at Pete and tell him she wanted to sit down and rest awhile when she caught sight of a man and woman coming toward them. They were dressed casually in jeans and shirts as were she and Pete.

She stopped, blinked and did a double take. The man was Burk!

He looked right at her, and she saw the blood drain from his face just before her head began to whirl and the lights went out.

Burk was trying to deal with the shock of running into Kate so unexpectedly after all these weeks of avoiding her when she suddenly crumpled and pitched forward on the ground.

Propelled by a force outside himself over which he had no control, he tore across the few feet that separated them and picked her up, cradling her in his arms. "Katie, Katie, Katie," he murmured over and over into her ear as he carried her unconscious body quickly across the campus toward the registration building while the man with her, looking perplexed, ran along beside them.

The building was open and the dispensary was staffed with two paramedics to take care of any injuries and illnesses that might occur during the festival. Burk headed right for it, and by the time he got there Katie was stirring weakly in his arms.

"Just lie quietly," he said, and sat down in one of the chairs with her across his lap.

"What happened to her?" one of the paramedics, a woman, asked.

"I don't know," Burk answered. "She was coming toward me and all of a sudden she crumpled to the ground."

The woman looked at him. "Are you a relative?"

"No, I'm her—" Dammit! He'd almost said *her fiancé.* "I know her," he finished uncertainly.

"Well, take her over there and put her on the examining table," the woman directed.

"No." Involuntarily his arms tightened around her. "That is, can't you examine her while I hold her?"

He knew he was making a fool of himself, but he couldn't bear the thought of giving her up. He'd needed her in his arms so desperately for so long. If he could just hold her a little while longer, maybe then it would be easier.

"Come on, fella, you know better than that," the other paramedic, a man, exclaimed. "And time may be imperative. Either you take her over there or I will."

With a massive effort of will Burk stood and carried Kate to the table and gently laid her on it. When he straightened up, his arms felt empty and ached for her.

"Okay now, if you guys will wait outside, this shouldn't take long," the man said, and it was only then that Burk realized the man Katie had been with was in the room, too.

Their gazes met. He was a good-looking fellow, blond with blue eyes, and quite a bit younger than Burk. A stab of jealousy knifed through Burk as they broke eye contact and turned to walk out into the hall.

There was no place to sit out there so they stood and glared at each other. Burk was the first to speak. "Who are you?"

"I think that's my question," the other man said angrily. "After all, Kate is my date." He looked around. "What happened to yours?"

Burk groaned. Damn. He'd forgotten all about Iris! "She'll be along. She knows her way to the dispensary. She's a professor here."

"Fine," he said grimly. "Now, suppose you tell me who the hell you are, and what right you have to simply take over. I'm perfectly capable of getting medical care for Kate."

Burk sighed. "I'm Burk Sinclair," he said wearily.

The other man stared at him with disgust. "You're the son of a bitch who left her practically standing at the altar?"

It was part question and part statement, and there was only one answer. "Yes," he said quietly, making no effort to explain or defend himself.

The man's fists clenched and his expression was thunderous. "In that case, I'd say you forfeited your right to come riding to her rescue on a white charger. I don't know what went wrong with the wedding plans. She won't talk about it to anybody, but I've known Kate all her life and I know she'd never do anything to deserve that kind of treatment, so take your heroics and get out of here. Go find your own date. You seem to have a penchant for abandoning women, but as long as I'm around, you're not going to hurt my Katie any more than you already have."

My Katie. Burk found it hard to breathe. What was this guy to her? She'd denied having anyone special in her life before she met Burk, but this man had a definitely proprietary attitude toward her.

"Before you start giving me orders, I suggest you tell me who you are and what you are to Kate," Burk snapped. He wasn't used to being ordered around. Especially by someone younger than he and a stranger besides.

"My name is Peter Vernon," Pete said, "and my relationship with Kate is none of your damn business. What the hell do you care anyway? You made it plain to the whole town that you didn't want her, so at least have the decency to leave her alone now.''

The anger drained out of Burk and he turned away. Peter Vernon, whoever he is, was right. Burk had no right to interfere in Kate's life even if it was to help. She didn't need his help. She had another man to love her and take care of her now.

The pain that thought brought was excruciating, and he started walking toward the door. He'd better find Iris. The very least he owed her was an apology.

When Kate came fully conscious she told the medics about her pregnancy, and the woman examined her.

''You seem to be all right,'' she said, ''but I strongly advise you to get off your feet. You've got a couple of men out in the hall growling and baring their teeth at each other. Get one of them to take you home. If you notice any bleeding, call your doctor immediately.''

''Oh, I will,'' Kate assured her. ''And please, don't tell those two men that I'm pregnant.''

The woman eyed her wryly and Kate knew she was wondering how many men Kate would have to sort through before she decided which one was the father, but all she said was ''Rest assured, it's not our place to make that announcement.''

When the male medic went out to tell the men they could come in, only Pete showed up. She was sitting on the edge of the table, and he must have seen the question in her expression because he quickly explained.

''Sinclair left, or to be more accurate, I threw him out. Sorry, honey, but I couldn't let the crumb hurt you again.''

Kate felt a worm of sadness curl up inside her and settle there. ''He's not a crumb,'' she said sorrowfully, ''and it's not his fault that he changed his mind about marrying me, but it's just as well that he didn't stick around. Do you mind bringing the car here? The medic said I was to go home and put my feet up.''

On the way home Kate leaned back in the seat and told Peter about her pregnancy and her inability to get in touch with Burk. When she finished, Pete was livid. She'd known he would be, but he'd have learned of her pregnancy shortly anyway, and she'd rather he heard it from her.

''Where does he get off treating you like that?'' he growled deep in his throat. ''His ex-wife is the one who disappeared with their child, and she'd have done that when he produced his little bombshell in court anyway. All you did was hurry it up by a day.''

Kate sighed. ''I know, but Burk doesn't think straight where Monique is concerned. You really can't blame him, Pete. Monique's sudden disappearance is agonizing for him. It's been five years and he hasn't found a trace of her.''

''The hell I can't blame him,'' Pete muttered. ''It's his wife who's responsible for that, not you. She's obviously scared to death that if she and Monique ever surface, with all his wealth and prestige he'll take the child away from her without even letting her have visiting privileges—and I think he probably could. Not because of her past indiscretion, but because she bolted once and no judge will want to be guilty of putting her in a position to do it again.''

Kate was quite sure he was right. Burk could be pretty impressive when he brought all his weight to bear on a subject.

''I suspect they are both behaving like vindictive children instead of responsible adults,'' Pete continued, ''and I doubt that she'll ever surface until she has some assurance that she won't lose the child altogether.''

As soon as she got home Kate went to bed and stayed there until the following morning when she awoke feeling not only rested but invigorated. She showered, dressed in blue jeans and a *Les Misérables* T-shirt she'd bought when she saw the touring company of the play last year, and she even kept her breakfast down, which gave her hope that the nausea was finally going away.

It was Sunday, and at ten-thirty Grandma's friends came by to drive her to church and Kate was left alone. She liked the solitude. She needed to think, and that was difficult to do with Grandma around. If Kate stopped talking for five minutes, Grandma was always sure she was either brooding or sick.

A smile lifted the corners of her mouth. Dear, sweet Grandma. Kate knew she was fortunate to have somebody who cared enough to worry about her even if it did break her concentration.

She'd just loaded the clothes washer when the doorbell rang. Who could that be? She wasn't expecting anyone.

She hurried out of the laundry room, across the kitchen and dining room to the entryway, then opened the door and stared.

It was Burk!

What was he doing here? Yesterday he'd left before she had a chance to say a word to him, so what did he want now? He hadn't cared enough to stick around and find out what was wrong with her. She'd have told him about her pregnancy if he had, but now she wasn't sure she wanted to share that bit of news with him. He didn't seem to be especially concerned about her.

For a long moment they stood there gaping at each other. Finally he broke the silence. "May I come in, Kate?"

That shook her out of her daze and she reached out to unlock the screen door. "Yes, I'm sorry, please do."

She'd been too well brought up to be rude.

He opened the door and she stood back to admit him. He looked classy even in cotton trousers and a pullover sweater, but he also looked stressed-out. There were dark circles under his eyes and tiny wrinkles at the corners of his mouth.

"Can we talk in the kitchen over a cup of coffee?" he asked.

"If that's what you want." She started walking toward the kitchen. She couldn't drink coffee anymore. Even the smell of it made her nauseous, but hot tea didn't bother her.

"Have a seat," she said, and motioned to one of the wooden chairs at the round table, then opened the cupboard door and reached for a couple of mugs.

Her hands were trembling, and she hoped she didn't drop or spill anything as she poured his coffee and set it before him. She knew he didn't take cream or sugar so she didn't offer it.

"Aren't you going to have any?" he asked as she went over to the stove and turned on the heat under the teakettle.

She shook her head. "I drink tea now."

Burk watched her carefully as she took the tea canister and a ceramic pot out of the cupboard. "I remember when you could drink a whole pot of coffee by yourself."

She almost dropped the canister. "If you just came here to reminisce then I'd like you to leave," she said tremulously. "I'm really not interested in reliving the past."

Before she could anticipate him, he got up and was standing beside her. "I'm only trying to put you at ease," he said softly. "I came to find out what's wrong with you. Are you ill? You have almost no color and you've lost weight. I noticed that especially when I was carrying you yesterday. You're all bones, and you feel so fragile."

She felt a thrill of relief. He was concerned about her. So why hadn't he stayed around yesterday to find out if she was all right?

"I didn't intend to leave yesterday until the medics were through examining you," he said, as though reading her mind. "But your boyfriend and I were coming close to blows so I decided I'd better get out of there. You didn't need the two of us brawling in the hall.''

"Pete's not my boyfriend," she snapped, and then could have bitten her tongue. She didn't have to explain who Pete was. It was none of Burk's business.

''If he's not your boyfriend, then who is he?'' Burk asked.

Her tone softened. "He's my next-door neighbor, my best friend, my brother.''

Burk's eyes widened. "Your brother? I thought you were an only child.''

"I am," she explained reluctantly, "but Peter Vernon is like a brother to me. We were practically raised together. He takes care of me, even when I don't want him to.''

"And I don't?" His voice was laced with pain.

Her first impulse was to put her arms around him and soothe his anguish; instead she stepped back and turned away. No, she wasn't going to get caught in that trap again. Burk was the neediest man she knew, and she was frighteningly vulnerable to him, but Pete had been right in his assessment of the disappearance of his wife and child. Kate had played only a small part in it and she was through taking all the blame.

"There's no reason why you should take care of me," she said forcefully. "I'm nothing to you. You've made that very plain since you called off our wedding. So why are you here?''

The teakettle began to whistle and she turned off the burner under it and poured boiling water into the pot then put in a tea bag.

"You couldn't be more wrong," he said wryly. "I'm here because I went a little crazy yesterday when I saw you blanch and fall to the ground. Hell, I acted like you belonged to me. Your Peter was ready to do battle, and I doubt if Iris will ever speak to me again.''

Kate's heart speeded up, but her mind spoke louder. *Don't let him do this to you. You'll only get hurt again.*

Burk picked up the teapot and carried it over to the table for which Kate was extremely grateful. Her hands were shaking so hard that she'd almost certainly have spilled it if she'd tried to do it.

"Well, as you can see I'm perfectly fine, so you don't need to worry," she said as they sat down—or in her case *dropped* down—in their chairs. Her legs were shaking as badly as her hands.

"You're not perfectly fine," Burk argued. "You're too thin, and you look tired and gaunt. What's the matter with you, Kate?"

Imagine that. What did she have to look gaunt about? Just a lover who didn't want her. A difficult pregnancy with no husband to share the anxiety. And a child to raise with no father to do his share of the parenting.

"You'll forgive me if I find this concern of yours a little hard to believe," she said sarcastically, "but I've been trying to get in touch with you for months and you haven't answered my calls or responded to my messages."

"I know," he admitted wearily. "I was afraid to talk to you."

Kate blinked. "Afraid? Of me?"

He shook his head. "Not of you, but of what you do to me. I was afraid if I talked to you I'd beg you to come back to me."

She was quite sure she'd never been so insulted. Now she was trembling with anger. Standing, she kicked her chair back and leaned over the table, bracing herself on the palms of her hands.

"Well, pardon me if I tempt you to do something so crass and beneath you," she sniped, "but you can relax. There will be no more attempts on my part to contact you, and even if you should run into me on the street and lose control enough to make such a demeaning and shameful suggestion, I'd see you in hell before I'd accept it. Now get out of here and leave me alone."

She started for the door but had only gone a few steps when he caught her and whirled her around to face him. "Katie, I didn't mean it that way! I want you. I love you! Have you forgotten that so soon?"

Now Kate was thoroughly rattled. "You...you love me?" She could barely get the words out.

"Of course I do." His eyes spit fire even as his grip on her arms gentled to a caress. "You should know that, I've told you often enough."

"Well, you've got a hell of a way of showing it," she grumbled and pulled away from him. If he was trying to confuse her, he was doing a masterful job of it.

"Why did you think I was so upset yesterday?" he asked. "I didn't stop loving you. You can't shut love off and on, but I stopped trusting you. I don't see how we could have a happy marriage without trust, and you lied to me, Kate. You lied about your part in something that was very important to me."

He still loved her, but he wouldn't marry her because of her part in the disappearance of his little daughter. But the point was that she didn't lie to him. She had to make him understand.

"Burk, I didn't lie to you. I admit I—"

"Now you're doing it again," he interrupted. "How can I marry you if I'll never know whether or not you're telling me the truth?"

She pulled out of his grasp, defeated. He wouldn't listen to her, and he wouldn't believe her even if he did. She might as well not even try.

"This is getting us nowhere," she told him. "Please leave."

He looked beaten, too, and started for the door. "I'll go, but please do one thing for me."

She nodded. "I will if I can."

"Go to the doctor, then call and tell me what he said."

She knew she had to tell him about the baby. It would be grossly unfair of her not to. After all, he had a right to know. He was the father.

"You don't answer your phone when I call, and I'm not going to talk to your machine. Besides, I'm already seeing my doctor once a month."

Fear and shock registered in Burk's expression. "You are! Then there is something wrong. Dammit, Kate, what does he say?"

She turned and looked straight at him. "He says I'm four months pregnant."

Chapter Fourteen

"Pregnant!" Burk stared at Kate, stunned. "But that's not possible! We always used protection."

"That was my first reaction, too," she told him, "but then it occurred to me. Remember the first time we made love?"

"How could I ever forget?" he murmured softly.

Darn! He was doing it again. Every time he spoke to her in that tone, her mind turned to mush.

"Well, there was one thing we did forget, and that was a condom. I thought of it later but I wasn't too concerned because it was the wrong time of the month. I was sure we were safe."

"You're pregnant," he said again with what sounded like wonder as his gaze roamed over her. "But why didn't you tell me?"

Slowly a sad look of understanding replaced the wonder. "You weren't going to tell me, were you?"

That brought her out of her fairy-tale dreamworld.

"Where do you get off making assumptions like that?" she demanded hotly. "I was going to tell you. Even though you refused all my efforts to talk to you after that scene with Evel Jensen. I thought it was only fair to let you know you were going to be a father, although I was pretty sure you wouldn't welcome the news."

He frowned and tried to protest but she didn't give him a chance. "I got the same rigmarole all over again, but you already know that. I have to tell you, Burk. You're really good at avoiding issues you don't want to confront. I finally gave up."

He looked thoroughly shaken. "I'm awfully sorry about that, but you could have left a message."

That incensed her even more. "Oh, sure," she snapped. Then she mimicked, "'Tell Mr. Sinclair that he somehow slipped up and is about to become a father.' No way! If you want to hide, that's fine with me. I don't need you. I don't even want your help. I can support and raise my baby by myself and don't ever think I can't."

"No, Katie, don't even suggest such a thing!" There was fear and urgency in his tone. "I couldn't survive losing another child! I'm sorry I've been behaving like such a jerk. I'd give anything if I could go back and correct my mistakes, but that's not possible. I don't know what more I can say."

He took her arm. "Come sit down with me in the living room and let's try to straighten this out. I feel like I've been hit with a double whammy, and I can hardly think, let alone reason."

She realized then that she had been pretty hard on him, and let him lead her to the sofa where they sat down. She could feel his hand shaking on her arm, and as always she had the urge to comfort him. She wasn't going to get over loving him so she might as well learn to live with it.

She put her hand over his where he'd moved it to his thigh, and he turned his over and grasped hers. She felt the tingling sensation all the way up her arm. "Forgive me for being such a shrew, and you're right, I had given up trying to contact you. Contrary to what you think, I would never have lied to you, but neither was I going to plead for your attention. Your message, after all, was very clear. You didn't want anything more to do with me."

He shook his head sadly. "I only wish that were true. Every time I heard your voice on my answering machine it tore me up. I had to leave the building to keep myself from calling you back. I can see now that it was childish. I should have accepted your calls, but I was so damn mad at you—"

"You had a right to be," she interrupted. "But just don't scold me for not telling you about the baby sooner."

He squeezed her hand. "I won't. It was my own fault. How far along did you say you are?"

"Four months. The baby's due in January."

His gaze searched her breasts, waist and hips. "You don't show it. Why are you so thin when you should be putting on weight?"

"I have trouble keeping food down, and I don't want to take too much medication that might hurt the baby. The nausea is easing up, though."

"We'll get you a better doctor," he said domineeringly, "and you'll have to quit working. We'll be married just as soon as it can be arranged and—"

Kate couldn't believe what he was saying. "Now slow down there," she interrupted, and pulled her hand out of his. "What gives you the right to start rearranging my life?"

He looked surprised at her outburst. "I'm the baby's father."

"So?" she said firmly. "All that entitles you to right now is visiting rights after it's born. And what's this about marriage? You just told me you don't trust me and we could never be happy together."

"But everything's different now," he pointed out. "We have the baby to consider."

"And you think I haven't been considering it? I'll hire a nanny. She'll baby-sit while I work—"

"A nanny is no substitute for a father," he insisted.

"Of course she's not," Kate agreed. "But my baby's father was sulking and wasn't around when I was making the plans."

He winced and she regretted her spiteful remark.

"Well, I'm around now and I intend to be a father in every sense of the word," he promised her.

He took a deep breath and lowered his voice. "Katie, I don't want our child to be illegitimate. I know that word is out of style, and that babies born out of wedlock are no longer considered wages of sin, but surely you want ours to have all the privileges of being born within the vows of marriage."

That made Kate stop and think. Was she being selfish to insist on trust and respect from a husband, as well as love? But what about Burk's declaration of love? Wasn't it really only a lingering lust that he felt for her? After all, they'd been a really hot couple, but wouldn't the fire have burned out even if he'd never found out what she'd done?

However, he had found out, and until he heard about the baby he'd had no intention of forgiving her. In fact he still hadn't said anything about forgiveness, just duty.

Was it possible to love a person you didn't even like?

Burk's voice interrupted her thoughts. "Kate. Are you going to answer me? Don't you want our child's parents to be married before he's born?"

He! It was the first time either of them had conferred a gender on the baby.

"He?" This time she said it aloud. "Is that what you want, Burk, a little boy?"

He looked confused and hesitated. "Did I say 'he'? I wasn't aware of it, but yes, I think I would like a son, although I'd be just as happy with a daughter. When can you have the test to find out which it is?''

She shrugged. ''The doctor will do an ultrasound routinely at five months just to make sure everything's going okay, but if the baby's positioned wrong to tell if it's a boy or a girl, my insurance won't pay for another one....''

He took her hand again. ''Don't worry about the expense, honey, but we're getting away from the most important subject. Let's deal with it first. I want to marry you. I want us to be a family.''

She couldn't shake her doubts. ''Why? Just because I'm pregnant?''

''What difference does it make?'' he asked irritably. ''It's the baby we have to think of now.''

''And that's enough for you? You're willing to marry me just to give my child your name?''

''Dammit, Kate, that's not what I said,'' he exploded. ''You keep twisting my words around and giving them meanings I never intended. Why are you being so stubborn? You were willing to marry me a couple of months ago.''

''Yes, and you called the wedding off without even doing me the courtesy of hearing my side of the story or notifying me in person.'' She was equally explosive. ''The first Grandma and I knew of it was when we each received an announcement in the mail.''

''She sent you an announcement!'' His tone was one of disbelief.

''I don't know who 'she' is,'' Kate raged, ''but I'd been going crazy trying to get hold of you or some of your family to confirm that the wedding was off and find out if the guests had been notified, and then we got the same printed announcement in the mail that everyone else got. I can't easily forget such unnecessary cruelty.''

Burk shook his head. ''Kate, I had no idea you'd been treated so insensitively. I was in France. I left a couple of days after the...the last time I saw you. I was still so upset,

I didn't attempt to confront you in person, but I asked Mother to call on you and tell you I'd...I'd changed my mind and was going to France to try again to find Monique. It never occurred to me she'd just send you an announcement." He dropped his face in his hands. "I'm sorry."

Kate shrank from the pain of hearing it was Burk's mother who had treated her so shabbily. She'd liked Jennifer, and she was sure Jennifer had liked her. They'd gotten along well together, but it only made sense that she'd take her son's side on this issue. She didn't have to be so mean spirited about it, though.

Kate believed Burk's explanation, but it seemed like a pretty lame apology. "Sorry doesn't do it," she told him. "You should at least have called me or written me a personal note. I admit I was wrong not to tell you I was the reporter you were looking for, but I think you've extracted your revenge. Did you learn anything new in France?"

He raised his head and looked at her. "I wasn't looking for revenge. I just wanted to get away and try to get my life back on track. Unfortunately, running away didn't help. It just made everything worse, and no, I didn't learn anything I didn't already know."

He straightened up. "Tell me what it is you want from me and I'll give it to you."

She looked away. Now he had her on the defensive again. She wasn't trying to blackmail him with the baby as a pawn. The very thought of such a thing was revolting.

Actually, all she'd ever wanted was for him to love, trust and forgive her, but that was beyond his control. He couldn't force feelings that weren't there, and she wouldn't want them if he could. Unless they were spontaneous they wouldn't be what she yearned for.

"I don't want anything you can't give willingly, happily," she said quietly. "So why don't we compromise? I'll marry you now and live with you until the baby is six months old if, at that time, you'll agree to a dissolution of the marriage and joint custody of the child with me as primary caregiver.''

That should give her time to get her fill of him and adjust to the idea of a temporary marriage. It would be easier for her if she called the shots instead of waiting for him to walk out on her again.

His eyes widened and a look of incredulity spread across his face. "You want to negotiate the terms of a divorce before we even get married?''

She nodded. "I guess you could say that, yes. That way you won't be tied for life to a woman you can't be happy with, but the child will be legally your son or daughter and you'll have an equal say in its upbringing.''

"How do you know I can't be happy with you?'' he muttered.

"Because you told me you couldn't,'' she reminded him.

"I've got a big mouth,'' he said, "and a habit of shooting it off. I sure as hell haven't been happy without you.''

She wasn't going to let him sweet-talk her into changing her mind. Especially when the only reason he wanted to preserve the marriage was so he could have the baby full-time instead of just having visitation rights.

"I'm truly sorry that I've caused you so much grief,'' she said gently. "I should have told you about my part in that newspaper article as soon as you remembered who you were, but I didn't lie to you. I just didn't tell you the whole truth.''

"You deliberately misled me.'' His tone was heavy with misery. "Don't you consider that a lie?''

She twisted her hands in her lap. "I don't know. I didn't think so at the time. In fact, I was careful not to lie to you, but maybe I was just deluding myself. I loved you so much, and I knew you'd never forgive me....''

"How could you have known that?'' he demanded. "You couldn't predict how I might feel in the future.''

"Oh, but I could,'' she insisted. "You kept telling me

how, when you found him, you were going to make life miserable for the unknown reporter whom you claimed was solely responsible for you losing your little girl.''

"He was...or rather, *you were* responsible," Burk said adamantly. "If you'd minded your own business and not spied on what was going on in mine—"

Kate couldn't stand to go over that argument again. "Stop it, please," she cried as she clapped her hands to her ears. "I don't want to hear any more about it—" A sob cut her off in midsentence, and she bent over and put her forehead on her knees. "Just go home and leave me alone," she pleaded as tears ran down her cheeks.

His response was immediate. "Katie, don't cry," he pleaded urgently, "I didn't mean to upset you." He picked her up and cradled her on his lap with her head on his shoulder.

"Dammit, I can't seem to say or do anything right with you," he chided himself as he stroked his hand through her hair. "No wonder you don't want to marry me anymore. I'm a clumsy oaf whose only talent is making you miserable. Don't cry, love. I'll do anything you want me to if you'll just stop crying."

That caused her to sob all the harder, and she put her arms around his neck and wailed. She hated to cry and almost never did. But now that she'd started she couldn't stop. It wasn't fair to use tears to get her own way.

He rocked her gently in his arms while he stroked tendrils of blond hair back and trailed kisses across her wet face and down her throat. She'd forgotten how tender he could be, how warm and loved she always felt in his embrace.

So what if he didn't like her very much? Few women got everything they wanted in a husband. Apparently Burk still desired her. He wouldn't be so anxious about her crying if he didn't care something for her. That had to be better than nothing, which is all she'd had since he walked out on her.

He'd told her he hadn't been happy without her, and she sure knew what that was like. She'd been desolate without him. If it hadn't been for the fact that she was carrying his baby, she didn't know how she'd have gotten through these last two months. Thank God for their one contraceptive oversight!

Carefully she disengaged one arm from around his neck and brought it down to place her hand in the middle of her stomach. There was no sign of it yet, either by movement or size, but when her alienation from Burk became more than she could bear, she knew the baby was there, and it comforted her.

His reaction was immediate and concerned. "What's the matter? Don't you feel well? Are you in pain?"

"Everything's fine," she assured him as she caught one of his hands and laid it on her flat abdomen. "You can't feel the baby yet, but in another month it will be moving around."

"Really?" Ever so gently he moved his hand over her belly. "How can you tell where it is?"

She chuckled. "I can't, but it's in there someplace. It has to grow a little more before it pushes me all out of shape, but once it starts I'll probably blow up like a balloon."

He continued his tender exploration. "I don't care. You'll be nurturing my son or daughter inside you and you'll be beautiful."

He lowered his head and captured her mouth. With a tiny gasp of surprise she put her arm back around his neck and parted her lips for his invasion. He sucked lightly on her lower one then outlined her mouth with his tongue and planted kisses on her moisture-filled eyes and back to her mouth.

Kate responded passionately, and his arms tightened

around her as he pulled her close and snuggled her against him.

"Oh, Katie, I've missed you so," he groaned. "My life has been pure hell without you. I've told myself I hated you, but that was utter nonsense. I'll marry you on your terms, but with one provision. I want nothing to do with a celibate 'marriage of convenience.' While you're my wife we'll sleep in the same bed and have sex as often as we want to unless your doctor says otherwise. What does he say about that, by the way?"

Kate winced. Burk had been doing fine until he mentioned "having sex." That sounded so cold and clinical. Couldn't he bring himself to call it "making love"? Apparently not.

"He says it's allowed up to the time I start dilating or until it becomes too uncomfortable, and for three weeks after delivery," she answered. "And it never occurred to me that we wouldn't sleep together once we're married."

He hugged her and found her mouth again, only this time it was a deeper, more passionate kiss and she could feel his arousal against her thigh.

"How soon can we be married?" he asked shakily as his hand roamed over her back and down to her buttocks.

She should have been thrilled, and she was, but not as much as she would have been if he'd wanted to hurry the ceremony because he loved her and not just because he lusted after her and wanted his discomfort relieved.

She sat up and slid off his lap. "Whenever is convenient for you. This time I'll let you make the arrangements. Just keep it as small and private as possible."

He looked troubled. "All right. Would next Saturday be okay?"

"Yes. Fine." Her tone was crisp and all business. "We should be able to get the premarital contract drawn up and signed by then. Also, I want the ceremony performed by a justice of the peace somewhere other than in a church. I won't take sacred vows before God when neither of us has any intention of keeping them.''

"Katie, I—" Burk tried to intervene, but she paid no attention and swept on.

"Oh, one more thing. I'm sure you have a high-powered lawyer who is terribly busy, but Peter is leaving on Thursday so we'll have to get together on the premarital agreement before then.''

"Peter?" Burk said. "You mean Peter Vernon, your neighbor and good friend. What does he have to do with this?''

"He's my lawyer. He'll be representing me.''

"But I thought you said he lives in California.''

"He does, but he also has a license to practice in Oregon so he can advise his family and friends should the need ever arise. I'll ask him to draw up the agreement and give your lawyer a copy to go over.''

"Dammit, Kate, it sounds to me like you've given this a lot of thought," he said suspiciously. "You've been planning it for quite some time, haven't you?''

She supposed she did sound pretty high-handed, but she'd learned from bitter experience to think on her feet and not let anyone take advantage of her.

"No, actually I haven't. I'm sorry if I come across to you as being hard-boiled and scheming. That's not the case at all. I never expected to see you again, at least not close up and personal, but I've seen how the Sinclair gang works. You'll never take my baby away from me! You've got the power and the money, but I've got the child and I intend to keep it. I'll marry you because I also believe that's best for the baby, but only if it's on my terms. There will be no loopholes, and you're not going to sweet-talk me into agreeing to anything without my lawyer's consent, so make up your mind. Do you want to marry me or not?''

"I don't seem to have much choice," he groused. Then seeing the gathering storm in her expression quickly amended, "I mean about the terms of the marriage, not the fact of it."

Burk left then, but he came back the following evening with his mother. She looked as spiffy as always in her three-hundred-dollar designer pants suit and matching gemstone jewelry. Kate felt a familiar twinge of admiration. Jennifer was a very beautiful mature woman.

Kate was also surprised. Burk hadn't called to tell her they were coming and she was caught off guard and unprepared to talk to his mother, who had treated her so shabbily.

However, Jennifer was going to be her mother-in-law for the next year and would always be the baby's grandmother, so she might as well try to get along with her.

She invited them in and seated them in the living room while Emily bustled around in the kitchen fixing tea and coffee.

Burk got right to the point. "Mother has something to say to you, Kate. Don't you, Mom?"

Jennifer squirmed uncomfortably, but her tone was clear and firm when she spoke. "Yes, I do. I owe you an apology, Kate. Emily, too, and I'll speak to her later. There is no excuse for the insensitive way I informed you that the wedding was canceled. I can only say I'm sorry, and I hope you are more forgiving than I was."

Kate could imagine how difficult it was for this proud woman to plead for forgiveness with the "girl" who had deceived her son as well as the rest of her family, but if Kate wanted to get back on an even mildly friendly relationship with the Sinclair family there were some questions she had to ask.

"Was it your idea or Burk's that you apologize to me?" She kept her tone free of bitterness.

He opened his mouth to interrupt, but Jennifer spoke before he could. "It was his," she admitted.

"Did he threaten you with dire consequences if you didn't?"

A tiny smile quirked at the corners of Jennifer's mouth. "I'm afraid he did. He said if I didn't, I probably wouldn't be welcome in the home you and he will establish."

Burk was trying desperately to get Jennifer's attention. "Dammit, Mother—"

Both women ignored him. "Did you believe him?" Kate asked.

Jennifer shook her professionally coiffed head. "No, I knew you wouldn't be that cruel, but I also knew that my relationship and that of my whole family would be pretty rocky with the two of you if I didn't admit to you that I'd been a witch and was sorry."

This time it was Kate who smiled. "And are you?"

"Yes, I am," Jennifer freely admitted, "and not just because you're going to be my daughter-in-law and the mother of my grandchild. I've felt rotten about myself ever since I pulled that nasty little stunt, but I was too proud to admit it. I'm glad he forced the issue."

Apparently he hadn't told his mother that the marriage was only a temporary one to assure the baby's legitimacy.

Kate's smile widened. "So am I," she said, and meant it. For the child's sake as well as her own she wanted to be on good terms with Burk's family.

Kate, Burk and their lawyers met on Wednesday evening in Burk's office to discuss the premarital agreement Peter had drafted, and none of them was happy. Surprisingly, Peter and Burk were upset about the same terms.

"You aren't even asking for child or spousal support in the event that the marriage ends in divorce!" Burk protested.

"You see," Peter said to Kate. "Even Burk doesn't approve of that."

He turned to Burk. "I've tried to tell her she's entitled

to support and it should be written in the agreement, but she refuses to let me include it.''

Kate looked at Burk, too. ''I explained when I told you I was pregnant that I'm more than capable of supporting myself and my child.''

He pushed back his chair and stood. ''I know you did, but you're forgetting something. That child is mine, too, and I'm entitled to support it. You can't take that right away from me.''

''I'm not trying to,'' she said quietly. ''If you want to send child support checks, I won't stop you, but I won't ask for it and I won't have an amount written up in the agreement.''

''All right, if that's the way you want it,'' he grumbled and started to pace the floor. ''But what about you? As my ex-wife you'd be entitled to support, too.''

Burk's lawyer tried to intervene. ''Burk, don't volunteer—''

He got no further before Kate made her feelings known, loud and clear. ''No way. I can work and support myself.''

''But wouldn't you rather stay home and take care of the baby instead of working and letting a nanny raise our child?'' Burk asked.

She started to seethe again. He was making her sound as if she thought working and being self-supporting was more important to her than raising her son or daughter.

''Yes, I would,'' she answered firmly, ''but I intend to do both. It's true I'll be away for eight hours a day during the week, but I'll give the child all my time on evenings, weekends and holidays. Millions of mothers have that same schedule.''

''Yes, and there are an awful lot of messed-up kids,'' he growled.

''That's not fair and you know it,'' she protested. ''One thing I promise you. My child will never want for loving care.''

"I've never doubted that, Kate, but why do you insist on leaving me out of the picture altogether?"

Kate blinked. "I'm not—"

"Yes, you are," he insisted. "You didn't tell me about the pregnancy until you were four months along—"

She was outraged. "That's not true—" she sputtered.

He held up his hand. "I know, it was my own fault. You tried to get hold of me and I didn't answer your messages. But the fact remains that if you'd really wanted to get in touch with me you could have. Except for the week I spent in France I've been right here in town all the time."

"That may be," she acknowledged angrily, "but I didn't know it. It was obvious that you didn't want anything more to do with me, and I wasn't going to beg."

He stopped pacing and looked at her. "I understand, and I don't blame you for that, but now you don't want me to support the baby, and you refuse to let me support you, which in the long run would be better for the little one, too. And you keep referring to the child as '*my* baby,' never 'ours.'"

Kate was astonished to realize he was right—she had been excluding him. That had never been her intention, but she could see how he would think it was deliberate.

She ran her fingers through her thick blond hair, loosening the knot at the top of her head and allowing a few long tendrils to escape and tickle her neck.

"I'm sorry, Burk," she apologized. "I honestly didn't realize how thoroughly I've been excluding your rights as my...that is, *our* baby's father. I didn't mean to. Or, maybe subconsciously I did. I've just been trying to establish the fact that it's *my* baby, and I'll never allow you to take it away from me." Her voice rose. "I'll do anything to prevent that!"

Burk looked perplexed. "Kate, what makes you think I'd do a thing like that? Why are you so afraid of me?"

"You tried to take Monique away from Fleur," she reminded him. "That's why Fleur bolted. She was afraid she'd never see her daughter again if you got sole custody."

"But that was different," he explained calmly. "She was going to take Monique out of the country."

"You don't know that," she insisted. "The way you told it to me, you just assumed that she would, and you were pushing ahead full tilt. She was scared to death of you, and then I came along and provided her with the confirmation of her worst nightmares. She took the child and ran, and I don't blame her. I'd have done the same thing!"

Chapter Fifteen

The wedding had been scheduled to take place at two o'clock on Saturday. It was to be held in the smaller of the two banquet rooms at the clubhouse of the country club where the Sinclair family belonged. Although at her own request Kate had taken no part in the plans, Burk and his family had done a great job on such short notice.

She'd seen the room for the first time during the rehearsal on Friday night, and it was exactly what she would have chosen herself. Both Burk and Kate had agreed that they wanted only family members as guests. Neither of them would have felt comfortable inviting the friends and business associates who would have attended the first ceremony that had been canceled at the last moment.

This room was big enough to handle the catered buffet luncheon reception, which would follow the taking of the vows, without seeming cavernous with only thirty some guests.

Kate spent Saturday morning packing her things to move

them into Burk's condominium and then getting dressed. She'd long ago given her wedding gown to the hospital thrift shop, and she hadn't bought a new one. It didn't seem appropriate since this wasn't going to be a real marriage.

Instead, she'd chosen a misty green chiffon loose-fitting dress with side panels cascading from the shoulders to the calf-length hem. After all, she was pregnant, and all the guests knew it, so it would be a sham to wear virginal white.

She didn't feel much like a bride. She'd seen Burk only three times since last Sunday when he'd asked her to marry him, and never alone. There was Monday when he'd brought his mother over to apologize, Wednesday when they'd gotten together with their lawyers to draw up the premarital agreement and last night when he'd taken Grandma and her to the wedding rehearsal.

Two of those times had been short, and they'd ended up quarreling, but last night had been nice. They'd had a rehearsal dinner afterward at his parents' house, and everyone had been friendly to her. It was obvious Burk hadn't told any of his family that this was to be a limited-time marriage for the benefit of the baby, but she'd let it slide. If he wanted his parents and siblings to think everything had been patched up between them, it was all right with her.

She'd found out when she'd told Grandma about it that it wouldn't meet with everyone's approval. Grandma had been shocked and had insisted that they were just buying trouble for themselves.

"You aren't even giving the marriage a chance," she'd said. "It's sacrilegious to take vows you don't intend to keep. You'll live to regret it—both of you."

Kate already regretted it. In fact, she'd regretted it even as she'd insisted on it, but she wasn't going to use the baby to tie Burk to her. If she did, he'd be miserable and come to blame her for it. That was no basis for a life together.

She'd tried to explain that to Grandma, but Emily wasn't

buying it. "Be careful what you ask for, Katherine," she'd warned, "because you might get it."

Last night, though, had been a happy time, and Burk had even kissed her good-night when he brought Grandma and her home. That was the first time they'd had any close contact since Sunday. Would he make love to her tonight after he took her to his home as his bride? Or would he decide he didn't want her after all? They seemed to strike more anger than passion between them.

They weren't going on a honeymoon. Kate couldn't afford the time off; she needed what little she'd accumulated for when the baby was born. Even so, she'd have to take some leave of absence without pay.

Burk wanted her to quit her job, but she wouldn't do that. For one thing, she'd need it after the divorce, and for another, she didn't want to be dependent on him. They'd finally decided to wait and go somewhere nearby for the four-day Labor Day weekend instead.

Burk sent a limousine for Kate and Emily with instructions to the driver to have them at the country club by one-thirty where they were ushered into the library by Burk's mother. She told them Burk had already arrived. He and his brother, Douglas, who was serving as his best man, were whiling away the time by playing pool in the game room. Emily was Kate's only attendant and would serve the dual roles of matron of honor and giving the bride away.

The guests started arriving shortly after that, and at exactly two o'clock the justice of the peace, Burk and Doug took their places in front of the fireplace, and the disk jockey started playing the tape of the wedding march. Kate and Emily walked hand in hand, and Kate thought how appropriate it was that her grandmother be the one to give her in marriage. After all, she'd raised Kate and given her as much love as her deceased parents ever could have.

As they approached their destination Kate's eyes widened. Last evening at the rehearsal she'd thought the big stone fireplace in front of which they would be taking their vows was perfect for the occasion, but now it was banked with white flowers of every kind—gladioli, chrysanthemums, roses and others she couldn't identify—plus the appropriate greenery. The scene was breathtaking!

Somehow she knew this had been Burk's touch, and she looked at him. He was wearing a black sheer wool suit that fit to perfection, a white shirt and a gray tie with a royal blue pattern. There was an orchid in his lapel that matched the bouquet she carried. No bride had ever had a more handsome groom.

He watched her as she came toward him, and there was no mistaking the pride and admiration in his expression. He certainly didn't look like the unwilling groom in a shotgun wedding.

She wore no veil, only a circlet of flowers sprayed a misty green to match her gown, so he could see her own smile widen as their gazes held. She mouthed "Thank you" to him, and he nodded and winked at her.

He really was thoughtful and considerate!

When Kate and Emily positioned themselves in front of the justice of the peace, Kate leaned over and kissed her grandmother on the cheek, then reached for Burk's hand on the other side of her. He took hers and held it as the vows were read and repeated.

They used the rings they'd picked out together for the first ceremony. She'd sent them back to him after it was canceled, but apparently he hadn't returned them. They vowed to love, honor but not obey each other, and when it came time for the kiss, he gathered her in his arms and took her mouth with an eagerness that told her their marriage would be passionately consummated as soon as they could get away by themselves. She was delighted and let him know it with her response.

For the rest of the afternoon he hardly left her side. The

buffet luncheon was delicious although neither of them was able to eat much, and afterward there was dancing. For the first time in over two months they strained their bodies against each other, this time on the dance floor, and were electrified by the ecstasy of being profoundly aroused, and the agony of not being able to appease it.

Kate throbbed with need as he danced her in back of a large plotted plant and pushed her groin against his. "Are you as fired up as I am?" he moaned as he nibbled her earlobe.

"At least," she whispered, and stood on her toes so she could rub against his most vulnerable area.

He groaned and dug his fingers into the fleshy part of her bottom. "How soon can we leave?" His voice shook.

Kate glanced at her thin gold watch, an earlier gift from Burk. It was nearly five-thirty. "I think we've fulfilled our social obligation," she said with a grin. "Shall we say our goodbyes and get out of here?"

"I thought you'd never ask," he muttered, and kissed her deeply.

"Did—did you bring your own car?" she stammered when she was able to catch her breath again.

"Damn right I did," he told her. "I didn't want a driver infringing on our privacy, that is if we ever managed to find any."

He released her then took her hand. "Come on," he said softly. "Let's go home."

Home. It sounded so…so permanent. For a while at least she was going to pretend that it was.

As soon as they'd driven away from the clubhouse Burk looked at her and took her hand. "You are such a beautiful bride," he remarked tenderly. "I hope you weren't too disappointed that it was such a small wedding."

She loved it when he spoke like that, so sincere and caring. "It was a perfect ceremony—I wouldn't have wanted it any different. Your mother did a marvelous job of arranging it in such a short period of time. I tried to thank her, but there really aren't words to express…''

He squeezed her hand. ''She'll understand. She still feels bad about the…the canceled wedding and the…the way she treated you…'' he stammered, both embarrassed and fearful of bringing up the subject.

Kate didn't want to hear about the canceled ceremony. It intruded on today's happiness. ''Please, Burk, let's don't talk about that. She's more than made up for it since.…''

He brought her hand to his lips and kissed it. His breath was warm and made her tingle.

''You not only look like an angel, but I think you must be one,'' he murmured. ''Not many people would be so forgiving.''

Including him? Was he warning her that he must be included in the group that couldn't?

''I'm not an angel,'' she said spiritedly. ''You should know that by now, but I don't believe that holding on to grudges brings one anything but grief and ulcers.''

He let loose of her hand supposedly to make a turn, but she noticed that he didn't pick it up again.

''Sometimes it's not possible for one to forgive and forget a grievous wrong,'' he contended sadly.

She sighed and clasped her hands in her lap. ''I'm afraid the two go together. If you can't forget a wrong then you can't forgive it, either.''

''That's true,'' he murmured more to himself than to her, and for the next few minutes they rode in silence until he turned into the condominium parking garage.

When they got out of the car, he put his arms around her and drew her close. ''I've upset you, and that was never my intent. Can we forget this conversation ever took place?''

She shook her head regretfully. He'd as much as told her he could never forgive her even though he'd also implied that he wished he could. ''I'm afraid not,'' she said mournfully, "for the very reason we were talking about, but maybe we can pretend it didn't."

He hugged her, then left one arm around her while they walked to the elevator and took it to his floor.

When they got to his door he opened it then swept her up in his arms and carried her across the threshold. She gave a surprised gasp, dropped her purse on the floor and flung her arms around his neck. "Burk, you'll drop me!"

He laughed. "Don't be silly. I've been looking forward to carrying you across the threshold of your new home. Now give me a kiss and maybe I'll put you down."

She put her hands on either side of his head and lowered his mouth to hers. Her lips were parted and she inserted the tip of her tongue between them and slowly ran it back and forth as he tried to capture it with his own. When he did he rained kisses over her face, then turned her and slowly slid her down his body until her feet touched the floor.

She couldn't miss the fact that he was again fully aroused, but he didn't rush her off to the bedroom the way she'd thought he would. Instead, he held her gently and murmured in her ear, "I'll bet you're tired. Why don't you sit down on the couch and I'll fix us both a drink."

"I—I gave up liquor when I found out I was pregnant," she told him. "It's not good for the baby, but you go ahead and fix one for yourself."

He chuckled. "I'm sorry," he murmured. "I'm afraid I'm not thinking very straight this afternoon. Would you...um, would you prefer to lie down?"

She was surprised by his hesitation. He'd never been bashful about taking her to bed before. "That would be lovely," she said lightly. "That is, if you'll lie down with me."

His arms tightened around her. "Are you sure, sweetheart?" he asked anxiously. "I don't want you to feel obligated to do anything you might not feel up to."

She stifled a giggle. "Are you up to it?"

He grinned and rubbed against her. "Katie, you little tease." He sucked on her earlobe. "Surely you don't have to ask?"

This time she rubbed against him and bit him gently on the neck. "Burk, my darling, I'm pregnant, not sick. I told you, the doctor said it was okay."

He looked skeptical. "I know, but I don't want to hurt you or the baby."

"You won't," she said, and reached between them to unfasten his suit coat. "In case you hadn't noticed, I'm as hot to trot as you are, and the baby is protected inside a sac of amniotic fluid."

"I'd noticed," he said as he pulled his arms out of the sleeves of his coat and flung it across the back of a chair, "and I'm overjoyed. It would have been pure agony to spend the night in the same apartment with you and not fulfill my 'husbandly duties.'" He snorted. "Duties, hell! I've been without you for so long that consummating this marriage with you will be pure bliss."

He offered her his arm. "May I escort you to our 'chamber,' my lovely bride?" His tone was formal but his eyes sparkled.

She curtsied then took his arm. "You may escort me to our 'chamber' anytime you have the urge, my husband," she teased back.

He leaned down and kissed her on the mouth, slowly and thoroughly. "Be careful what you promise, Katie." This time he was serious. "I found out early on that I'm insatiable with you."

Kate wondered if insatiable lust was as lasting as enduring love. Probably not, but she'd take whatever she could get for the next eleven months and try to be content.

In the master bedroom Burk led her across the spacious area and sat her down on the side of the bed, then knelt down in front of her.

"I'll undress you first, then you can lie down while I get out of my own clothes," he said as he picked up her right foot and removed the sea green pump.

"You mean I don't get to undress you?" she asked with a pout. "But that's part of the fun."

He removed her other pump and looked up at her. "You can undress me anytime you want to, sweetheart, but I thought—"

"Well, think again." She reached down to untie his tie.

He came up to sit on the side of the bed with her while she tackled the small pearl buttons of his shirt. "These things are such a problem," she grumbled good-naturedly. "I'll bet a lot of them get ripped off when their wearer is in a hurry."

Burk smiled. "You have my permission to rip, love. It's going to take you all night to unbutton each one."

She leaned over and kissed him. "But I wouldn't think of ruining that expensive garment," she whispered against the corner of his mouth.

"Well, I would," he said impatiently, and tore it the rest of the way open with one jerk, scattering custom-made buttons in all directions.

"My goodness," she said quaintly as she fingered his belt buckle. "Now look what you've done. Don't be so excitable, dear."

"You excite me to the point of madness, and you know it. You do it on purpose, don't you." It wasn't a question.

"But of course I do," she admitted as she loosened the buckle and the snap beneath it. "That's what makes it so erotic."

She started pulling his shirt out of his trousers. "Besides, you like it, too. You just don't want to admit it."

"I'll admit to anything if you'll just hurry up," he grated as she tugged on his shirtsleeve then stopped.

"Now what?" he grumbled.

"I forgot you were wearing cuff links," she told him as she grabbed one wrist and fumbled with the link.

"Let me do it," He reached for his wrist, but Kate pushed his hand away.

"I can do it," she said patiently, and with a little more fumbling got the jewelry undone, then reached for the other wrist. "You see, I just had to figure out how it worked," she said happily and slid the shirt off his arms.

Suddenly, without warning, he leaned over and untied his shoes and kicked them off, then stood and unzipped his trousers and stepped out of them.

"Burk! That's not fair," Kate cried. "I was looking forward to unzipping that fly."

He grinned and, taking her hands, pulled her to her feet. "I know you were, and I'd never have withstood it. Now, how do I get you out of this dress?"

With a little instruction from her he found the zipper and hooks and managed to undo them. After guiding the gown off her shoulders it fell gracefully to the floor and left her standing in cream-colored satin panties and bra and thigh-length stockings.

He paused and stepped back to look at her. "Oh, how I've missed you, Katie." His voice was husky and his eyes clouded with passion. "I couldn't get you out of my mind. I thought about you during the days and dreamed about you at night, and I wanted you so bad that it nearly drove me crazy."

He reached out and cupped her face with his hands. "Now I'm afraid to touch you for fear I might do something wrong."

He stepped closer and lowered his head to kiss her. It was sweet and restrained and sent tingles down her spine. She wanted to reassure him, but couldn't seem to find her voice.

Slowly he ran his hands down her neck and over her shoulders to come to rest on either side of her breasts, then leaned down farther to kiss both rises of the bare flesh exposed by the low décolletage of her bra.

She shivered and felt her nipples harden, but when he rubbed them with his thumbs she winced and cried, "Ouch!" He immediately removed his hands and straightened up.

"Did I hurt you?" he asked fearfully. "I didn't mean to."

She raised her arms and put them around his neck. "I know you didn't, but my breasts have gotten awfully tender, especially the nipples."

He put his arms around her waist. "Do—do you want to stop?" he asked, and she knew how difficult that would be for him. For her, too.

"No, please, there's no need for that," she assured him, then chuckled. "Just remember to go a little easy on the bust."

He smiled but it was a little shaky. "Is it all right if I take off your bra?"

"Sure."

He brought his hands up to the middle of her back and unhooked the garment then carefully removed it. It landed on the floor with her dress, and he carefully cupped the bottoms of her breasts.

"They're bigger, too, and heavier," he observed, and kissed each one more widely now that the restraints were gone. "Are you going to nurse the baby?"

She let her hungry hands roam over his muscular back. "I intend to, at least until I go back to work."

"Lucky baby," he murmured, and covered one nipple with his open mouth then sucked very gently. "Tell me if I hurt you."

It wasn't hurting, it felt good. After a while he moved to the other one and repeated the erotic caress, sending blasts of heat to her most intimate places.

She shuddered with need and dug her fingers into his

back as he released her breasts and stripped off his briefs, then put his hands on her hips underneath her panties, peeling them off, too, as he lowered himself to a kneeling position. With her hands on his shoulders she stepped out of the undergarment, but instead of standing up, he put his arms around her waist and his head against her belly.

The fire that had been igniting in her blazed as he placed moist kisses in a straight line from her waist to the nest of hair at the junction of her thighs. She gasped and twisted her fingers in his dark hair as she struggled to contain the tide of rapture that threatened to overwhelm her. She was wet and wanting, but he seemed intent on taking it slow and easy. She knew it was out of concern for her, but she didn't need concern, she needed release.

Taking him by surprise she dropped to the floor beside him and pushed him off balance so that he was sitting on the floor with his back against the bed. Before he could react she climbed on his lap and straddled it.

"Now let's see how long you can hold out," she said, and wrapped her fingers around his swollen organ.

"Oh, Kate, I need you so." He groaned and raised her up, then lowered her on his throbbing hardness.

The penetration was all it took to light their fuses, and the world spun out of control, taking them to heights they'd never imagined.

Chapter Sixteen

Kate fingered the ornaments on the department store Christmas tree and could hardly believe that Christmas was less than two weeks away. She and Burk had been married almost four months and their son was due to be born in less than six weeks.

Where had the time gone? When she'd agreed to this marriage she'd known it was only temporary and would last less than a year, but that had seemed like a long time. She was still young enough that a year out of her life was a big chunk, but even so, time had a way of creeping up on her.

She'd celebrated her twenty-ninth birthday on the day she'd had the ultrasound and found out she was giving Burk a son. He'd been delighted, although she knew he'd have been just as happy with another daughter. Not that it would have taken the place of the one he'd lost, but it might have helped to heal the open wound he still carried. On the other hand, another girl could have just been a constant reminder of Monique.

She picked up one of the small fancy boxes that contained the decoration she'd been admiring and headed for the cashier. "Waddled" was a better way of describing her gait. She was getting fat and slow, in that order, and it annoyed her that she tired easily. She'd been shopping for only three hours but already she was exhausted.

Burk was always after her to stay off her feet and let the part-time maid he'd employed to supplement the weekly house cleaner do the work, but she felt so useless just sitting around. Her maternity leave from work would start in two more weeks, right after Christmas, and then maybe she wouldn't feel so washed out.

The thought of Burk made her smile. He was so attentive and afraid she'd overdo. She knew his concern was mainly for the child she carried, but even so it was nice to be hovered over.

They'd gotten along so well since their marriage. Their sex life, as he continued to call it, couldn't be better. He was a passionate lover, not only needy and always ready, but also considerate of her. No matter how aroused he was, he always asked her if she felt like it, and insisted they could stop if she didn't.

Felt like it? It was all she could do not to jump his bones the minute he came in the door!

There was a darker side to her happiness, though. Sexually they radiated white-hot heat, but they couldn't spend all their time in bed. The other times they were together their compatibility was somewhat forced. He was aloof, silent and unwilling to share his thoughts and problems with her.

They never quarreled, but sometimes she wished they would. At least then he might spew out the rage and distrust he still harbored against her. As it was, if she nagged him about their lack of communication, he just made some excuse and left the apartment. He always returned later, smiling and acting as if there had never been any discord.

Kate paid for her purchase and put it in one of the filled shopping bags she carried. Then she headed in the direction of her car in the store's parking lot. She wanted to get home before Burk did so he wouldn't see how tired she was.

Even though it was Saturday, Burk was working at his office. He did this frequently since he'd married Kate, and he hated himself for it. Every day that passed put them a day closer to the one when she would leave him. The thought was unbearable, but still he couldn't forgive her.

Did he love her? Lord, yes, he did, or maybe he just lusted after her, but whatever it was, he couldn't get away from it. It invaded his heart and soul.

But almost as strong was his rage at what she'd done to him. She'd caused him to lose his little girl, and he could never forgive her for that.

He might not like her much, but neither could he leave her alone. Every night he could hardly wait until bedtime when they would curl up together and make exciting, mind-bending love.

She deserved better than just being the object of his carnal desires. She was the mother of his son! Why didn't that balance out her part in Monique's disappearance? Logically it should, and it had softened his attitude toward her, but it wasn't possible to replace one child with another. They were both equally precious to him.

He glanced at his watch, then ran his fingers through his hair and looked at the papers scattered around on his desk. Dammit, it was almost three-thirty and he should be home with Kate. He sure wasn't getting much work done here.

He gathered up the papers and put them in a drawer. He'd take her out to dinner tonight. She enjoyed eating in the high-priced restaurants she'd never been able to afford on her own salary, whereas he'd grown up taking them for granted.

It was unnaturally quiet when Burk let himself into the condo. No radio, television, or tapes filling the air with soft music. Kate loved his wraparound stereo and usually had one of the systems playing.

He called her name but got no answer, then remembered she'd said she was going shopping this morning. Still, it was—again he glanced at his watch—ten after four. He hadn't noticed whether or not her car was parked in its assigned space in the underground parking garage, but surely she'd be home by now. She'd said she was going early to avoid the worst of the crowds.

A feeling of unease assailed him, and he started searching. Dining room, kitchen, family room, bathroom. It was in their bedroom that he finally found her sound asleep in bed. The shopping trip must have worn her out because she never napped in the daytime. Again, the uneasy feeling pricked at him.

The thick carpet absorbed his footsteps as he walked over to stand beside the bed. She seemed to be sleeping normally. Her breathing was soft and regular, and she was lying on her side with her back to him and one hand under her cheek.

Smiling, he reached down and smoothed her hair away from her face, then bent over and kissed her on the exposed cheek. He was strongly inclined to waken her but stifled it. She needed the rest. He'd be so glad when her maternity leave started and she could take it easier. If only she'd let him take care of her instead of being so damned independent!

He decided to let her sleep for another half hour then waken her. If she napped longer than that she'd have trouble sleeping tonight.

He went into the family room and settled down with the

Wall Street Journal, but it was only a few minutes later that he heard a sharp cry of distress coming from the bedroom. He dropped the paper and rushed down the hall to find Kate stretched out on her back, shaking violently all over and uttering shrill little shrieks that vibrated around the room.

"Kate! Katie! What's the matter!" Terrified, he sat down on the side of the bed and gripped her shoulders. Immediately she sat straight up, as if released by a spring, then dropped back down again, all the while emitting the shrieks.

Burk recognized it as a seizure but didn't know how to handle it. He reached blindly for the phone and knocked it off the nightstand, then dialed wrong twice with his shaking fingers before getting 911.

The ambulance with three paramedics, one the driver, arrived within minutes, but it seemed like forever to Burk as he tried to quiet Kate without success.

The medics strapped her on a stretcher and loaded her into the ambulance. Burk started to climb in, too, but was stopped. "There's not enough room for another person in back," one of the medics told him. "You can ride in the front seat, but I'd advise you to get in your own car and follow us to the hospital. Otherwise you won't have anything to come back home in."

Burk reluctantly agreed. He didn't want to leave Kate, but he would need a car later.

By the time they got to the hospital she'd stopped convulsing but was still unconscious. She was wheeled into the emergency room and transferred to a gurney. The physician on duty was summoned and her obstetrician was notified. The ER doctor and Burk kept calling her name in an effort to waken her.

Much to Burk's intense relief she finally opened her eyes and asked the age-old question, "Where am I?"

Before he could answer, the doctor interrupted. "Do you know him?" he asked her and pointed to Burk.

"Sure," she said drowsily, "that's Burk."

"And what's your name?" the doctor persisted.

"Katherine Brown Sinclair."

The doctor smiled and patted her shoulder. "That's fine. You fainted, so we're going to do some tests. Dr. Young is on his way, but while we're waiting for him the nurse is going to draw some blood while I talk to Burk. Okay?"

Her expression suddenly changed. "My baby!" Her tone was charged with concern.

"Your baby's all right. You just relax and Dr. Young will examine you when he gets here." The doctor motioned to the nurse to begin then asked Burk to come outside with him.

"What's wrong with her, Doctor?" Burk asked anxiously. "That was no faint."

"It was a convulsion," the doctor agreed, "but I didn't want to upset her. It could be very serious, Mr. Sinclair, but since I don't have access to her medical records I don't want to draw any hasty conclusions— Oh, here's Dr. Young now." He hailed the man just entering the area.

Dr. Nick Young hurried over and shook hands with Burk then turned to the other doctor. "Has she stopped convulsing?"

"Yes, but she was a little hard to wake up. She's alert now, though. The nurse is getting her prepped for you."

"Good," Dr. Young said, then turned to Burk again. "Has she ever done this before?"

"Not that I know of," Burk told him. "Certainly not since we've been married."

Dr. Young left then to examine Kate, and the other one directed Burk to the waiting room, but he didn't want to get that far away from her, so instead he paced the area outside the examining room. After what seemed a lifetime,

Dr. Young opened the door and beckoned to him. He looked grim, and Burk panicked.

"For God's sake, Nick, tell me what's wrong with her," he demanded as he joined the doctor. "All I've been getting is evasions. Dammit to hell, I want some answers."

"I'm going to give you some," Dr. Young told him, "but come back in here where we can have a little privacy."

A curtain was drawn around the bed where Kate lay, and the doctor led Burk to the corner farthest away from it and lowered his voice. "Kate has toxemia, a fairly rare but dangerous complication of pregnancy caused by poisons circulating in the blood."

Fear and rage struck twin blows to Burk's midsection. "How could you have let this happen?" he demanded.

"I didn't *let* it happen—it just did," the doctor explained patiently. "Usually it comes on slowly and we can divert it, but Kate had none of the symptoms the last time I saw her, which was not quite three weeks ago."

Burk was wild with impatience. "What's going to happen? Will she be all right? Dammit, man, do something!"

"I'm going to do something, but you're going to have to calm down and understand what I'm telling you. You're a strong, intelligent man and I'm not going to pussyfoot around about this. It's an extreme emergency. We might have to do a cesarean section and take the baby, but Kate's only seven and a half months along. I can't guarantee the child will survive. On the other hand, if we don't do it we might lose Kate—"

He was interrupted by a high keening sound coming from the bed. "She's having another convulsion," the doctor muttered, and hurried to the curtained-off area with Burk right behind him.

This one didn't last as long as the first one, but it was just as terrifying to Burk. Kate was restrained by tubes and straps and bars, and he was tortured by the knowledge that if he'd been less self-indulgent and more responsible about birth control, his sweet and loving Katie would never have been pregnant and therefore subjected to this life-threatening illness.

Lose Kate! No way in hell was that going to happen! How could he have been so blind, so stubborn, as to not recognize how much she really meant to him? Well, he recognized it now and there would be no more blaming her for his mistakes. No one was responsible for him losing his daughter but himself, and he wasn't going to lose Katie, too, no matter what.

When they again had the seizure under control Dr. Young turned away and was stripping off his rubber gloves when Burk touched his shoulder and got his attention. "Do what you have to do, Nick, but don't let anything happen to Kate. She's my life. If it's necessary to make a choice, just remember, Katie is more important to me than anyone or anything."

Kate woke slowly but couldn't quite manage to open her eyes. She must have been sleeping more deeply than usual and she was uncomfortable lying on her back, but when she tried to roll over onto her side, bolts of pain ripped through her.

Her eyes flew open and she cried out as she relaxed onto her back again. Immediately someone came to her bedside and took her hand, but it was a few seconds before she could focus and see who it was.

"Don't try to move around, sweetheart," said a voice she recognized as Burk's at the same time as she saw him. "You'll be stiff and sore for a while."

He's talking nonsense, she thought and ran her tongue over her dry lips. Her throat was dry, too, and she was thirsty.

She blinked and he came into sharper focus. What was

the matter with him? He looked as if he'd been sleeping in his clothes.

She'd never seen him so disheveled before. He was wearing suit pants and a wrinkled white shirt, but no tie, and the shirt was unbuttoned several buttons at the throat. It was also pulling out of his trousers in some places, and the sleeves were rolled up to the elbows.

He leaned over the bed, which she now noticed had metal side bars on it, and smiled at her. "Wake up, Katie, and come back to me. You've been on a long, hard journey, and you scared the hell out of me in the process." He spoke softly and there was a quiver in his voice.

He was still talking gibberish. Nothing he said made sense, and it wasn't only his clothes that were disheveled. His hair stuck up as though he'd been running his fingers through it, and there were dark circles under his eyes. His face was gray under a stubble of beard and lined with weariness. Where was she anyway? Certainly not in her big comfortable bed at home.

"Burk, where are we?" Her own voice was raspy and came out barely above a whisper. "I remember lying down to take a short nap, but not here."

He brought her hand to his mouth and kissed the palm. "That was yesterday," he said, "and a lot has happened since."

He folded her fingers into her palm and kissed her fist, then laid it across her chest. "There's something I've been waiting to show you." He grinned and touched the tip of her nose with his finger. "Don't go away, I'll be right back."

Very funny, she grumbled to herself. And just where was she likely to go when she couldn't even turn over in bed?

She gazed around, and for the first time it registered that she was in a hospital room. But what hospital and how had she gotten here? She didn't remember a thing after she went to sleep when she got home from shopping, but Burk said that was yesterday—

Then she made the connection, and cold chills ran down her spine. If she was in the hospital then it had to have something to do with the baby!

Instinctively she ran her hand under the sheet to her stomach. It was flat and heavily bandaged! There was no baby there!

"Burk," she screamed and tried to sit up before jagged shards of pain knocked her back down. "Burk, what happened to our baby?"

The door flew open and a nurse rushed in, followed by Burk who was carrying something in his arms.

"Lie down, Mrs. Sinclair," the nurse said, and wrestled Kate back down. "The baby is just fine. See, your husband has brought him to you."

Kate stopped struggling and looked at Burk standing beside the bed holding something wrapped in what she now recognized as a small blue flannel baby blanket. He leaned down and pulled the blanket apart so she could see what was inside.

"Mrs. Sinclair," he said pompously but with a twinkle in his eyes that lit his whole face, "I'd like to introduce you to your son, who insisted on arriving before we were ready for him. So he has no name. But I think you'll agree to keep him anyway."

Kate melted. Her baby! Their baby! He was beautiful, but so tiny. She'd never seen such a little infant before.

"Do you want to hold him?" Burk asked.

"Oh, yes. Please. Is it...is it all right?" She looked for the nurse, but the nurse was gone.

"Of course it's all right," Burk answered for her. "He's just been waiting for his mommy to wake up and cuddle him."

Tenderly he laid the bundle in the crook of Kate's arm. Her son felt so warm and soft, and his tiny mouth was making sucking motions as his equally tiny fist waved awkwardly in the air.

Her heart pounded so hard, she was afraid it would burst. She hadn't known that being a mother would be such an euphoric experience. She looked up at Burk and smiled. "He looks just like his daddy," she lied happily. Actually, his features were so small that you couldn't tell what he was going to look like, only that he was the most beautiful baby in the whole world.

Burk leaned down and kissed her. "Maybe he'll grow out of it," he teased.

She returned his kiss enthusiastically, but she also had questions that needed answers. "Burk, this baby wasn't due for another six weeks. What happened? I don't remember anything about coming here. Did I go into labor?"

He stroked a strand of hair back from her forehead. "No, sweetheart, you developed an emergency complication called toxemia and the doctor had to deliver the child by cesarean section. It was touch and go there for both of you for a while, but the little guy is just fine and so are you."

It was all so confusing. "But why don't I remember?"

"Dr. Young will explain it all to you later, but right now all you need to know is that loss of memory surrounding this type of event is not unusual, and your son is a strapping four pounds three ounces and measures fifteen inches in length."

Fear clutched at her. "So tiny. Will he...will he be all right?"

Burk cupped her cheek. "Actually that's pretty good size for a preemie at this stage. He's confined to an incubator and will have to stay in the hospital for a while until he gains another pound, but the pediatrician says he'll probably grow up to be a husky football tackle."

The door opened just then and the nurse bustled in. "Sorry, but I've come for the baby. We can't have him out of his incubator for very long at a time, but when you're feeling up to it your husband can take you to the nursery in a wheelchair to see him."

"Oh, I hate to give him up," Kate said sadly as Burk took the child from her and handed him to the nurse.

"We'll take good care of him," the nurse assured her and left, letting the door shut behind her.

"My arms feel empty already," Kate said on a sigh.

Burk put down the bars on the side where he was standing and sat down on the edge of the bed. "Would you like to try filling them with me?" he asked huskily.

"I'd love to," she replied, and opened both arms to him.

He leaned down and gently embraced her, and she clutched him to her. No wonder he looked so done in, he was exhausted. She must have given him quite a scare. She didn't need to have it spelled out that the baby could have died.

Involuntarily she shuddered and he held her closer. "Burk, I'm so sorry," she murmured.

"You have nothing to be sorry about," he said against the side of her neck.

"But maybe if I hadn't continued working, or if I'd—"

He raised up and kissed her on the mouth, effectively shutting off her words. "Listen to me, Kate, and listen carefully. Nothing you did or didn't do would have made any difference. Toxemia is a poison in the blood. No one is to blame. I'll ask Nick to explain it to you more fully, but I won't have you blaming yourself for anything."

He relaxed again and buried his face in her shoulder. "You've been the most loving and most careful expectant mother it's possible to be, and I love you so much that it's like the lash of a whip against my bare skin when you apologize to me. I'm the stubborn, self-righteous bastard who owes the apologies."

His declaration of love was like a soothing balm to her tattered ego, and she was tempted to accept the lie and pretend it was the truth, but she loved him too much to bind him to her with his own good intentions.

She kissed the top of his head and stroked his bristly cheek. "Burk, I don't expect expressions of undying love from you," she said, trying to keep the tremor out of her voice. "We both know our marriage is one of expediency, not love...."

He raised himself up and looked down at her wearily. "That may be how it is with you, but if so, I'm going to let you down again, Kate, because I have no intention of honoring our prenuptial agreement."

She stared, then blanched. "You what? You mean you're not going to let me have physical custody—"

He sat up straight and put his finger across her mouth. "I'll gladly give you anything you want, my darling. Anything but a divorce. If you're still determined to have our marriage dissolved in six months you'll have to fight me for it."

She couldn't believe what she was hearing. "But why? You married me only because I was pregnant. You don't even like me."

Again he leaned down and captured her mouth, making her head swim and her senses reel.

"I adore every luscious inch of you," he insisted. "From the top of your angelic head to the tips of your sexy little toes. If you'll give me a second chance, which I know I don't deserve, I'll do my best to convince you of that by actions as well as words."

That declaration was nourishment for her soul and she so badly needed to believe it, but how could she? Their relationship was tenuously based on the fluctuating stability of sand and the uncertainties of the appearance and disappearance of children.

She was sure he'd never have spoken to her again after he found out about her involvement in his older child's disappearance if she hadn't been pregnant with this baby.

Because she'd agreed with his wish that their child be his legally she'd married him, but she'd also given him an out. So why was he now trying to convince her that he loved her?

"When did you have this sudden change of heart?" she asked, still unconvinced.

He nuzzled her neck. "It wasn't a change of heart. In my heart I've always known that no matter how upset I may be with you I'll always love you. It was my stupid pride that got in the way."

He sat up, breaking their embrace, then took her hand and held it to his cheek. "You may not have noticed, sweetheart," he said facetiously, "but we Sinclairs tend to be a mite bullheaded, strong-willed, stiff-necked and unrelenting. Especially me. I've always been given everything I wanted—all I had to do was ask. No one ever seriously refused me anything because my family had the money and the power to force the issue."

He was speaking lightly, but Kate could tell by the way he gripped her hand that he was speaking the truth as he saw it, and it was difficult for him.

"Then I met Fleur," he continued, "and she was different, an exotic French beauty with a mind of her own. She dared to say no to me now and then and that whetted my appetite. I thought I loved her, but I knew I wanted her as a prize to show off to my envious friends.

"The first time I proposed to her she said no, and that made her even more desirable. She was a challenge, and I wasn't used to being challenged. I knew how to handle one, though. I just turned up the charm and hinted at all the things I could do for her."

He made a disparaging face. "It wasn't long after we were married that I realized I'd been bested at my own game. She didn't want me, she wanted what I could give her. I guess you could say we deserved each other."

He leaned down and kissed her, and she had to admit he

was starting to make a believer of her. Men like Burk had to have a compelling reason to admit their shortcomings the way he was admitting his to her. Maybe he did love her after all.

He sat up and folded her hand in both of his. "After Monique was born we tried to make the best of our unhappy marriage for her sake, but then without consulting me, Fleur filed for divorce and custody of our daughter."

Again he was gripping her hand more tightly than he realized. "I was outraged! How dare she! I had no objection to the divorce, but no way was she going to get custody of *my* child!"

He shrugged. "You can imagine how well that went over. I think we wound up fighting more for power than for our daughter. Instead of sitting down with Fleur and making an honest effort to resolve our differences, I kept threatening her with more and direr consequences if she didn't agree to letting me have physical custody of our daughter.

"As you so wisely pointed out, I scared her so badly that she was left with no choice but to grab the child and run when she realized I intended to use her past against her."

He kept her hand in one of his and used the other to run his finger lightly down the side of her face. "Yesterday when the doctor warned me that toxemia is sometimes a fatal complication of pregnancy and you might not survive the surgery, I almost went out of my mind...."

Even after all this time his lips quivered and he had to stop for a moment and get control of his emotions. "That's when I learned all about the fires of hell!"

Kate's heart swelled and she again held out her arms to him. A small window in her memory was opening. She remembered Burk and her doctor talking as she slept nearby, or at least she assumed it was sleep. Anyway, she heard Burk say...

Her teeth worried her lower lip as she held him to her again. No, she couldn't have heard that. It must have been a dream.

"I...seem to remember you saying something," she stammered, but... Oh, never mind—"

He raised himself up on his forearms and looked down at her. "I told Nick that, if he had to make a choice before that nightmarish night was over, he was to do everything in his power to save you."

That's what she'd heard, but she still found it hard to believe. "But the baby is your son, and you'd already lost one child...."

He looked infinitely sad as he lowered himself and rubbed his cheek against hers. "And you thought you'd be lucky to run a distant third in my priorities?"

A sob escaped from deep in his throat before he could control it. "Oh, sweetheart, I'm so sorry I've let you believe that. Actually, there was no contest. It would have broken my heart to lose our son but, Katie, you're my love, my life, my soul mate. I can't envision life without you. It's too painful to even think about."

Carefully he relaxed against her again, and she stroked her fingers through his hair. "I hope you believe everything you've just told me because I gotta tell you, buddy, there's no way in hell I'm going to fight you for a divorce. You're stuck with me for the rest of your natural life. You've made your bed, now you're going to have to sleep in it."

Very carefully he stroked her breast. "I'm all for that," he whispered. "Just as soon as they let you out of here so you can come home and sleep in that nice, big, comfortable bed with me."

Kate's cup runneth over with love.

Epilogue

Burk's hand shook with excitement as he unlocked the door to the condominium and let himself in. It was early for him to be home, only a little after four o'clock, but he couldn't wait to show Kate the e-mail he'd received less than an hour ago at the office.

The apartment was quiet and for a moment he thought she'd taken the baby and gone birthday and Christmas shopping. It didn't seem possible but Billy was going to be a year old tomorrow with his second Christmas following shortly after that.

A childish squeal from the gaily decorated living room sent Burk striding down the hall and to the left where he found that his young son had pulled himself up onto his feet in the playpen and was gnawing happily on the plastic-coated rim. Burk's heart flipped over as it always did when confronted by his child.

"Hi, guy," he said as he took off his coat and flung it into a chair before picking the shrieking baby up and lifting him high in the air. "How's my boy, and where's your mommy?"

"Burk?" Kate's voice came from behind him. "What are you doing home at this time of day? Is something the matter?"

He put the child back in the playpen and swept his wife into his arms. If anything, childbirth had made Kate even more beautiful. There was a soft madonna quality about her that was irresistible.

"Not a thing," he said as he swung her around. "In fact, something is very very right. My private investigator in France has found Monique and Fleur!"

Kate looked as stunned as he felt. "No! Really? Where? How do you know?"

He put her down but kept her close in his embrace. "I got an e-mail letter. Here, read it." He fished a folded piece of paper out of his pants pocket and handed it to her.

"Why don't you go sit on the sofa in front of the fireplace," he suggested. "I'll bring Billy."

He picked the baby up and got a sloppy openmouthed kiss on his cheek as he carried him to the couch and sat down next to Kate with Billy on his lap.

"It says here that Fleur has agreed to let you see Monique but you'll have to go to France," Kate pointed out.

"I know," he said, refusing to let anything diminish his high spirits at the prospect of seeing his young daughter again. "She's still wary and doesn't completely trust me, but you were right, sweetheart, she was terrified of me. She never would have come out of hiding if I hadn't had my attorney draw up that agreement that I wouldn't try to get full custody of Monique or have Fleur prosecuted for kidnapping or any other related crime."

Kate snuggled against him and he put his arm around her and held her close while he anchored Billy on his thigh with the other hand.

"Oh, Burk, I'm so happy for you," she said and rubbed

her cheek against his shoulder. "Will you be leaving soon?"

"Just as soon as you can get yourself and Billy boy here ready to go," he murmured into her hair.

She pulled away from him. "You want Billy and me to go with you?"

He blinked. "Well, of course. I'm not going anywhere without you. Besides, I want Monique to meet her stepmother and her half brother."

He put his arm around her and settled her against him again. "It may be pretty awkward this time. After all, it's been over six years since she last saw me, and she was only three at the time. She won't remember me, and God only knows what her mother and grandparents have told her, but meeting the three of us at once might break the ice and make things easier next time. I don't delude myself this will be a cinch, but I'll do almost anything to win her trust again."

Kate put her arms around his waist and rubbed her face against his chest. "I love you," she murmured seductively, sending hot prickles of testosterone surging through him.

He shivered with the intensity of his passion for her. He suspected that on their fiftieth anniversary they'd still be making excuses to go home early so they could curl up together in bed.

"And I love you, more than I can say," he murmured into her hair, and relaxed with her against the back of the couch.

The fire in the fireplace crackled and threw dancing shadows into the rapidly darkening room. Light from the Christmas tree that Kate had decorated so resplendently was the only other illumination, and Billy bounced on his knee and chortled with glee.

His life was finally in order. He was married to the woman he adored, their son who had come into the world so tiny and fragile was now robust and healthy, and his long-lost daughter had finally been found. In a matter of days he would be reunited with her.

No man could ask for anything more!

* * * * *

Take 4 bestselling love stories FREE

Plus get a FREE surprise gift!

Special Limited-time Offer

Mail to Silhouette Reader Service™

3010 Walden Avenue
P.O. Box 1867
Buffalo, N.Y. 14240-1867

YES! Please send me 4 free Silhouette Special Edition® novels and my free surprise gift. Then send me 6 brand-new novels every month, which I will receive months before they appear in bookstores. Bill me at the low price of $3.34 each plus 25¢ delivery and applicable sales tax, if any.* That's the complete price and a savings of over 10% off the cover prices—quite a bargain! I understand that accepting the books and gift places me under no obligation ever to buy any books. I can always return a shipment and cancel at any time. Even if I never buy another book from Silhouette, the 4 free books and the surprise gift are mine to keep forever.

235 BPA A3UV

Name	(PLEASE PRINT)	
Address	Apt. No.	
City	State	Zip

·This offer is limited to one order per household and not valid to present Silhouette Special Edition® subscribers. *Terms and prices are subject to change without notice. Sales tax applicable in N.Y.

USPED-696   ©1990 Harlequin Enterprises Limited

Welcome to the Towers!

In January
New York Times bestselling author

NORA ROBERTS

takes us to the fabulous Maine coast mansion
haunted by a generations-old secret and introduces
us to the fascinating family that lives there.

Mechanic Catherine "C.C." Calhoun and hotel magnate
Trenton St. James mix like axle grease and mineral
water—until they kiss. Efficient Amanda Calhoun finds
easygoing Sloan O'Riley insufferable—and irresistible.
And they all must race to solve the mystery
surrounding a priceless hidden emerald necklace.

Catherine and Amanda

THE Calhoun Women

**A special 2-in-1 edition containing
COURTING CATHERINE and A MAN FOR AMANDA.**

Look for the next installment of
THE CALHOUN WOMEN with Lilah and Suzanna's
stories, coming in March 1998.

Available at your favorite retail outlet.

As seen on TV!
Free Gift Offer

With a Free Gift proof-of-purchase from any Silhouette® book, you can receive a beautiful cubic zirconia pendant.

This gorgeous marquise-shaped stone is a genuine cubic zirconia—accented by an 18" gold tone necklace.

(Approximate retail value $19.95)

Send for yours today...
compliments of ▼ *Silhouette®*
™

To receive your free gift, a cubic zirconia pendant, send us one original proof-of-purchase, photocopies not accepted, from the back of any Silhouette Romance™, Silhouette Desire®, Silhouette Special Edition®, Silhouette Intimate Moments® or Silhouette Yours Truly™ title available at your favorite retail outlet, together with the Free Gift Certificate, plus a check or money order for $1.65 U.S./$2.15 CAN. (do not send cash) to cover postage and handling, payable to Silhouette Free Gift Offer. We will send you the specified gift. Allow 6 to 8 weeks for delivery. Offer good until December 31, 1997, or while quantities last. Offer valid in the U.S. and Canada only.

Free Gift Certificate

Name: _____

Address: _____

City: _____ State/Province: _____ Zip/Postal Code: _____

Mail this certificate, one proof-of-purchase and a check or money order for postage and handling to: SILHOUETTE FREE GIFT OFFER 1997. In the U.S.: 3010 Walden Avenue, P.O. Box 9077, Buffalo NY 14269-9077. In Canada: P.O. Box 613, Fort Erie, Ontario L2Z 5X3.

FREE GIFT OFFER   084-KFD

ONE PROOF-OF-PURCHASE

To collect your fabulous FREE GIFT, a cubic zirconia pendant, you must include this original proof-of-purchase for each gift with the properly completed Free Gift Certificate.

084-KFDR

CHRISTINE FLYNN

Continues the twelve-book series—36 HOURS—in December 1997 with Book Six

FATHER AND CHILD REUNION

Eve Stuart was back, and Rio Redtree couldn't ignore the fact that her daughter bore his Native American features. So, Eve had broken his heart *and* kept him from his child! But this was no time for grudges, because his little girl and her mother, the woman he had never stopped—could never stop—loving, were in danger, and Rio would stop at nothing to protect *his* family.

For Rio and Eve and *all* the residents of Grand Springs, Colorado, the storm-induced blackout was just the beginning of 36 Hours that changed *everything!* You won't want to miss a single book.

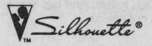

Available at your favorite retail outlet.

Look us up on-line at: http://www.romance.net

36HRS6

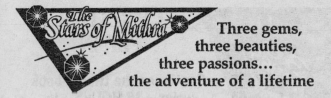

**Three gems,
three beauties,
three passions...
the adventure of a lifetime**

SILHOUETTE·INTIMATE·MOMENTS®
brings you a thrilling new series by
New York Times bestselling author

Nora Roberts

**Three mystical blue diamonds place three close
friends in jeopardy...and lead them to romance.**

In October
HIDDEN STAR (IM#811)
Bailey James can't remember a thing, but she knows
she's in big trouble. And she desperately needs private
investigator Cade Parris to help her live long enough to
find out just what kind.

In December
CAPTIVE STAR (IM#823)
Cynical bounty hunter Jack Dakota and spitfire
M. J. O'Leary are handcuffed together and on the run
from a pair of hired killers. And Jack wants to know
why—but M.J.'s not talking.

In February
SECRET STAR (IM#835)
Lieutenant Seth Buchanan's murder investigation takes
a strange turn when Grace Fontaine turns up alive. But
as the mystery unfolds, he soon discovers the notorious
heiress is the biggest mystery of all.

Available at your favorite retail outlet.